The Clockmaker of Perth

Barbara Stevenson

This first edition published in 2024 by
FMN Publishing

ISBN 978-1-7385720-1-4

Copyright © Barbara Stevenson

The moral right of the author has been asserted.

All rights reserved
No part of this publication may be reproduced in any form or by any electronic or mechanical means, including Information storage and retrieval systems, without permission in writing from the publisher.

The Clockmaker of Perth is a work of fiction.
Any resemblance to people alive or dead is purely coincidental.

Cover artwork copyright © Anna Gardiner 2024

Special thanks to Kathleen Stevenson for her time and expertise, without whose help this book may never have been published.

Thanks also to Anna Gardiner for the cover design

The Clockmaker of Perth

Perth, Scotland. 1885

Winnie was snoring. She sounded more like a hog bound for the knacker's yard than a squeaking piglet and Alfie decided that was an apt comparison. He sat at the dressing table with his pocket watch in his left hand. He screwed his eyes, but was forced to move the watch nearer his nose to read the time. Eight minutes to five. In the mirror, behind his reflection, he could see the bed covers rise and drop, tick-tocking in time to Winnie's stertorous exhalations. He also saw that his necktie wasn't sitting right. Winnie could sort it for him, but he was loath to wake her. She was never at her best before half past six. He returned the watch to his waistcoat pocket then re-knotted the tie. His fingers twitched, and his lack of the required skills rendered the task a fiddly one. Winnie's snoring reached a record height.

Stop that infernal cacophony, woman.

He rubbed an over-zealous dollop of ambergris into his hands to slick down his hair. There were more grey hairs than black, but at least he held a full head. Satisfied with his grooming, Alfie rose and lifted his jacket from the peg attached to the door. Winnie rolled over with a drawn out grunt.

A pillow held over the snout for several minutes was an infallible cure for snoring. Peace.

Alfie gave a snort and left the room, catching the door before it slammed. His tread down the stairs was light, avoiding the loose board on the third step. By the time he reached the seventh step he could hear the familiar ticking of old Charlie's grandfather clock. His father-in-law used to joke that it kept better time than his heart. For years it seemed an even race. In kirk, every Sunday, Charlie sang of claiming his mansion in glory, but he wasn't keen on taking up residence there. It took pneumonia, a delayed call for the doctor and a snow drift, before Alfie could inherit the business, as promised when he married the old watchmaker's daughter.

He reached the bottom step with a slight tweak in his left knee. He gave it a rub through the wool of his trousers then removed his keys from his pocket. The shop key was the heaviest. He fumbled to turn it in the lock. The door opened without a creak and Alfie looked in satisfaction at the array of timepieces arranged on shelves, in display cabinets, on the wall or, as was the case with the grandfather clock, on the polished floor. Their individual rhythms never failed to thrill him. Wall clocks, cuckoo clocks, desk clocks, mantel clocks, grandmother clocks, grandfather clocks - they all had their own music. He considered watches to be the strings in his horological orchestra. They were the ones that carried the tune, and they were aware of their importance.

Fob watches and pocket watches sold well. Watches set in etched cases and jewelled watches for ladies took longer to shift, but they were priced accordingly. The curios in the cabinet behind the counter weren't for sale. There was a gold watch that showed the movement of the stars, a watch that had belonged to Napoleon Bonaparte, allegedly, and a watch with a hidden compartment which held a capsule of poison.

Alfie stopped to correct the hands of a Swiss wall clock as he headed to the shop counter. A carriage clock was waiting to be parcelled up and returned to its owner. The buffoon had requested ridiculous alterations: mechanical figures dancing a gavotte on the hour, a complex chime, gold etched dials. It didn't concern the owner that the clock hadn't kept time since leaving its workshop. The workings were from an establishment in Glasgow and that, to Alfie, said enough. The fault wasn't his, but he baulked at the thought of returning a shoddy timepiece to a customer. He had made an excuse to keep it longer than his original estimate, allowing him to send for a two and a quarter inch cog from the metalsmith. He had completed the repair free of charge.

At the counter he bent to remove a locked box from the drawer, holding his back as he rose. The key wasn't attached to the fob with the others, but kept in his jacket pocket. He opened the box and removed two banknotes and a handful of coins then re-locked it and replaced the box in the drawer. It was necessary to side-step oak framed cabinets containing watches and pens to reach the front door of the shop. His hand moved to the handle, but he stopped and clicked his fingers.

He wove a reverse path to the counter and retrieved a parcel, roughly the size of a matchbox, wrapped in coloured paper and tied with a red string. Dotty would not be happy if he didn't bring her a present. Small things were important to children, and Dorothy was still very much a child. He twiddled with the string, arranging the bow in the centre of the parcel then slipped the package into his jacket pocket. At the door he collected his hat from the stand, brushed down the felt and positioned it on his head. Outside he locked the shop door and glanced up at the new sign.

ALFRED PETERS ESQ., MAKER OF FINE TIMEPIECES AND WRITING IMPLEMENTS.

The writing was in gold with a red shadow. He didn't need to advertise his services. Although there were other watchmakers in the city, he was the best. Five years ago, he had taken over Charlie's well-respected and thriving business. Charlie was a gifted craftsman, and had been a patient teacher. Using trusted methods, combined with modern equipment, Alfie had built up the business, so that now he had more customers than he could cope with. It was Winnie who convinced him that two feet high, gold letters were essential to show the civic worthies in the city hall that he was someone to take notice of. His choice of wording had been:

Alfred Peters – watches, clocks and pens.

It was to the point and significantly cheaper, but Winnie said it made him sound like a sheepdog.

The sun crept up from behind Kinnoull Hill and it was a pleasant walk along the river and down to the railway station. Alfie kicked aside the autumn leaves, a childish pastime, but he didn't expect to be spotted at such an hour. He jumped when, passing the bridge, he heard a cheery voice.

'Good morning to you, Mr Peters. I hope you are keeping well.'

'As to be expected,' Alfie answered, touching his hat to Walker Squires, joint owner of the new and extravagant West Tay Hotel overlooking North Inch Park.

'And your wife?' Walker asked.

Alfie gave a wry smile. 'As to be expected,' he answered.

'Good, good.'

Alfie didn't inquire after Squires' family although he knew Walker had a plump wife and two daughters ripe for the market. In his opinion, men should marry younger women, who had the vigour to care for them in older age. Squires' wife was three years older than he was and a permanent fixture on her velvet settee thanks to one ailment or another. At least the younger girl was plain enough to be left at home to care for her parents, unless Squires was foolish enough to offer a dowry.

Squires headed in the opposite direction and Alfie continued his walk to the station. The train was on time and he took a seat in the second class compartment opposite a respectable-looking gentleman with a white beard and spectacles. The man was reading a newspaper and he lowered it two inches to bob his head in greeting before returning to the news. Alfie understood that to mean the man didn't want disturbed by inane chatter. This was to Alfie's liking. He wished he had purchased a paper in the station kiosk before boarding.

The doors slammed closed, the guard blew his whistle and the train chugged out of the station. Admiring the autumn colours amused Alfie for ten minutes, until he found himself peering over at his travelling companion's paper. The man had folded the pages for easier reading and Alfie thought he could make out a photograph of Adam Farquhar. A coincidence, since Farquhar's business partner was Walker Squires. He leaned forwards in his seat to get a better view. As the train rumbled on the track he was jerked into the man's knees.

'Terribly sorry,' he muttered and sat back.

'Was there something in my paper that interested you?' The man emphasised the possessive pronoun.

'The photograph of Adam Farquhar caught my eye. I was curious to know what the old fox is up to,' Alfie replied.

'Farquhar?' The man turned the paper over to examine the photograph. 'Is he a friend of yours?'

'Not a friend,' Alfie realised he needed a reason for his interest. 'A possible business associate.'

'I see, and you want to make sure he isn't being investigated for skulduggery before you commit yourself.'

Alfie gave a thin smile and the gentleman tapped the side of his nose with a stumpy finger. He prodded the writing beneath the photograph and read aloud. 'Farquhar and Squires, owners of the newest luxury hotel in Perth, the West Tay…' the man skipped a few lines. Alfie watched his finger blur the ink as he did so,

'...have commissioned a clock for the grand entrance hall.'

'A clock?' Alfie squinted at the print.

'To show the time, I imagine.'

'What else would a clock do?' Alfie couldn't hide his sarcasm.

'You might ask. Apparently this won't be any old clock. This will be a "spectacular merging of modern art and mechanical engineering", or so it says.' The man read from the article. 'No expense will be spared. People will come from miles to admire it. A shortlist of designers has been drawn up and… ah, this is my station.' The man stood up and handed Alfie the paper. 'Here, you'd better have it. I've read the share prices, which is all I'm interested in.'

Alfie accepted the paper. He waited until the man had left the compartment before reading. He had received a letter from Farquhar and Squires the previous week, asking him to visit their office on a matter of mutual advantage. He had stowed the letter in a drawer, intending to reply at his leisure, but he had no time for leisure and had forgotten to respond.

He read the caption under the photograph of Farquhar. The clock was to be the centrepiece of the hotel lobby. The frontrunner to design the casing was a young American, Giles Templeman, although according to the reporter, Walker Squires would prefer to commission a local man. Alfie relaxed into his seat. Whoever they chose would design a casing for the clock, but he would be the man to figure out the mechanical workings and make sure everything fitted inside.

He read the rest of the paper as the train made its way through Fife towards the Forth and left it on his seat for the next occupant when he alighted. There was a crowd of passengers catching the paddle steamer across the river, but Alfie minded his business and they minded theirs. The crossing was rough, and the wooden hull of the ferry creaked as it withstood the waves battering in from the North Sea. Despite this, they made it to South Queensferry without incident. The sooner work was completed on the railway bridge over the Forth the better, Alfie thought. On the Lothian side of the river Alfie boarded a coach to take him to his destination.

There was a final walk of half a mile to the hospital. Snuggled between a glue factory and a junkyard, the smoke-choked stone walls of the building rose to block out any remaining light. Alfie felt a coldness creep towards him. He chapped on the weathered oak entrance gate and waited as the locks were unfastened.

Snap, snap, snap.

'Mr Peters, how are you?' the warden asked, stepping aside to allow Alfie in.

'Fine,' Alfie answered, choking as the carbolic in the air hit him. 'How is Dotty?'

'Much the same, sir, much the same. If I could ask you to empty your pockets before you visit her.'

'Why? You know who I am. I haven't had to do this before.'

'No sir and I'm sorry for the inconvenience, but there has been an incident.' The warden lowered his voice.

'An incident? With one of the patients?'

'Aye, with Lady Amelia, sir. Her husband had her confined here because she wouldn't let him touch her. Well, a man likes more than a look, especially after he's bought the goods, if you know what I mean.' The warden swept the sleeve of his filthy tunic across his nose and sniffed. As he did, Alfie spotted a pistol jutting out from his belt. He was used to the wardens carrying wooden batons, but a firearm seemed excessive. 'Dr Lutheral diagnosed a blockage and instigated a course of massage treatment to the feminine organs,' the warden continued. 'In here please sir, and take your hat and shoes off, if you don't mind.'

Alfie took off his hat and lowered his head to enter the small chamber. There was a table in the centre and he laid his hat on it before emptying his jacket pockets: a handkerchief, a railway timetable, his wallet, watch and the parcel. He then removed his shoes, lining them up side by side.

'Much appreciated, sir. Where was I?'

'Massaging the feminine organs.'

The warden fluttered his fingers in the air and leered. 'Lady Amelia objected at first, but after two or three sessions it seemed to be doing the trick and she lay still while Dr Lutheral applied the lubricant. That's when he got sloppy, didn't think it necessary to tie her hands to the bed frame.'

'Whatever happened?'

'She had a visit from her maid that morning and seemed in good spirits. The doctor was about to begin – I was holding the petticoats – when she sat up, seized a vial from beneath the mattress, opened it and tossed half the contents over Dr Lutheral's face and the rest where a lady shouldn't.'

'That doesn't sound like the behaviour of a lady.'

'Indeed not, sir, the doctor screamed in agony. Acid it was. Strong stuff too. I did well to get my fingers away. The police were called and the maid was arrested, but she swore she had no idea what her mistress intended.'

The warden searched the lining of Alfie's shoes. Satisfied there was nothing concealed, he handed them back.

'That's hard to believe,' Alfie said.

'Foreign girl,' the warden answered. 'French or Russian. What's in the parcel?'

'Toffee, the same as usual.'

'Of course, but I'll have to check.' The man pulled open the carefully wrapped package and poked a dirty finger round the sweets. He lifted one and popped it in his mouth. 'Pretty good toffee it is too,' he said through stuck teeth. He used his thumb to dislodge a slither of candy from his molar.

'If that will be all?' Alfie re-wrapped the parcel and tied the bow. He replaced his personal items in his pocket, put on his shoes, lifted his hat and walked to the door.

'There's a new doctor now. Dr Matthews. He'd like to see you after your visit. Nurse Horton will escort you to the room.'

Nurse Horton was a dour-faced woman with cropped hair and a stained apron. She took wide strides down the corridor and Alfie struggled to keep up. He paused for breath under the broken clock on the wall, halfway along the corridor. The clock ticked, but the hands forever jerked on their spots at five minutes to two. He was tempted to fix it, but everything else in the asylum was broken, why should the clock be different? The nurse had reached the room, unlocked the door and was standing with her hand on the handle. Alfie hurried to catch up, puffing for breath.

'If you could be finished before two,' Nurse Horton said. 'The patients have their physical exercise in the yard then. We don't like their routines being upset.'

'Of course.'

The nurse opened the door and Alfie entered the dimly lit room. There was an unmade bed at the far end, with a plain nightshirt strewn across it. A nursery bookcase was against the wall at his side, holding a few tattered volumes of children's books. Dotty was sitting on a chair by the window, looking out. He sat on the chair opposite her, but didn't speak. Her hair was brushed back and plaited. She wore a navy hospital dress with a shawl over her shoulders. Alfie was relieved there was no need for the straight jacket.

'I'm glad you are here,' Dotty said, not turning to look at him. 'I've been so lonely.'

'I come as often as I can, you know that,' Alfie said.

'I wish you could stay here with me.'

Alfie ignored her plea. 'What has happened to your hands?' he asked. There were red weals across her knuckles. She tried to hide them, but he took hold of her arm.

'It's nothing,' she answered. 'The warden hit me because I bit his hand.'

'You bit the warden's hand?'

She turned to face him. Instinctively, he looked away. He had tried, but he could never bring himself to look at her face. He reminded himself the blemish was merely a birthmark, but that didn't improve matters. A knot of over-ripe flesh bulged from beneath her left ear and swarmed over her cheek and nose, distorting her upper lip, until it covered her right eye. Perhaps if it wasn't for the bristles of hairs growing from the lesion, he could at least glance at it.

'He put his hand beneath my blouse. Surely that isn't right?' she said.

'The warden assists the doctor in his examinations. He was checking your chest, child. Promise me you won't misbehave like that again.'

Dotty turned her gaze back to peer out of the window. 'There's a little bird on the currant bush,' she said, jumping in her seat.

'Promise me you won't misbehave,' Alfie repeated.

'I think it's a chaffinch.'

'Promise.'

'Very well.'

'Say, "I promise".'

'I promise.'

'Good girl.' Alfie patted her on the knees. 'I've brought you a present.' He took the parcel of toffee from his pocket. In his haste he hadn't re-wrapped it properly and some of the sticky confection had fallen out into his pocket. Dotty reached round and took the parcel and spare lumps of toffee from him. She put one piece in her mouth then knelt down to hide the rest under her mattress.

'Thank you. You are very kind to me. What is happening in Perth? Tell me the news, please.'

'Business is good,' Alfie said. 'It is likely I will be asked to build a clock for the new hotel.'

'A giant clock?'

'An enormous clock,' Alfie said with a smile.

'A ginormous clock,' she laughed. 'I wish I could help you make it. When can I come home?'

'This is your home, Dotty,' Alfie said.

'Why can't I return to Perth?'

'Don't whine, woman. I've told you why.' Alfie stood up. His voice was hard. 'I have to go now. It's time for your exercise and I have to see Dr Matthews.'

'Please stay. I didn't mean to upset you.' She reached for his jacket, but he pushed her away. Feeling guilty, he looked for something to say.

'Make your bed girl, it's a disgrace.'

She didn't seem to hear. 'Dr Matthews is kind,' she said. 'He has a handsome smile.'

'Don't be having thoughts about some young doctor,' Alfie warned.

'He listens, not like Dr Lutheral. I hate Lutheral. I wish he were dead.' She gasped and held her mouth. 'That is an evil thing to say.' She picked up the hem of her dress and lifted it above her face. Alfie watched in dismay as she jerked her feet in a grotesque dance and chanted a silly ditty. 'I wish he were dead, I shouldn't have said, I'll hide under the bed.'

Alfie closed his eyes. Every time there was a chance Dotty would be able to act as a young woman should, things like this happened. He opened them to see Dotty squatting on the floor. 'Get up,' he ordered.

Dotty began to laugh, a titter at first, growing into a hysterical snigger. Alfie banged on the door and Nurse Horton entered.

'You've upset her, sir,' the nurse said. 'I think you should leave.'

Alfie left as Nurse Horton took hold of Dotty and twisted her right arm behind her back. Walking along the corridor past rows of closed doors, he heard Dotty scream. His heart was racing and he took out his pocket watch. He had no need to check the time, but the feel of the metal casing and regularity of the movement settled him. As he walked farther along the corridor, the voices faded. He closed the watch and returned it to his pocket.

The doctor's office was on a lower floor, down damp, mould-smeared steps, hardly conducive to good health. Dr Lutheral's name plaque had been replaced by one advertising the qualifications of Dr John Matthews. Alfie knocked on the office door and entered before being called. Dr Matthews was writing at his desk and looked up. Dotty's description of the doctor, although accurate, had not prepared Alfie for a man barely older than Dotty herself. He had smooth cheeks, framed by dark sideburns and soft brown eyes, not what Alfie expected in a psychiatric doctor.

Dr Matthews got to his feet and offered Alfie his hand. He had a weak handshake.

'The warden told me about Dr Lutheral,' Alfie said.

'Ah, a bad business.' The doctor spoke with a refined Edinburgh accent.

'It's an ill wind that blows nobody any good,' Alfie countered. 'Early promotion for you.'

'I don't see it that way, however, I asked to see you to talk about Dorothy.' The doctor sat down and gestured to Alfie to take the seat in front of him. Alfie remained standing, but he put his hat on the desk. 'I'm afraid she has suffered two fits since your last visit.'

'Her condition continues to deteriorate,' Alfie said.

'Your last visit was three months ago. Dorothy has undergone a minor setback, but I see signs that lead me to believe she could respond to different treatment. With your permission, I plan, along with a high fat diet and oily fish, to introduce potassium bromide to her medicine. You need have no concerns about it. The regime is perfectly safe and has been used for over twenty years in similar establishments.'

'Dr Lutheral didn't feel there was a need for it. You said, with my permission? What if I refuse? Dotty doesn't need her hopes raised by wonder cures, only to be crushed when your fancy pills prove to be as useless as the previous ones.'

'Dorothy is a young woman. She deserves to be given a chance to lead a normal life.'

'A normal life,' Alfie snorted. 'Even if you could stop the fits with your diet and medicine, how can she lead a normal life with that monstrosity covering her face? It is an abomination.'

'I believe, with modern surgical techniques…'

'No, I refuse. The girl has suffered enough without having her face cut apart in the name of medical science.' Alfie picked up his hat. Dr Matthews stood up and moved to open the door.

'I can understand your concern, Mr Peters,' the doctor said, 'but I have spoken to Dorothy and I believe it is her wish to try. Shouldn't it be your wish also? After all, we are talking about your wife.'

Chapter 2

On the coach back to the ferry, squashed between one of Her Majesty's infantrymen and a pipe smoking schoolmaster, Alfie had time to reflect on the peculiarities that led to the preposterous position he and Dotty were in. He should have joined his father in the tannery, but he had no interest in leather. The smell was repulsive and his father's hands were worn rough before he reached thirty. It may not have been the reason his mother refused to let him touch her, but it was the one she gave. Clocks, on the other hand, fascinated Alfie and after cajoling his parents he was apprenticed to Dotty's father at the age of twelve. Charlie was a patient teacher and, combined with his own curiosity, he developed a flair for clock making.

'You need to have clockmakers' fingers.'

He often heard Charlie's voice in his head. Without such heavenly digits, the highest endeavour would prove groundless. Fortunately, Alfie had them. He served his master without complaint, from apprentice to journeyman then a full member of the guild and expected to inherit the business once Charlie was in his grave. By all accounts this would have happened, if Charlie hadn't taken it on himself to acquire a wife late in life and talk of having sons. This, thankfully, was not to be. His wife died of a fever four days after giving birth. The baby was a girl. She was weak and deformed, but a wet nurse was found, and she survived to become a particularly ugly child. A fleshy birth defect consumed half her face.

Alfie had known Dotty since she was a cocooned squidge of pink in Charlie's arms. Her father indulged her, allowing her into the workshop when she was teased by the children in the streets. Her features were no less repulsive to Alfie than to the city urchins, and he too turned his head away from her. He did admit she had beautiful hands. Delicate hands, with skin as smooth as planed chestnut and slim, candlestick fingers. Clockmakers' hands.

She proved to be a natural and by the age of fifteen was equal to her father, whose eyesight was failing and whose fingers were stiffened with arthritis. It seemed inevitable that Charlie would bequeath the business to his daughter. Alfie had to come up with a plan. He had a long term sweetheart, Nancy, but he believed her to be unfaithful, the evidence being a young daughter. He proposed to Dotty on her sixteenth birthday and they were married three months later.

The marriage was never consummated and Alfie intended a swift divorce once Charlie was gone, but the old clockmaker was no fool, as was made plain when his will was read. Charlie did indeed leave his workshop and business to Alfie, but only on the condition he remained married to Dotty until one of them died. Since he was twenty seven years Dotty's senior, and despite her poor start she had grown into a strapping lass, it was unlikely she would precede him to the grave. If he divorced Dotty, the business would transfer to her.

While Charlie was creaking along, they lived in a rented room at the edge of the town, away from prying eyes. It wasn't convenient and when Charlie was gone they moved into the larger apartment above the shop. Being near the workshop had a disadvantage. Dotty wished to resume her work of making pocket watches and artisan pens for prosperous clients. Alfie could not tolerate ugliness around him while he restored intricate clock mechanisms. Apart from his own sensitivities, clients would be nauseated by such a face. He confined Dotty to the flat and soon afterwards the fits started.

Minor incidents at first, but after the accident with the lamp that almost annihilated the business, he couldn't leave her unattended. Dr Lutheral's private clinic was the answer. Alfie had hoped it wouldn't be for long, as the fees weren't inconsiderable. Despite Dr Matthews' optimism, he could tell Dotty's mind was deteriorating, but in keeping with her father, she was proving to have a strong constitution.

Two fits since his last visit. However long it might have been, Dr Matthews couldn't deny two seizures were two more than normal people had.

The coach jolted to a halt and Alfie was brought back to the present. His stomach rumbled and he received a dour look from the woman opposite, who clearly managed to keep regular meal times. He had foregone breakfast in anticipation of the river crossing, but it was now past time for lunch. There was an inn near the ferry pier that served a medley of whelks, mussels and scallops that the chef called his 'seafood extravaganza.' A case of overzealous advertising, but it was reasonably priced, and edible if covered in oil and downed with the local ale. He waited until the infantryman, the schoolmaster and the miserable spinstress got out of the coach before stepping down. The inn was emptying and he selected a table in the corner. The serving girl was a comely lass, if a little stroppy. She made a face when he pinched her bottom and he could see her whispering to the innkeeper.

The man came over. 'Everything all right, sir?'

'Acceptable,' Alfie answered. The man's pock-marked face put him off his food.

'Lizzie is new. My sister's girl.'

Alfie sensed a warning in the words, not to mess with family. He left the remaining mussels swimming in oil, but finished his ale before leaving.

The ferry was busy and he had no wish for conversation in the lounge, so despite the breeze he remained on deck, looking towards the islands in the estuary and the building work on the bridge.

'Sure is a wonderful sight, sir. That is some piece of engineering. There is no limit to what man can do - with God's help, of course.'

The words caught in the wind. Alfie turned to see a young man with a tweed jacket and deerstalker hat. He was trying to light a pipe, but his match wouldn't stay lit.

'You have to face away from the wind,' Alfie advised.

The man turned away until his pipe was lit. 'Thank you. That did the trick.'

'American?' Alfie asked.

The man sucked on his pipe before answering, 'New York.'

'Then you must be familiar with the New York and Brooklyn Bridge, an outstanding construction by all accounts, with or without the Almighty's assistance. I heard that elephants were led over it to prove its strength,' Alfie said, chuckling at his pun.

'Indeed, by Mr Barnum himself, although not an entire herd.'

Alfie didn't ask who Mr. Barnum was. 'What brings you to Scotland?'

'I would love to say I have always wanted to visit your beautiful country, but on this occasion it is business,' the man answered. 'The name's Templeman. Giles Ichabod Templeman the third.'

Alfie got the impression he was meant to recognise the name. His interest in the building of the bridge may have been a clue. 'Are you an engineer?' he asked, pointing at the metal pillars springing out from the river bank.

'I would like to think I am, of sorts,' Templeman replied. 'I design magnificent constructions.'

'An architect, and you are over here on business, you say?'

Templeman tapped the side of his nose with the stem of his pipe. 'I can't talk about it. Things are under wraps. What about you? Whom do I have the pleasure of addressing?'

'Peters,' Alfie replied. 'Alfie Peters.' It was tempting to add "the first", but he resisted. 'From Perth.'

'Ah, Mr. Peters,' Giles wagged his right index finger as if he was placing the name. 'I am heading for Perth myself. Perhaps we could share a railway carriage.'

'I'm afraid I'm not returning directly to Perth,' Alfie said. 'I have business elsewhere.'

'Pity.' Giles balanced his pipe on the top of the railing and removed a silver case from his inside pocket. He opened it and offered Alfie a card. 'I'll be staying at the West Tay Hotel. Look me up.'

'The West Tay?' This was too much of a coincidence. 'Do you know the owners, Mr Squires and Mr. Farquhar?'

'I haven't met them, but I have corresponded with Adam and Walker.'

'Adam Farquhar and Walker Squires, aye - and you said your name is Templeman?'

'You've got it.'

The boat whistle informed them the ferry had docked and the wagons, carriages and passengers should disembark. Alfie accepted the man's card.

'I shall certainly "look you up". Good day sir.' He raised his hat and walked towards the landing ramp. He felt the young American's eyes were on him, but he didn't look round.

He watched from a distance as Templeman took a seat in a first class carriage then boarded the train further down, in second class. Adam Farquhar had got his way. Templeman was the man to make the clock casing. He couldn't be going to Perth for any other reason. He was younger than Alfie imagined, but just as American.

Sharing a carriage for over an hour would have been testing, but Alfie hadn't lied. He had business in one of the villages before returning to Winnie. There would be opportunities over the coming weeks to discuss the West Tay commission. He liked time to measure a man's calibre, and he had a feeling Templeman would take some weighing up.

As the train slowed to approach his station he scanned the platform to see if Nancy was there to meet the train. He spotted her on a chair with her pretty pink hat on. She had only just departed from wearing her widow's weeds although it had been five years since her no-good husband passed away. She rose and ran alongside the train to arrive at his carriage door as the train stopped. She had her arms around his neck before he stepped down.

'Are you here for long?' she asked as they made their way to her house, arm-in-arm. 'Can you stay the night?'

'I'm afraid not. I have a business dinner in Perth. It's to do with the new West Tay Hotel.'

'I heard about the hotel from Mrs. Wilson,' Nancy interrupted. It was a habit he deplored, but it saved him from expanding on his lie. 'They say it has a hundred and fifty bedrooms, each with its own bathroom and balcony. There is a ballroom, a conservatory, three restaurants and a grand hall with marble pillars and palm trees.'

'The only thing it doesn't have is a magnificent clock to catch the eye,' Alfie said.

'A clock?' Nancy was slow to understand, but when she did she gasped and held her hand over her mouth. 'You are building the clock for the West Tay Hotel?'

'It's hush-hush. I can't speak about it yet. How is little Teddy?'

'A typical boy, he is always in trouble.'

'Not with the law?' Alfie stopped. Nancy kept walking. They were still arm-in-arm and she swung back towards him and banged against his chest.

'He's four years old,' she said when she got her breath back.

'I'll have a word with him,' Alfie said.

'He needs his father at home.'

'Shh, not so loud.' Alfie looked round to make sure no-one had heard. The nosier in the village had already done their sums over the timing of Teddy's birth and her husband's death. 'I come as often as I can. You know the problem. I am married to Dorothy, whether she is in her right mind or not.'

'I know. How is Dotty? Potty as usual?'

'She enjoyed the toffee you made.'

'I'm glad o' that. It wasn't too sweet for her? I had to add extra treacle.'

'She has a sweet tooth,' Alfie said. He paused for a second and sobered his voice. 'She's had two fits since my last visit.'

'It seems to be taking so long. George died three months after the fits began.'

'Your husband's liver was already soaked in booze.'

'When Dotty is gone, we will marry, like you promised me before you had to marry her?'

'After a suitable period of mourning.'

'We wouldn't want tongues to wag.' Nancy gave him a kiss on the cheek and released her arm from his. They had reached her end cottage and a grubby lad ran up, tripping as he reached them. He grabbed Alfie's trousers to stop himself falling. A few paces behind were two older boys. They pulled up when they saw Alfie and Nancy. Teddy hid behind his mother.

'Get away, you're terrifying Ted.' Nancy waved her hands at the boys.

'He stole our apples,' one of the older boys shouted.

'We'll tell the policeman,' his friend said.

'Constable Thompson won't believe a lie from you, James Neil,' Nancy called back.

'He will so, he's my mum's cousin.'

Alfie could see a slither of apple skin lodged between Ted's teeth when he grinned. He reached in his pocket for a couple of pennies. 'Here.' He tossed them towards the boys. 'Now get going.'

The boys picked up the coins and headed off.

'You shouldn't have given them anything,' Nancy said. 'You are too soft hearted.'

'Maybe Teddy would like to tell us where he got the apple that is stuck in his teeth.' Alfie stared at the boy. Teddy puckered his lips, looked at his mother and began to cry.

'My baby.' Nancy picked him up in her arms. She frowned at Alfie.

'Open the door,' Alfie said. 'It's freezing out here.'

Nancy fished in her pocket for the key, balancing Teddy on her opposite arm. The boy took it from her, but was unable to turn the lock. Alfie grabbed the key from him.

'I want to do it,' Teddy yelled.

'Let him,' Nancy said.

Alfie glared at the boy, but handed him the key. 'I don't have all day,' he mumbled.

Teddy stuck the key in the lock and with Nancy's help he unlocked the door. Nancy entered first and Alfie followed.

'I opened the door, dad.' Teddy shoved his hand in Alfie's face.

'Good for you,' Alfie strode past Nancy towards the sitting room.

Teddy was a disappointment. He had his mother's fair skin, beneath the dirt, but he also had her chubby milkmaid's fingers. Even at four he was proving to be deceitful and not altogether bright. There was little chance of him taking over the business.

'What are you gaping at? I can see you,' he called towards the young girl peeking at him from behind the kitchen door. She stepped out and stood in front of the fireplace, holding onto the folds of her skirt.

'Maggie, I told you Mr. Peters was coming,' Nancy said. She had put Teddy down and removed her coat.

'Why do you call him Mr. Peters? He's my da', isn't he?' Maggie said.

Alfie snorted. 'I'm no father of yours. You were abandoned as soon as your father realised what a snide little cur you are. Your mother was lucky to find someone, with you clinging to her petticoat. I have often thought that drunkard must actually have been your father, or he wouldn't have taken you on.'

Maggie's eyes watered, but she stood her ground.

'Don't stand there like a cold pudding. Alfie's had a long journey. Fetch him a beaker of ale while I wash Teddy and ready him for bed,' Nancy instructed. She breezed out of the room.

Maggie didn't move. Alfie looked her up and down. At fifteen, she was developing into a woman, ready to tempt the village lads into sinning. She had fair hair, like her mother, and pert breasts announcing themselves beneath her blouse. He took a step towards her and she shuffled away.

'It is time you started earning your keep,' he said.

'I want to stay at school. I want to be a doctor.' She stuck out her chin. Alfie slapped the back of his hand across it.

'You, a doctor. Since when have women been doctors?'

'Times are changing. There is a school in London, and Edinburgh allows women into medical classes. It won't be long before there are female doctors all over Scotland.'

'You are from the gutter, girl. More talk of schooling and that is where you will return.'

'You are my father and you know it, no matter what you say,'

Maggie persisted. 'You don't like me because I'm not a boy like Ted.'

Alfie was about to slap her again, but he heard Nancy approach and stepped back. He fiddled with the position of an ornamental figure on the mantelpiece as Nancy entered.

'I've put Ted to bed. He's such a sweet child.' She looked round for the ale jug and beakers. 'Haven't you brought the ale yet, Maggie?'

'Your daughter would do better if she had a domestic position and formal training in how to serve,' Alfie answered before Maggie could speak. 'I know a family in Edinburgh, a clockmaker, his wife and five children, who are advertising for a maid. I shall speak with them on Maggie's behalf and arrange an interview.'

'You would do that? Isn't that wonderful, Maggie?' Nancy put an arm around her daughter. Maggie couldn't hold her tears any longer. She pulled away from her mother and dashed from the room.

'Ungrateful wretch,' Alfie said.

'She'll come round. Edinburgh is so far away and she'll miss Teddy,' Nancy said. 'They are close. She's a good girl.'

'Enough talk about Maggie. I don't have time for chitter chat.'

His voice softened as he reached for Nancy's hand. She giggled and unbuttoned the top of her blouse.

'I feel like a girl myself, when you are here.'

****

It was dark by the time Alfie waved goodbye to Nancy. She came with him to the railway station, although he told her not to. He promised to visit again soon.

'Don't leave it so long next time.'

Nancy held his hand as he leaned out of the train. The guard blew his whistle, but Nancy didn't let go.

'The train is leaving, miss,' the guard said. Alfie wriggled free and raised the window, narrowly avoiding amputating Nancy's fingers. He made a hurried retreat to the compartment.

It was raining when he stepped out of the station in Perth. He considered calling a cab, but he had given Nancy what was left of his money. His trouser legs were soaking by the time he reached his shop. There was a light on and the door was unlocked. Winnie was waiting for him.

'What time do you call this?'

She pounced before he had taken off his hat and returned it to the stand. He stretched out a hand to demonstrate his wares. 'We have a room full of clocks, all at the exact time, if you need to know.'

'Where have you been? The shop has been busy straight from opening and there have been gentlemen looking for you.'

Alfie walked towards her without answering.

'There's money missing from the till, too. Should I call the constable?'

He put his arms around her waist and drew her towards him. She didn't resist. He could smell honey on her breath. 'It is my money. I took it,' he answered. 'I had to go to Edinburgh.'

'You should have left me a note,' Winnie pouted.

'Don't do that,' Alfie said. 'It makes you look ugly.'

He released his hands and pushed her aside. She knocked against one of the shelves and rubbed at her bruised wrist.

'I'm sorry, dear. Don't be cross with me,' she whined.

'You are the bad-tempered one,' Alfie accused. 'I haven't heard a kind word since I got in. I'm going to bed.'

Winnie moved to bar his way to the upstairs apartment. She twirled her fingers round the bottom of her hair in the teasing manner he couldn't resist.

'I'll find someone to help out in the shop, if you find it too taxing,' he allowed. 'You don't want to stress yourself in your condition.' He forced his lips into a smile and patted Winnie's expanding stomach. 'I think we'll call the baby Freddie.'

'It may be a girl,' Winnie said. 'Sylvia is a nice name for a girl.'

Alfie grunted and moved his hand away. 'Did you sell any clocks while I was out?'

'Yes, a pocket watch and two pens. Mrs Finley left a carriage clock to be mended. I told her it would be ready by Friday.'

'Why did you say that? I may not have time this week,' Alfie snapped.

'Then you should tell me what you are doing,' Winnie replied. 'I never know when you are coming or going. What were you doing in Edinburgh?'

'That is none of your business.'

'I'm your wife, Alfie. I'll soon be the mother of your child. Don't I have a right to know where you are?'

Alfie huffed. He ran his tongue round the inside of his mouth. There was a segment of shellfish lodged at the back of his palate. He tried to shift it and was reminded of the hospital warden and his toffee. 'If you must know, I was in Edinburgh paying my respects to Dorothy. It has been three years since she died.'

'Oh, I'm sorry,' Winnie moved to take his hand. 'You were

always thoughtful towards her, but I don't see why she couldn't have been buried here in Perth.'

'She died in Edinburgh. There were regulations regarding moving the body, not to mention the cost. It didn't bear thinking about.'

'Do you miss her?' Winnie asked.

'What sort of stupid question is that, woman?' Alfie spoke harshly and he could see Winnie was upset by his tone. He put his hand out to stroke her cheeks and softened his voice. 'I have you now, don't I? Dotty was a child, but you are a woman.'

'I've made you supper,' Winnie smiled. 'Periwinkles and scallops fresh from the market.'

Alfie felt his stomach twist, but he didn't complain. 'You go upstairs. I'll check a few things here and lock up,' he said.

'When can we buy our own house, away from the shop?' Winnie asked. 'We'll need more space when the baby is born. We could have servants.'

'A cook would be nice,' Alfie muttered.

'What was that?'

'I said you can start looking whenever you like.'

'Really?' Winnie jumped with excitement and clapped her hands.

'Those gentlemen who were looking for me - I'm expecting them to offer me a lucrative commission.'

'They want you to make them a watch?'

'A clock, my dear. The like of which has not been seen before. It is to adorn the entrance of their new hotel.'

'Ooh.' She grabbed hold of his hands and tried to make him dance with her.

'Careful,' he warned as she avoided knocking against a table of expensive pens by less than an inch.

'You'll need a new suit and I can wear a silk dress and we'll parade the streets on Sundays. People will look at us and doff their hats and say, "he's the gentleman who made the amazing clock in the hotel".'

'An American artist is designing the casing. It will be his name people remember, so there will be no parading, but it will bring in a substantial sum.'

'And commissions from other hotels.' Winnie was getting beyond herself.

'I think you should lie down, dear,' Alfie said. 'I'll join you upstairs in a bit.'

He edged Winnie towards the door at the back of the shop and opened it for her, watching as she made her way up the stairs. She turned to blow him kisses, as if she were a drunken dock girl. Closing the door behind her, he wondered if her moods would swing for the duration of her pregnancy. If she gave him a son eager to learn his clock making skills and make him proud, then it was worth the inconvenience. If by a disaster of fate she produced a baby girl... there were childless couples in Edinburgh who would take the brat off his hands. If Winnie kicked up a fuss, there were empty rooms in Lutheral's asylum, just waiting for women with imbalanced minds.

Chapter 3

Alfie stood behind the counter of his shop tapping his fingers to the rhythm of The Piper of Dundee. There was no point starting anything until after the post arrived. A week had gone by since his trip to Edinburgh and there had been no news from Farquhar or Squires. Surely a letter would arrive that morning. He saw the postman march past the door, without entering. There was always the afternoon post, but he was losing faith, unlike Winnie who had lost no time in seeking out an agent to find a suitable house. She had arranged to visit several properties, all well above his budget.

'The baby is due in February. I want us to be settled in our new home by then,' she told him.

'What do women know about buying property? These matters shouldn't be rushed,' Alfie reminded her. 'I shall require the proper surveys and structural reports. These procedures take time, as they should.'

Winnie wasn't convinced by his excuses. Her list of potential properties was growing. Much to his chagrin, Alfie realised it would be necessary for him to make the first move in approaching the hotel owners. He wouldn't go directly to them, though. Walker Squires and his family were regular church goers. Alfie had no time for hypocritical humility, but a casual encounter would give him an opportunity to sound out their plans for the hotel clock. Winnie was pleased at the chance to wear her best dress and coat.

'Can't you fasten it up? People will notice.' He nodded towards Winnie's expanded abdomen.

'And why shouldn't they? There is nothing improper about a married couple expecting a child,' Winnie countered.

'There is no need to flaunt it in public.'

'I can't fasten it any farther, not unless you want your son or daughter to have a flat head.'

'Here, wear this shawl.'

Winnie huffed, but she took the shawl and arranged it round her shoulders and over her midriff. It was a short walk to church, but Alfie escorted Winnie the long way round, passing the Squires' town house. They circled the block three times, admiring the view of the river until the Squires emerged. Walker Squires and his wife strode out first, with their arms linked. Their two daughters followed behind. Alfie linked arms with Winnie and strolled towards the party.

'Who is that?' Winnie asked, gesturing towards a young man in the company of the younger daughter.

'Don't point.' Alfie pushed her hand down. He screwed his eyes to see the man. It was the American, Giles Templeman. He was wearing a morning suit, rather than tweed, and had swapped the deerstalker for a top hat.

'Ah, Mr Peters, and Mrs Peters.' Squires spotted them and stopped. 'I didn't expect to see you here.'

'Good morning to you. My wife and I are heading to church,' Alfie answered.

'Indeed? I didn't realise you were a religious man.'

'I have lapsed somewhat in my faith, but Winifred is keen to have me brought back into the fold.'

'In time for the Christening,' he heard the Squires' elder daughter whisper over-loudly to her sister.

Winnie was about to say something, but Alfie squeezed her fingers and she smiled awkwardly instead.

'Splendid,' Walker Squires said. 'You must join us in our pew. You won't have met Mr Templeman, he hails from New York.'

At the mention of his name, Templeman looked up. 'Why, I believe I have met this gentleman,' Templeman said. He clicked his fingers. 'But Lord knows where.'

Alfie gave him a nod in recognition, but didn't remind him of their meeting on the ferry.

'Mr Peters is a clockmaker. The best the city has to offer,'

Squires said. 'You may get to know him very well in the next few months,'

'I see, you've put in a bid to make the workings for the clock, have you?' Templeman asked.

'No,' Alfie replied, more brusquely than he intended.

Templeman looked at Squires, who gave an embarrassed laugh. He released his wife's arm and strode ahead, leaving Templeman with the ladies. He gestured for Alfie to do the same.

'You will have heard of our intention to have a clock built for the reception hall of the West Tay?'

'I saw something in the newspaper,' Alfie agreed.

'Giles has been chosen to make the casing.'

'We have good clock designers in Scotland.' Alfie felt he should champion his countrymen although he was glad Squires didn't ask for specific names.

'He was Adam Farquhar's choice,' Squires admitted. 'He seems to know what he's about.'

It hadn't taken Templeman long to wrangle his way into the Squires' household. It wouldn't be long before he was in one of his daughters' beds, Alfie mused.

'And you are looking for bids from clockmakers to devise the workings. I wish you well in your enterprise,' Alfie said.

'You will be putting in a bid?' Squires sounded concerned. 'The process is purely a formality…'

'I can't say that I will, no,' Alfie said. 'I have sufficient work to keep me out of mischief until well after Easter.'

'I appreciate you are a busy man, but Mr Farquhar and I are busy too. We wrote you a letter. When we didn't hear back, we took time from our schedules to visit your workshop. You weren't at home and your wife could not say when you would return. Farquhar feels snubbed by your lack of enthusiasm and, I may say, manners.'

'Your letter said nothing about a proposed commission, merely a matter of mutual advantage, and indeed, it is on my desk to be answered. Mr Farquhar must learn to stand in line, like everyone else. We are all Jock Thompson's bairns, as the kirk minister will preach. No man is better than another.'

'Of course, that is why, should you care to send us an official proposal, it will be looked on most favourably. You have my word on that, Mr Peters.'

Alfie smiled and re-joined Winnie, taking her arm. They walked behind the Squires to the church in a silent procession, broken only by the stifled giggles of Miss Emily. On two occasions Templeman looked round to stare at Alfie, trying to place him. The church bells were ringing as they arrived. The building was as dusty as Alfie remembered and the sermon as stale. He didn't indulge in communal hymn singing and during the prayers he took the opportunity to scrutinise his fellow worshippers, with their heads bowed.

Giles Templeman was clearly not an overly devout man. During the prayers he twiddled with the fingers of Squires' younger daughter, trying to make her laugh. The girl wasn't as plain as he had pictured her, but she did have hair suited for a scarecrow and too many freckles.

After church he and Winnie strolled in the park. He ignored her jabbering as he considered what Squires had said. If he put in a bid, he had Squires' word that he would be chosen, but it irked him that he should have to ask. Wasn't he the best craftsman in the county? They wouldn't find a better man in Edinburgh or Glasgow. Part of him felt he should leave them to struggle, employ a second-rate fellow who would produce a second-rate clock to mock the reputation of their hotel. Another part was tempted by the money and prestige involved and a third part was horrified at the thought of a less than perfect clock being displayed in a public position in his town.

'Penny for them,' Winnie nudged him from his thoughts.

'They're worth more than that, woman,' he answered, but he kept his voice light-hearted.

'You didn't answer my question,' Winnie said. 'I asked if you wanted to view the house near the river. It has two bedrooms and a reception room, with basement space for three servants.'

'Two rooms, a cupboard and a flooded cellar, more like. Besides, we could never afford three servants,' Alfie grumbled. Winnie made a face. 'Very well, we can take a look tomorrow.'

'Monday, oh but that is impossible,' Winnie said. 'I've been invited to take tea with Mrs Squires and her daughters.'

'Have you, now? Going up in the world.'

'We were talking about France and Mrs Squires squeaked like a mouse when I told her that I can speak French. She is keen to have someone she and her daughters can practise their language skills with,' Winnie answered.

'I didn't know you spoke French,' Alfie remarked.

'There you see, you learn something about me every day.'

'I can't see how speaking French helps you in Perth. No matter, we can view the house on Tuesday, when I've finished with Mrs. Finley's carriage clock.'

Winnie leaned over and gave him a kiss on the cheek. He shooed her off.

'Not in public, woman.'

After dinner that evening Alfie set about composing a suitable correspondence to send to the hotel owners. He outlined his capabilities over several pages, reminding Farquhar that he had been presented with a civic medal for his services to clock-making in the city, by no less than the hotel magnate's father, William Farquhar. He let the letter sit overnight, but was satisfied with it in the morning and had it sent off before breakfast.

Winnie made no mention of his letter having arrived when she came home from speaking French with the Squires' ladies, but that evening he received a reply on official hotel writing paper. It requested him to attend a meeting with Messrs Farquhar, Squires and Templeman in the hotel on Friday morning.

"Requested" he noted, not "invited".

No doubt Farquhar would try to wrangle his services on the cheap, but he had cards to play. He would give a shilling to know how much Templeman was being paid for his pie-in-the-sky design.

'You'll never guess who was at the Squires' house this afternoon,' Winnie said as they sat together in the evening. Winnie was making a shawl for the baby while Alfie smoked a pipe and read the local newspaper. 'Well?'

'You said I would never guess,' Alfie objected.

'You could at least have a shot.' Winnie put down her needlework. 'It was Mr Templeman, the American gentleman. He does have some tall stories to tell.'

'In French?'

'In English, silly, or as near to English as a gentleman from across the ocean can manage,' Winnie giggled. 'You know, I think he has taken a fancy to young Emily Squires.'

'I knew Americans had no taste.'

'Granted, she is plain, but she has a pleasant manner and plays the piano beautifully.'

'What more could a man ask for - except a dowry?'

'Don't be naughty, Alfie. Ouch,' Winnie held her abdomen and smiled. 'The baby is kicking.'

'Isn't it a little early for that?'

'What do you know about babies?' Winnie laughed.

'I know they are expensive, messy and disrupt the household. That's not to mention the bawling.'

'The house we're viewing tomorrow has an attic room. We could convert it into a nursery, away from the living room,' Winnie said. 'Ooh, I can't wait to show you.'

'Sounds like you've already decided we're buying it,' Alfie said.

'Wait until you see it. You will love it as much as I do.'

'I doubt that, but we'll see.'

The house was in a quiet neighbourhood, but still within walking distance of his workshop. Winnie insisted on linking arms, to lead him to it. Alfie stopped in front of the property to look at the stretch of lawn, bounded by a well-trimmed hedge.

'You didn't say it had a garden. What am I supposed to do with that?'

'We can hire a gardener to tend it. We could grow roses.'

'More expense,' Alfie mumbled.

'Or potatoes, I suppose. We could eat those.'

'You want me to be a farmer?'

'It will be good for Freddie, or Sylvia, to get out the house and have somewhere safe to play.'

'I'm not paying a gardener to tend a lawn for it to be churned up by a child playing,' Alfie said.

Winnie unlocked their arms and took him by the hand to lead him up the cobbled path to the house. She knocked on the door and it was opened by an older lady, dressed in widow's black.

'How nice to see you again, Mrs Peters. This must be Mr Peters.' The lady hesitated.

He was old enough to be Winnie's father, a fact that didn't escape the widow, but Alfie decided against making a comment. He greeted the woman and stepped in. The house was warm and despite his preconceived ideas, once inside, Alfie was forced to admit that it pleased him. There was an elegant stone fire surround in the lounge and a window overlooked trees at the back.

'Stephen always did admire the view,' the woman said. 'Would you like a cup of tea?'

Alfie accepted in order to get the woman out of their way while they looked round.

'We could have a chair here, and your desk in the corner.' Winnie organised the room in her head.

'Let's see the bedrooms, before the widow comes back,' Alfie said.

He heard the owner rattling cups and saucers in the kitchen as he followed Winnie upstairs. The two bedrooms were both of a good size. The master bedroom was airy, with a view across the South Inch Park.

'Ah.'

'Is there a problem, dear? Is it your arthritis?' Winnie asked.

'No, I was thinking there is too much space.'

'When the baby arrives and we have a cook and a maid…'

'I won't have any excuse to put your mother off visiting,' Alfie said. Winnie pouted. 'I'm teasing you, dear. Now, I have to get back to work. I'm already behind schedule this week and it's only Tuesday.'

'You haven't seen the attic?'

Alfie glanced up the winding staircase. The banister showed signs of woodworm.

'Tea is ready,' the widow called.

'I'd forgotten about tea,' Alfie admitted.

They were forced to listen politely as the lady of the house recounted stories of life with her late husband. 'Our daughter is married and with Stephen gone the house is too large for me. I'm going to stay with my sister and her husband in Stirling.'

'Do you have servants?' Winnie asked.

'I have one girl, Rose. She doesn't have a family and is happy to come with me to Stirling.'

Alfie gulped down his tea, burning the back of his throat. It was worth the discomfort to escape before he had to listen to more tales.

'Did you like it?' Winnie asked as she cosied up to him on the walk home.

'It may suit. I'll consider it.'

Alfie thought about the house while he unscrewed watches and fiddled with broken cogs. It wasn't as large as Walker Squires' town house, and he had a country pile as well, but a house like that would show the people of Perth that he was going places. Servants too – he had forgotten to examine the basement, but presumably the girl Rose slept there with no complaints. It wasn't cheap though. If he were to make an offer, he would have to make sure he bargained for a good deal from Farquhar and Squires.

He rose early on Friday morning to prepare for the meeting at the hotel. Winnie had starched his collar and she tied his neckerchief for him.

'What are you doing, woman?'

'Spraying you with eau de Cologne. The gentlemen in the hotel won't appreciate it if you smell of oil from the workshop. I hope you've scrubbed the lead filings from your nails.'

'Stop fussing, Winnie.' Alfie examined the dark lines beneath his nails. 'I'm a clockmaker, not some Beau Brummell, dandy.'

'It does no harm to make a good impression.' Winnie brushed down his jacket.

'Away with you! What impression will it make if I'm late?'

He arrived at the hotel ten minutes before the scheduled

appointment. Giles Templeman was waiting in the reception hall, talking to the lady behind the desk. They were both laughing. Alfie walked up and the laughing stopped.

'Mr Peters. It sure is good to see you again.' Templeman offered his hand. He had a weak handshake, much like Dr Matthews.

'How does this compare to the grand hotels in New York?' Alfie asked.

'This place has class,' Templeman admitted. 'Real marble columns and gold chandeliers. Walker told me they brought in an artist from Milan to paint the ceiling stucco. The orange and lemon trees were shipped from Spain.'

'They won't thrive in our climate. More important that the beds are comfortable,' Alfie answered. He looked round the hall. There was a white, grand piano at the far end, surrounded by palms and an archway through to an orchestra platform. 'Where do they want the clock to go?' he asked.

'Over there, beside the fountain,' Templeman pointed.

Alfie sucked his bottom lip and shook his head. 'No good. Half of it will be hidden behind that pillar and it will be ignored by guests as they make for the stairs. The chimes will never be heard if the door to the dining room is open.'

'Gee, I hadn't thought about that,' Templeman said, 'You're right, I see now. Where would you put the clock?'

Alfie looked around. The hall was busy and it was important to keep the access to the stairs clear, in case of fire. 'There doesn't seem to be anywhere suitable...unless…'

'Yes?'

Alfie pointed.

'Where? You don't mean up there?' Templeman's laugh was in disbelief, but it changed to one of awe as he pictured the possibility. 'Suspend it from the ceiling?'

'If the beams can take it. There may need to be structural adaptations, but I'm not an architect.'

'You know, I have had a brilliant idea…'

'And what is that Giles, old boy?' Squires asked. He and his partner Adam Farquhar had emerged from Farquhar's office without being heard and were standing behind them.

'A clock in the shape of the city coat of arms,' Templeman said, turning to Walker Squires.

Adam Farquhar groaned. 'Not highly original, I was expecting something more avant-garde.'

'This won't be any old clock.' Templeman used his hands to demonstrate. 'Imagine the double-headed eagle hanging from the ceiling, bearing the coat of arms.'

'Hanging from the ceiling?' Farquhar repeated.

'It sounds magnificent, but will people be able to tell the time?' Squires asked.

'Of course,' Templeman put an arm on Squire's shoulder. 'What is more, the clock will open up to reveal mechanical figures, portraying scenes from local industries.'

Alfie looked at Farquhar, who rolled his eyes heavenward.

'Not only will the clock open on the hour, but panels will open at every quarter,' Templeman expanded. Farquhar cocked his head to the side. 'At the first quarter we will show linen workers, on the half hour leather workers and at the three quarters the whisky industry will be represented. We can have a bit of fun with a drunken beggar or children playing tricks.' Farquhar puckered his lips then nodded, picturing the hotel guests watching on in admiration. 'On the hour, the whole clock will come alive with noise and light and...and…'

'Smells?' Alfie suggested.

'This will all fit into your casing?' Farquhar asked.

'No problem, sir.'

It was Alfie's turn to roll his eyes.

Farquhar turned to Alfie. 'Will you be able to make it work?'

55

'I'm a clockmaker, not a toymaker,' Alfie said.

'In that case, I have a proposal from a firm on John Street…'

'They could barely mend a cuckoo clock,' Alfie snorted.

'It is a clock we're commissioning. I'm sure Mr Peters will be able to devise the mechanisms. ' Squires looked round, hoping to reassure all parties.

'We can work on it,' Templeman drawled. 'It was Alfie's idea to put the clock up there.'

Farquhar eyed Alfie, who was frowning at Templeman over the familiar use of his first name. 'I think we should retire to the office to discuss matters,' Farquhar said.

The negotiations took longer than Alfie hoped. Farquhar drove a hard bargain, but by the end he had a signed contract. All he needed was an advance to secure a deposit on the house.

'I shall require funds to order new equipment before I can begin,' he asserted.

'Out of the question.' Farquhar didn't look up from writing his notes. 'Application for funding has to go through official hotel channels. It will take weeks to get approval.'

'If there is no rush to start work on your clock, I shall concentrate on my established business, in the meantime.' Alfie stood his ground. He was sure Templeman would get whatever he

56

needed for his gold casing and mechanical dolls. They seemed to have reached an impasse until Squires came up with a solution.

'I shall pay the advance from my own pocket and claim it back on hotel expenses in due course.' He gave a smile.

'Very well,' Farquhar agreed. 'We shall expect progress reports every fortnight.'

They shook hands on the agreement and Farquhar opened the office door for them to shuffle out with doffed caps. Walker Squires followed Alfie and Templeman into the hall.

'How about a spot of lunch?' Templeman said, eyeing the dining room which was beginning to fill with guests.

"I'm afraid I have work to attend to,' Alfie said.

'Another time,' Squires answered.

Alfie watched as Squires and Templeman made their way to the restaurant. The smells wafting from the plates were tempting. He could taste the prime beef and dumplings, but clocks did not mend themselves and he had customers waiting. He turned to the hotel exit.

'Why, if it isnae ma old da'. Whit are you daein' here?' A coarse voice behind him asked.

Alfie turned and his face drained. Maggie was standing beside him, dressed in a hotel maid's uniform. He glanced back to make sure Squires and Templeman had gone in to dine and that no-one was watching them. He fluttered his hand to indicate she should be quiet.

'Ashamed of me, are you?' Maggie asked. 'You did tell ma I should go into service. She thocht Edinburgh was too far away and she had mind o' you spouting aboot this fancy new hotel. Hotels are aye looking for servants. Voila - that's French. I gave your name as a reference. It disnae look like anyone bothered following it up.'

'If you don't leave immediately I shall tell the proprietors you are here under false pretences.'

'And I'll tell them you're my father.'

'They won't believe you.'

'Doesn't matter. If you send me home, what will mum say? She wants me here to keep an eye on you.'

'You cheeky hussy. I shall have words with your mother about this. In the meantime, you'd better stay out of my way.'

'Or else what?'

'Or else you will live to regret it.'

Chapter 4

The purchase of the house went through without ado. Winnie kept herself busy instructing builders and decorators in the way she wanted the rooms laid out. It got her out of the flat, giving Alfie time and space to work on the construction of an astronomical clock for a professor in Edinburgh. It was no mean feat to be selected over watchmakers in the capital and Alfie was keen to ensure the academic's faith wasn't misplaced. He couldn't start on the West Tay clock until Templeman got his head round the mechanics of clock making and came up with a realistic design. If recent communications were anything to go by, that wouldn't be until well after the railway line crossed the Forth on the new bridge.

'His ideas are preposterous,' he moaned to Winnie. 'The man may have created spectacular sculptures in the States, as he claims, but he has never worked with watchmakers.'

'Especially not Scottish ones,' Winnie added, stopping her sewing to consider the point.

Alfie wasn't sure if she meant her words as a criticism of Templeman or himself. He let the matter rest and she continued making her baby garments.

The latest plan Templeman had sent round was something

little Teddy could have drawn; fancy mannequins, model birds, bells ringing. Infantile flippancy. His casing was crammed full of gewgaws and he was as puffed up as a popinjay about it. It was a delight to see his face drop when asked where he intended the numerous wheels, dials, cogs and springs, sprockets and gears to go. That was without mentioning the pendulums.

'Perhaps I should visit your workshop to get a feel for the science,' Templeman suggested.

Alfie agreed, without offering a specific time and was somewhat annoyed when the American chose to arrive on the morning he was devising a method to link the orbit of Jupiter, the solar solstice and the time in New York. He had mastered the calculations, but the workings were fiddly and Alfie struggled with stiffness in his fingers. The swelling of his joints worsened in winter, not helped by the climate in Perth. He had managed to elevate the dial into position and was about to hook it in place when the shop bell broke his concentration. He jolted his elbow and the dial shot across his bench.

'Howdy do, Peters?' Templeman called across the room, as if Alfie were on the other side of the Grand Canyon. 'I'm not disturbing you, am I?'

'Not at all.' Alfie put his screwdriver down and stood up. 'You haven't seen a quarter inch dial, have you?'

'A dial?' Templeman glanced round the room then up at the ceiling. 'Sorry. Hey, is this what you're working on? That looks like the sun.'

'It is an astronomical clock and that happens to be Jupiter.'

'Gee, who'd have known? What is the point of an astronomical clock? Who needs to know the time on the moon? A Martian?' Templeman guffawed.

'Very droll,' Alfie answered. 'This particular piece is a novelty item, but astronomical clocks were popular in mediaeval times. Of course, the earth was the centre of the universe then.'

'What happened?'

'We discovered America, which is at the centre of everything.'

'Huh? I didn't know you Europeans had clocks back in the Middle Ages.' Giles lifted one of the small parts on the bench to examine it.

'Granted, most of the clocks were water driven and couldn't be considered accurate,' Alfie admitted, 'but ahead of their time, nonetheless.'

'Clocks, ahead of their time. That's good.' Templeman wagged his finger.

'It wasn't meant as a pun.'

'You don't use water now?' Giles asked, looking as though he were trying to figure how to fit a small reservoir into his design.

'Weights and pendulums,' Alfie informed him.

'Sure, I knew that.'

'You don't seem to appreciate the intricacies involved in clockmaking, if I may say.' Alfie took the cog Giles was fiddling with from his hand.

'The workings are necessary, sure, but it's time itself that I find fascinating,' Templeman said. 'You know at this moment, while our systems are digesting breakfast, my family and friends in the States are still in their beds.'

'Exactly,' Alfie agreed. 'And if you could miraculously be transported to Japan at the click of a finger, you would find it was time for supper. Indeed, some parts of the world could be a day ahead of your friends in the States.'

'That is something to get your head around,' Giles said. 'I was thinking, if we could invent a machine that travelled as fast as…'

'Sunlight?' Alfie suggested.

'Faster than that.' Templeman wrestled with the idea. 'If we could do that, why, it would be a time machine.'

Alfie nodded. 'And if someone invented a way of slowing down time, or reversing it…'

Templeman stared at Alfie. 'We could go back into the past. You sound like a man who knows what he is talking about.'

Alfie tapped the side of his nose.

'Is that what you're working on? Time travel?' Templeman queried.

'That would take a better man than me. This is a mere bauble.' Alfie decided to change the subject. 'Have you brought your plans for the West Tay clock?'

'Sure have.' Templeman had a leather satchel slung over his shoulder. He opened the bag and pulled out a rolled-up parchment. Alfie cleared the bench and Templeman spread the plan out. 'You can see here, I've altered the lay-out to leave room for your mechanics.'

'Yes,' Alfie rubbed his chin. 'Perhaps I didn't explain clearly that the workings have to be spread throughout the clock. There is no use asking for a moving whisky taster unless the platform he is glued to is connected to the wheels. I can work with springs for the arm movements, but anything else requires wooden rods which will need to be placed out of sight.'

'Crikes, I don't want the workings visible from the front. The models should be seen to work by magic, not… clockwork.'

'We are constructing a clock,' Alfie reminded him. 'You will need to adapt the front of the casing to house the main pendulum.' Alfie ran his thumb over the diagram. He stopped over a shaded area. 'This is new.'

'You bet it is, Alfred,' Templeman tapped the page. 'It is space for a miniature organ.'

'A pipe organ? In a clock?'

'You've got it.'

'Why?'

'Clocks chime the hour, don't they?'

'Normally with bells.'

'This will be no normal clock.'

'It doesn't seem like a clock at all. I assume you have more than one copy of the plan. If you leave this with me, I'll see what I can do.' Alfie rolled the paper up until he reached Templeman's hand.

'Sure.' Templeman raised his hand and Alfie finished scrolling. 'I'd be obliged if you didn't kick your heels over it. Farquhar is clinging to my back like a rodeo cowboy on a bronco. He wants the clock in place by Easter.'

'Six months.' Alfie did a rapid calculation in his head. 'Mr. Farquhar will have to dig into hotel funds for that.'

'Squires is the man paying, from his own pocket,' Templeman

said.

'I hope it is a deep one.'

'Mr Squires is a gentleman of substance. I'll catch up with you in a few days. Good morning.' Templeman touched his hat and left.

Alfie ran his fingers over the parchment, pondering whether to examine the plans in greater detail while the ideas were fresh or to return to the astronomical clock. His enthusiasm for astrology had vanished, but excitement for the hotel clock didn't take its place. He decided to break for coffee and was on the first stair to the apartment when the shop bell rang.

A customer? Where was Winnie when you needed her?

'Just a moment,' Alfie called. He returned to the shop, closing the flat door behind him. The diagram of the clock was on view and he slipped it beneath the counter before stepping out to greet the person entering. His forced smile faded. 'What are you doing here? How did you find me?'

'A "nice to see you" would be fine,' Maggie chirped. 'You weren't hard to unearth. Your name is in giant golden letters above the door. It didn't take Inspector Bucket to work it out.'

'Who?'

'He's a detective in a book.'

'Who has been giving you books?'

'Nobody.'

'What do you want?'

Maggie lifted a watch displayed on a shelf at her side. Alfie grabbed it from her. Before she could react he gripped her by the shoulders and dragged her out of sight of the shop door.

'Ouch, let go of me.'

'What are you doing here?' Alfie repeated, shaking the girl.

'You'll rip my uniform. If you don't let me go, I'll scream.' Maggie struggled free. She stood shaking a couple of feet from him. 'I don't want nothing,' Maggie said. 'It's my morning off. I've brought a poke of toffee for you, from mum. She wants to know when you'll be dropping in to see her next.'

'I'm busy,' Alfie said. 'I'd have more time if I wasn't constantly being interrupted.'

'Busy with the hotel clock? Everybody is talking about it at work. They're talking about Templeman though, not you.'

'Templeman is young, good-looking and American,' Alfie said. 'Naturally, silly girls want to talk about him.'

Maggie had got her breath back and was nosing around behind the counter. She stopped at the door to the upstairs flat. 'Is that where you live?'

Alfie didn't answer.

'Alone?' Maggie probed.

'Give me the toffee and clear off,' Alfie said. 'I don't want you coming here again, do you understand?'

'Why not? Scared somebody will see me?' She offered Alfie a paper bag. He snatched at the packet and she drew her hand back. 'Manners.'

Alfie put out his hand and she passed over the bag. He opened the top and peered inside.

'Toffees, like I told you.'

Alfie shook the bag. 'Have you eaten any of them?'

'Maybe you'd like me to, but I'm not as stupid as you think.'

'Tell your mother I will be visiting Dotty in a week or two. I'll visit her and Teddy then.'

'Mum says I've to keep an eye on you while I'm in Perth. She doesn't trust you.'

Maggie stared at the flat door, willing it to open.

'Really? Maybe somebody has been feeding her untrue stories,' Alfie countered. Maggie screwed her face and stuck out her tongue.

'Insolent wench.' Alfie took a step towards her with a fist raised. Maggie jerked out of the way, knocking her arm against the counter. She hurried towards the front door of the shop before Alfie could stop her and was rubbing her elbow when the door opened. Winnie breezed through.

Maggie was thrust forwards and steadied herself by grabbing at a shelf of pocket watches.

'Watch what you're doing, girl,' Alfie shouted.

'What is going on, Alfie?' Winnie demanded.

Maggie regained her balance and glanced at Winnie. 'Nice to meet you, Ma'am.' She smiled knowingly at Alfie, straightened her uniform and marched out of the shop, slamming the door behind her.

'Was that one of the hotel maids?' Winnie asked. 'Hardly West Tay standards. What did she want?'

'Nothing. She brought a message from Squires.'

'He could have given it to Mrs Squires. I'm visiting Maude and the girls this afternoon.'

'On first name terms, are you?'

'Don't be like that, Alfie. You want us to move up in the world, don't you? Mr Templeman will be there.'

'Mr Templeman seems to be "there" more often than the postman.'

'You could be too, if you put in the effort. It wouldn't take much to smarten up and engage in polite conversation. Surely a clean shirt and a "how do you do" isn't beyond you? Goodness, is that the time? I shall have to go and change.'

'You're not forgetting to make lunch, are you?' Alfie called after her. She was half way up the stairs and didn't answer.

With Winnie making herself up in the apartment, Alfie decided against coffee. He pottered around the shop, re-arranging his displays until the post boy arrived. There was a letter addressed to Winnie in her mother's handwriting and a more formal letter for him from Edinburgh. It was from the asylum. Dr Lutheral only sent letters if the patient happened to be deceased or his bills hadn't been paid. In the case of a death, the envelope would be edged in black. This one wasn't. He was up to date with his payments, so what could Dr Matthews find so urgent to warrant a letter before his next visit? A decline in Dotty's condition? A plea for him to visit before she departed this life? Or an entreaty to allow his new-fangled treatments?

Alfie took his time opening the envelope with a silver letter opener. He drew out the paper. Dr Matthews had an untidy hand and the writing was difficult to decipher.

In regard to your wife, Dorothy Peters, nee Harris, I would be obliged if you could attend the hospital at your earliest possible

69

convenience.

There were a few more sentences, mere medical etiquette. There was nothing to explain why Alfie needed to re-arrange his schedule and visit Edinburgh with winter on the doorstep. He read it again, mindful that he might have missed something and wondered if Winnie would be able to make anything more of the scrawl.

'Winnie,' he opened the side door and called up the stairs.

Fool.

He gritted his teeth. How could he show Winnie a letter beginning "in regard to your wife Dorothy Peters"?

'What is it, dear?' Winnie shouted down.

'Nothing, a letter has come from your mother.'

He put the doctor's letter back in the envelope and concealed it below the counter with the toffees, but there was more than a chance Winnie would find it. She was always snooping around his things. He recovered the letter and burned it over the gas light. The ashes were crumbling in his hand when Winnie appeared in the shop.

'What's that you're burning?' she asked, sniffing the air.

'Not your mother's letter. It's on the counter,' Alfie said. He watched as Winnie retrieved it. She sniffed the perfumed envelope then secured it beneath the top of her dress, supported by her cleavage. 'I may have to visit Edinburgh again this month,' he said.

'That is excellent,' Winnie answered. 'There is a haberdashery in the New Town that I would like to visit. You can attend to your business while I shop and we can meet up for dinner.'

'I'm afraid that is out of the question,' Alfie blurted the words out.

'Why?'

'Why? Why?' Alfie struggled to speak, never mind come up with an excuse. 'What does your mother say?'

'I haven't opened the letter yet.'

'No doubt she will want to visit and disapprove of the house,' Alfie said. 'Why don't you amuse her while I am safely out of the way?' He could see Winnie was dithering over the suggestion. 'Besides, a trip to Edinburgh at this time of year would not be good for you in your condition.'

'But if I wait until spring, the baby will be here and it will take all my attention.'

'By then, we will be able to afford a nanny to look after little Fred while we enjoy ourselves.'

'Really? A nanny?' Winnie waltzed round the shelves, as

clumsily as Maggie.

'It's pointless trying to get any work done when you're in this kind of woman's mood,' Alfie grumbled. 'I shall go for a stroll while the weather remains mild.'

'Where will you go?'

'As if that matters to you, gallivanting with your new rich friends. I might take a stroll past the new house and see if our future neighbours are about.'

'There's a weird chap in the house opposite,' Winnie offered. 'He looks out of his window all day. The house on the right is empty and the old woman in the house on the left keeps cats. Lots of cats.'

'They'd better not dig up my garden. Pity we can't report her to the council and have her burnt as a witch.'

'Don't be nasty, Alfie. She's on her own. She must get lonely.'

'Even with a hundred cats?'

'I didn't say a hundred.' Winnie stepped towards the door to the flat, passing behind the counter. 'Oh, what are these?' She lifted the bag of toffees Maggie had brought and was about to take one when Alfie snatched the poke from her.

'They aren't good for you, in your condition,' he said.

'Nothing is good for me in my condition, according to you. Just as well the doctor doesn't agree, or I'd be stuck in bed eating nothing but vegetable broth,' Winnie complained.

'There is nothing wrong with vegetable broth.'

Winnie made a face before departing up the stairs. Alfie collected his coat, hat and scarf. He needed to clear his head. If Dotty's condition had deteriorated and she was near to death, it would make his marriage to Winnie legitimate before the birth of his son.

He hadn't intended to become a bigamist. He would have waited until Dorothy had departed, but Winnie's father was weeks away from greeting St Peter at the Pearly Gates. He was offering a reasonable dowry, but her mother had the modern idea that marriage should be based on love. Her romantic notions were fuelled by her own greed. Once she got her hands on her husband's money, there was no chance of a settlement. Everyone knew Dotty was ill and in hospital in Edinburgh. She had no family apart from him. Abetted by Dr Lutheral's dubious ethics, it hadn't been difficult to convince people of her premature death.

On the other hand, if Dorothy did die, what excuse could he give to Nancy for postponing their promised nuptials? With Maggie in Perth snooping around, the situation was becoming awkward. The girl would have to be got rid of.

It shouldn't be difficult to persuade Squires she wasn't suitable as a hotel maid. If he could arrange to have her caught in a compromising position with another member of staff...or better, one of the guests...

The thought grew as he walked towards the river and as he passed the bridge over the Tay he realised the hotel wasn't far away. Strike while the poker is hot, his mother always said. His father kept away from her when she had it in her hand. If it was Maggie's morning off as she said, he was unlikely to meet her. Templeman was safely entertaining the Squires' ladies. Excellent.

The reception hall was bustling. Alfie couldn't help but glance up to where the clock would go. He pictured Templeman's design and had to admit it fitted well into the space. According to his pocket watch - which kept perfect time - it was one minute before eleven o'clock. Across the hall were a dowager in her feather hat, a bickering couple, two businessmen and a gentleman in his plus fours who was creaking across towards the bar.

Alfie pictured them stopping to look up at the horological wonder: the organ prelude, the casing parting like the Red Sea, a puff of smoke as the city's industries and its railway came to life in mechanical magic, then the chimes and the city once more falling asleep, perhaps with the appearance of the moon. That wasn't a bad idea. He would suggest it to Templeman.

He wanted to grab the dowager's arm and tell her he had made it, he was the genius behind the workings, but of course there was only an empty space with nothing there. Not yet.

'Can I help you, sir?' The reception clerk noticed him looking blankly into space and came over.

'Why yes, I'm looking for Mr Giles Templeman. I believe he is staying here. Suite... em...three two seven or is it eight?'

'Mr Templeman is in suite two five one,' the reception clerk said, 'but I'm afraid he has gone out for the morning. I can't say when he will be back. Who would you like me to say has called?'

'An old friend. I think it would be better if I left him a note. Do you have a sheet of writing paper?'

'Of course, sir.'

Alfie returned with the man to the desk and was given a sheet of hotel writing paper.

'I shall also need a pen and ink?'

The man obliged and Alfie took the writing material to a nearby table and chair. He sat down and began to compose his letter.

Dear Mr Templeman, he began. Was that how a young girl in service would address a gentleman? Maggie had been allowed something of an education, so he let it stand, although dotted the rest of the short message with spelling errors and common terms. Without being explicit, he wanted to make sure that Giles knew exactly what 'Maggie' was offering. He ended by suggesting a time and place when the floor manager would be engaged elsewhere. *Yours expectantly, Maggie.*

Templeman was vain enough to think any young girl would swoon at his feet, but as an extra touch, Alfie visited the wash room and smeared a finger of soap on the paper to make it smell alluring. Suite two five one was on the second floor. Alfie felt a twinge in his back as he made his way up the steps and along the empty corridor. Bending to slip the note under the door caused a spasm to run up his spine. He groaned as he stood up and rubbed the muscles.

'Are you in trouble, sir?' The floor manager appeared from what had seemed to Alfie to be a laundry cupboard.

Alfie spotted the edge of his letter poking out from beneath the door and shuffled over to push it further into the room with his heel. The floor manager straightened his tie.

'My back,' Alfie said. 'Terrible twinges.' He moved to admire one of the paintings on the wall. The portrait was signed by Raeburn. 'Is this an original?'

'We don't have imitations here, sir.' The floor manager took his question as a personal insult.

'Nor taste,' Alfie said, pointing at the unashamedly brash landscape next to it.

'That is by Mr. James Guthrie,' the manager said, as if he were meant to know who the gentleman was. Alfie mumbled a few words which he didn't intend the manager to understand and headed for the stairs. He took them as fast as his arthritis allowed.

'Would you like me to give your letter to Mr Templeman when he returns?' the clerk asked as Alfie tried to slip unseen past the reception desk to the main door.

'No, I've...actually, I've decided I should speak to Giles in person. I'll return this evening. I've left the pen and ink on the table.' He hurried towards the door without giving the young man time to respond.

The next task was to make sure Maggie was in the place he suggested at the right time. That might be tricky, although getting the floor manager there as a witness wouldn't be difficult, not if the man made a habit of hanging out in cupboards. Alfie took another stride and laughed. He had smelt lavender on the manager's collar. No wonder he was annoyed at being disturbed. The maids weren't the only ones up to mischief.

Chapter 5

Alfie re-arranged his schedule before posting a letter to Dr Matthews informing him he would visit the hospital the following Tuesday. He had been unable to set up the desired liaison between Templeman and Maggie, but no matter. The scene was set for a future encounter. Life was a waiting game. Templeman would be flattered and aroused by the maid's proposal. With luck, fate might snatch things out of his hands. His current problem was with Winnie.

'I have made up my mind, Alfie dear. I shall have a day in Edinburgh,' she declared in a voice that could have been her mother's.

'My business will take all day,' Alfie tried to dissuade her. 'I shall have to leave early, before quarter to seven.'

'I find it difficult to sleep these days.' Winnie held her grossly enlarged abdomen. 'I shall be out of bed well before you.'

'Several times,' Alfie muttered, thinking of his wife's frequent nocturnal trips to relieve her bladder.

'What was that?'

'I said, it will be a long day for you. It's unlikely I'll be free before seven in the evening.'

'Don't worry about me. Maude Squires has a friend in the

capital. I can visit her for tea.'

'Then it hardly seems necessary for you to come with me,' Alfie tried one last card. 'You could arrange your own day out.'

'I like to have company on the train,' Winnie answered.

There was no putting her off, although Alfie wondered why she needed company when on the day she snored her way from Perth to Burntisland. Her noise made it impossible for Alfie to concentrate on his clock makers' journal. She woke in time to alight for the ferry and suffered from seasickness for the duration of the short crossing.

'They aren't very far advanced with their work on the bridge,' Winnie complained.

'The weather doesn't help in winter. I wouldn't fancy being up there when the wind blows.'

'The construction workers are used to that,' Winnie answered.

'Maybe so, nonetheless, I have heard there have been injuries with men falling from the icy rails.'

Alfie hadn't meant to frighten Winnie, but she shivered and was silent for the rest of the trip.

When they reached the south side of the Forth, Alfie helped his wife onto a train for Edinburgh. 'I shall have to leave you here,' he said. 'Make sure you behave.'

'Of course.' Winnie slapped his hand playfully, her cheerfulness recovered. 'Where and when shall we meet?'

'In thunder, lightning or in rain?'

'It looks like it will remain dry.' Winnie looked to the sky.

'I was quoting Shakespeare's MacBeth,' Alfie started to explain, but decided it wasn't worth the bother. He promised to join her in the lounge of a stated hotel near Waverley railway station, at a time that allowed him a fleeting visit to see Nancy. He baulked at the expense of travelling most of the way to Perth, to return to Edinburgh before journeying home again, but it was a spit in the wind compared to the bills he could expect Winnie to present him with after her day shopping. She blew him a kiss which he didn't return.

Winnie found a window seat in the carriage and Alfie fixed his eyes on her hat as the train left the station. He made sure she was gone before he caught his coach. Sitting next to him on the train, her increasing weight had pushed against his side. The toffee in his pocket was squashed and melted. He salvaged the best ones as he approached the hospital.

Dr Matthews was at reception to greet him, strumming his fingers on the desk diary.

'I didn't expect you to be waiting here. Not bad news, I hope?'

Alfie asked, trying to sound upset.

'Rather to the contrary.' John Matthews shook his hand. 'Your wife is responding better than I expected. Her regulated food intake and fitness regime…'

'Exercise? Is that suitable for the female frame?'

'… are doing her a power of good,' Dr Matthews finished his sentence.

'Ah. Good.'

'The warden tells me that you bring your wife toffee when you visit.'

'Damn good stuff too,' the warden put in.

'I'm afraid it is squashed.' Alfie took the bag from his pocket. 'Still, I'm sure it will taste the same.'

'I shall take charge of it.' The doctor held out his hand.

'Why?'

'As I said, Dorothy is on a special high fat and low sugar diet. I wouldn't want this countered by toffee.'

'Of course not.' Alfie gave the bag to the doctor. 'But everything in moderation, surely? Dotty is particularly fond of toffee. She will be allowed moderate portions, won't she?'

'In a controlled method, yes,' the doctor agreed, accepting the sticky bag and handing it to the warden. 'I expect you'll wish to speak with Dorothy now. She's anxious to see you. Believe me, you will be amazed.'

Alfie followed the doctor along the corridor. The clock was still struggling to make its way past five to two, which re-assured Alfie. The doctor stopped outside a door on his left.

'This isn't Dotty's room,' Alfie remarked.

'This is a workshop,' Dr Matthews said. 'Since she's been feeling better, Dorothy has become interested in handicraft.'

'Working with needles? You feel she is up to that?'

'Certainly.' Dr Matthews opened the door. Dorothy sat in a circle with three other women, embroidering a tablecloth that was spread between them. She didn't look up at first and Alfie watched her chat and laugh. After a minute one of the other women spotted the two men and nudged Dorothy. She turned round and in her excitement jabbed herself with the needle. A spot of blood dripped onto the material.

'There you see,' Alfie said to the doctor, 'She can't even control a sewing needle.'

'Dorothy, would you come here, please?' Dr Matthews said.

Dorothy tied off the thread and set her part of the needlework down. She stood up, excused herself, and walked over. The blue skirt and fawn blouse she wore flattered her figure. Alfie appreciated it as she approached. Her hair was brushed until it shone and hung loose over her face.

'Where did she get those clothes?' Alfie asked.

'They belonged to my sister,' the doctor answered. 'Margery has no need for them and they fit Dorothy as if they were tailored for her.'

'What is wrong with hospital clothing?'

'It is dull, ill-fitting and depressing,' Dr Matthews said. 'Not conducive to the encouragement of mental freshness.'

'You should have informed me,' Alfie said. 'I am capable of providing clothes for my wife.'

'Please, we can discuss matters in private, if you'll both follow me.' He smiled at Dorothy and she returned the gesture. Alfie scowled.

'Whit aboot us, doctor?' one of the needlewomen called, an older woman with teeth like a knacker's yard nag. 'When is ma Jimmy coming tae see me?'

'I have written to your son, Mrs Johnson, but he is in India and won't be home this year.'

'Or ever, if that's what he has to look forward to,' Alfie said.

'Wha are ye tae talk?' the woman shifted in her seat. Dr Matthews edged Alfie out the door before the woman created a disturbance.

'Aren't you going to lock the door?' Alfie asked as they walked from the workshop.

'This isn't a prison.'

'These women are a danger to themselves and others.'

'You seem to have a poor impression of our establishment,' Dr Matthews said.

'Dr Lutheral kept the doors locked,' Alfie reminded him.

Dr Matthews thought it wiser not to reply, not wishing to criticise his predecessor or remind Alfie of the result of Dr Lutheral's methods. He led them into a lounge where three comfortable chairs and a settee surrounded a fireplace. The fire was lit and gave a rosy glow. 'Please, take a seat.'

Alfie waited until Dotty sat down before positioning himself so as not to see her face. Dr Matthews sat opposite them.

'What's this about?' Alfie asked.

'I would like to discuss provisions for Dotty's release,' Dr Matthews said.

Alfie smirked at the choice of word – release, not discharge. 'That is hardly likely to be soon,' he said. 'Granted, Dotty may be making temporary progress, but this has happened before. We get our hopes up only for them to be dashed.'

'I believe things are different this time,' the doctor said.

'I imagine you would, but you don't have the experience of Dr Lutheral.'

'Alfie, I feel much better,' Dotty put in, leaning over to take hold of his hand. Alfie drew it away.

'Don't interrupt our conversation,' he said curtly.

'If Dotty could be in a safe environment, in familiar surroundings, I believe...'

'That is not possible,' Alfie cut in before the doctor could finish. 'What if Dotty came home and had a fit in my workshop, while I was out? Who can say how much damage might be caused to Dotty, as well as my clocks and watches?'

'I can assure you…'

'Besides, even if we say Dotty is cured of her epilepsy, there is the question of her face.'

'I'm sorry, I don't understand,' the doctor said pointedly.

'How can I protect my wife from the ridicule she will receive outside of these walls? The distress and humiliation would be too much to bear. No, I cannot allow it.'

'Very well,' the doctor said after a short pause. Dotty gave a small gasp. 'I intended postponing this part of the discussion until a more suitable time, but since you are adamant I shall mention it now. I have a friend who is an eminent surgeon in the city. I have spoken with him about Dotty's affliction and he believes that surgery would be possible.'

'What, you mean cut Dotty up like a piece of butcher's meat?' Alfie got to his feet. 'Over my dead body.'

'It is hardly butchery. My friend has operated on lords and ladies. If you would permit me to invite him to visit Dorothy...'

'Lords and ladies, eh? I can't imagine I shall be able to afford his fees. No doubt you get a healthy slice as commission. I should have guessed it would come down to money.'

'I take offence at that, Mr Peters.' Dr Matthews got to his feet and glared at Alfie. Dotty cleared her throat and stood up.

'Can I speak with Alfie alone?' she asked.

'Yes, of course.' Dr Matthews moved to the door. 'I shall be outside, should you need me.' He was speaking to Dorothy, not Alfie.

Alfie waited until the doctor departed and the door was closed before speaking. 'Surgery, indeed,' he snorted. 'What would he say if somebody suggested cutting up his wife?'

'Dr Matthews is not married,' Dotty said.

'That explains everything.' Alfie walked over to the fire to warm his hands and Dotty sat back on the sofa.

'I would love to see the workshop again,' she said.

'It has changed since you were last there. I have brought in sophisticated equipment from the Continent.'

'Wonderful. Tell me about this clock you are making for the West Tay hotel, please.'

'You remember that?'

'I remember everything you tell me.'

'I haven't started work on it yet. The plans won't be ready for weeks,' Alfie huffed. 'Not until Templeman gets his head around mechanical engineering and comes up with something workable.'

'Templeman, is he the American gentleman? What has he planned?' Dotty was on the edge of the cushion.

'Moving figures, smoke, and why, he even wants a real organ inside the casing.' Alfie warmed to the subject.

'It will have to be a large clock,' Dotty said.

'Ginormous,' Alfie joked. Dorothy didn't laugh.

'You will need new staking tools and precise screwdrivers. Oh, I wish I had the taps and dies and I could make them for you. That would save you so much time.'

'Needlework is one thing, making a clock is something else,' Alfie reminded her.

'I haven't forgotten what my father showed me,' Dotty said. 'I could easily learn how to work the new equipment. I do wish I could help you. What pendulums will you use? How will you balance the weights across the casing? What else has Mr Templeman devised to test your skills?'

Dotty was full of questions; sensible, clock making questions. Alfie sat next to her and they discussed techniques and instruments as they had in her father's workshop before they were married.

'Why, is that the time?' Alfie looked up to see the mantel clock. It was past the time he had hoped to be on the train to visit Nancy. 'I have to go.'

'Must you?'

He stroked her hair. 'I'll come again, soon.'

'Promise?'

Alfie smiled, but didn't answer.

'I would like an operation on my face, if it is possible,' Dotty said.

Alfie pulled his hand back. 'That doctor is filling your head with dangerous nonsense. It is unprofessional. Dr Lutheral may not be practising, but he still owns this hospital. I shall write to him and complain.' He put his hand in his pocket and felt a toffee stuck to the lining. He pulled it out, rubbed away the threads on the side of his jacket and offered it to Dotty.

'Dr Matthews says it isn't good for me,' she said.

'Dr Matthews says,' Alfie mimicked a high pitched voice. 'Here, take it.'

Dotty reluctantly took the sticky sweet and popped it in her mouth.

'Good girl. I'll be back when I can.' He waited until she finished the sweet then left the room.

He didn't speak with Dr Matthews before leaving. He had made his viewpoint clear and he was short of time. The coach journey to the ferry was unremarkable, although he did have longer than expected to wait on the boat due to a technical problem with the paddle. It was raining, contrary to Winnie's forecast, and he regretted not bringing an umbrella. The soles of his boots were in need of repair, a fact he was reminded of when he stepped backwards into a puddle. Eventually the ferry departed and he was across the Forth and boarding the train.

'Why, it's Mr Peters.'

Alfie heard the voice of the elder Squires' daughter. He pretended he hadn't and snatched at the carriage door, pulling it closed leaving Lucy Squires on the platform with her sister. The train was busy and he was squashed in a compartment with a pipe smoking fishwife and two unwashed sailors. He opened the window, but one of the sailors closed it five minutes later.

'Heading to Perth?' he asked.

The sailors were, although the fishwife got off at the next stop. Nancy wasn't on the platform to meet him when the train arrived at her station. It irritated Alfie although it didn't surprise him. She would have expected him an hour ago. As he walked along the road to her cottage, he felt a thump on his lower leg, followed by a child's laughter. Looking down at his trousers, he saw a patch of mud where he had been hit.

'You little hooligan.' He rushed towards the side alley and caught a glimpse of a dark green jumper and blue shorts, but the child was too fast for him. 'I'll tell your father,' he called into the wind.

Alfie was still fuming when he arrived at Nancy's cottage. 'Look what some little tinker did.'

He demonstrated his stained clothing. Nancy hung up his jacket then brought a wet cloth. She tried to remove the stain on his trousers, but the mud was wet and refused to be brushed off.

'Let it be.' He pushed her away and sat down. 'Where's little Teddy?'

'He's playing with his friends. He'll be in soon. How was

Dotty?'

'Remarkably well.'

'I thought…'

'Then you would do better not to think.'

'Here's Teddy now.' Nancy went to the door to greet her son. 'Your father is here. You had better go and wash.'

Teddy's hands were smeared with mud. So were his green jumper and blue shorts.

'Why, you ungrateful wretch.' Alfie stood up and stepped towards the boy. Teddy ran to hide behind his mother.

'You're frightening the babe,' Nancy reprimanded.

'He deserves to be more than frightened,' Alfie grunted. 'He's the rogue who dirtied my trousers.'

'He's just a boy.'

'You didn't say that a minute ago when you thought it was one of the village brats.' Alfie realised he wouldn't win against Nancy where Teddy was concerned. He sat back down and moved his chair nearer the fire. Nancy ushered Teddy from the room and Alfie heard the splashing of water and squeals from the boy. Alfie removed his shoes and damp socks and warmed his toes.

'Feeling happier?' Nancy asked when she returned with a mug of ale.

'That boy needs a sound thrashing,' he said.

'He needs a father's hand,' Nancy repeated. 'Did you take the toffee to Dotty?'

'The doctor has banned her from eating sweets,' Alfie replied. 'He is talking about surgery.'

'Well, we know how dangerous that can be.' Nancy plonked herself on his knees and put her arm around his neck.

'Have you heard from Maggie?' Alfie asked.

'I had a letter today. There is a gentleman staying at the hotel who has taken an interest in her.'

'A gentleman? That can only lead to trouble,' Alfie said.

'I have brought her up to be a good girl.'

'Just like you,' Alfie gave Nancy a nip on her behind and she laughed.

'Maggie is a good girl, but gentlemen feel they have a right to take advantage of maids, especially in a large hotel where staff are hired and fired at will,' Nancy said. 'What Maggie needs is a position in a respectable household. One where the master of the house is well into his eighties and confined to a chair.'

'That is no guarantee against hanky-panky,' Alfie retorted. 'Although, I suppose there might be money in it. If you remember, I offered to place Maggie with a good family.'

'Yes, but Edinburgh is so far away.'

'Has Maggie said anything else about Perth?' Alfie queried.

'She told me your workshop was in need of a good sweep,' Nancy answered. 'You should employ Maggie to keep things in order. She's good with figures. She could keep your books for you.'

Alfie jumped at the suggestion, sending Nancy flying towards the fire. The end of her skirt caught in the flames and there was a short kerfuffle while she tried to stamp them out. Alfie tossed the remains of his ale on her skirt. The flames hissed and died.

'My skirt is ruined.' Nancy held out the end of the material to examine it.

'Better take it off then,' Alfie leered. Nancy's frown changed to a laugh.

'I'd better see to Ted. We don't want to be disturbed.'

Alfie helped himself to more ale while Nancy was gone. He noticed that the clock on her mantelpiece was fast compared to his pocket watch, but he didn't adjust it. He removed his waistcoat and neckerchief and undid the belt of his trousers.

'He's settled now, but we don't want to make too much noise,' Nancy said when she returned.

'I don't intend changing my behaviour because of a four year old child,' Alfie moaned.

'It would be nice to have a large house,' Nancy said. She retook her place on his knee and fiddled with the buttons of his breeches. 'We could buy a house in Perth, once we're married.'

'Once we're married,' Alfie said, grabbing Nancy round the waist.

His delay at the hospital gave little time for Nancy's company. After a short period of her kisses he stood up.

'Is that the time?' he pointed at the clock. 'I have to go.'

'That clock hasn't been working properly since Ted dropped it in the laundry tub.'

'Ted again. I'm fed up hearing about Ted.'

'You're being silly.' Nancy handed him his neckwear as he re-buttoned his trousers.

He took the neckerchief, but didn't put it on. Nancy took it from him and fastened it round his collar. He leaned over and kissed her on the cheek. 'Once Dotty is gone, we'll buy a nice house with a garden. Ted can go to school and we'll promenade through the park together.'

'And people will look on and say "that is the famous watchmaker". We could start a new family. I am still capable,' Nancy continued. She paused before adding, 'What about

Maggie?'

'What about her? Surely you'll have found a husband to take charge of her by then?'

He left Nancy pondering over who would take her stubborn minded daughter off her hands.

The train and ferry back to Edinburgh were running to schedule and Alfie estimated he had plenty of time to wash Nancy's cheap soap from his skin before meeting Winnie. It was a short walk from the ferry pier to the railway station and thankfully the rain had gone off.

'Where do you think you are going?'

Alfie jumped. It was Winnie's voice and she didn't sound happy. He turned to see his wife arm-in-arm with Lucy Squires.

'We had arranged to meet in town,' Alfie said, biting back the words he would have said if Lucy hadn't been there.

'I thought you had business in Edinburgh.'

'In Fife, dear. I said Fife.'

Winnie screwed her eyes and nose. It was clear, if Lucy Squires had not been there, she too would have had more to say and her language would have been agricultural.

'Here's Emily now,' Lucy said. 'We can catch the ferry together.'

Emily came up with a bag of sweets. She offered them around.

'I would love one,' Winnie said, 'but Alfie says sweets are bad for me.'

'Really, I thought sugar was needed for growth,' Lucy said.

'Which is why women will never make scientists or doctors,' Alfie said, hoping to put an end to the conversation.

'That's unfortunate, Mr Peters,' Lucy said brightly, 'because I fear we already are.'

Chapter 6

Alfie's new house was a good half mile from his workshop. No doubt, in summer, the walk would provide a pleasant start to the day, but in winter when the ice turned the pavements into curling rinks and the sun didn't rise until well after seven, the prospect of setting out for work was not a cheery one. Alfie had no wish to risk life and limb in the process and his caution meant the journey to work took almost fifteen minutes. It was a comforting habit to go upstairs to the vacant apartment, light the fire to warm his fingers, make a pot of tea, then settle in his favourite armchair to read the morning newspaper before attending to the shop.

The horsehair from the chair poked through his trousers, the springs were broken and the upholstery was burnt and stained. Winnie would have divorced him sooner than have it transported to their new house and displayed in her tidy lounge. Winnie had ideas about renting out the two rooms and kitchen above the shop, but he had put his foot down. The only access to the flat was through the shop and it would have cost as much to alter that as the rooms would bring in payment in a year.

As usual, there wasn't one article of good news in the local paper, unless you counted the funeral notice for the local excise man. The river had flooded and there was talk of reinforcing the bank, as there was every December. A school teacher's son had been caught stealing. That was something of a scandal, but he didn't know the man and apparently the son had moved to Glasgow. There was no accounting for what that city could do to a body. He was about to fold the paper, ready to put on the fire, when a picture of the West Tay Hotel caught his eye. The article was an excuse for a cheap advertisement to entice visitors to the town, but no mention of the West Tay could be complete without a reference to the clock. Templeman's name cropped up two paragraphs down.

According to the report, the design was 'ground-breaking,' 'gargantuan' and a 'wonder of modern science and horology.' The man had spelt horology incorrectly, with two 'r's, making it sound like a torture instrument from a Gothic novel. There was no reference to Alfie Peters, a citizen of Perth born and raised. Anyone reading the article would come away with the impression that Giles Templeman, the 'brilliant American' was responsible for every intricacy the clock had to boast.

'Pah.' Alfie tore the page out. 'Amateur drivel.' He scrunched the paper up. 'Calls himself a reporter.' With a swift arm swing, the paper flew across the room.

The distaste left by the columns in the paper wouldn't leave.

Alfie went downstairs to mend a crooked wheel on a pocket watch, but he couldn't concentrate. His fingers shook and the tiny fragment wouldn't balance on his tweezers. Farquhar had demanded a meeting to discuss the progress they were making on the hotel clock, or the lack of it, later that morning. It wasn't inconvenient, but Alfie disliked being called to attend at short notice, like some cap-touching hired man.

He had worked long hours, burning his own gas to light the room, in order to perfect the workings of the miniature organ Templeman outlined so descriptively in the newspaper. What other watchmaker in the town, in the country, could do that? He was confident Farquhar would give a satisfied nod when he saw the comprehensive diagrams. The pneumatic system took up more space than Templeman allowed for, but the casing could be expanded, as he demonstrated in the addendum. The hotel reception hall was large enough to accommodate two such clocks with ease.

He returned the watch to the box it had been delivered in. There was no point trying to work, with his mind distracted and rushing to finish a job was for cut-price charlatans who advertised their services from travelling wagons. He spent five minutes re-arranging his displays before returning upstairs to collect his satchel with the drawings for the clock. He set off towards the hotel, dawdling along the street, yet still arriving at the hotel ten minutes before the scheduled time. Farquhar and Templeman were waiting.

'What time do you call this?' Farquhar tapped his pocket watch. 'I expect punctuality, especially from a clockmaker.'

Alfie checked his watch. 'You did say ten thirty?' he asked.

'Ten fifteen,' Templeman answered before Farquhar could speak. 'I told you that when we met yesterday.'

Alfie was sure he hadn't, but he didn't argue. He followed the two men into Farquhar's office. The room wasn't arranged for work. The carpet was of thick pile, the curtains velvet and the wallpaper had been brought up from London at two guineas a roll. Farquhar took his seat behind his oak desk. Templeman and Alfie stood on the other side.

'Should we wait on Mr Squires?' Alfie asked.

'We would have to wait some time,' Farquhar answered.

'Walker is at the dentist,' Templeman explained.

'I don't envy him.' Alfie rubbed his cheek.

'You're not here to gossip like fish wives. What do you have for me?' Farquhar positioned his elbows on the desk and leant across.

Alfie opened his satchel and removed his drawings, setting the parchments on the desk and unrolling them to face Farquhar. The cut crystal ashtray would have been handy to prevent the edges rolling back, but Farquhar frowned at any of his possessions being touched by plebeian hands. Templeman cocked his head like a chicken to see over Alfie's elbows.

'I see what you've done.' Giles pointed to the tiny bellows. 'Pistons, in tune with the clock wheels.' He paused, as if expecting applause for using a technical word. Alfie turned his head to glare. 'It looks good,' Templeman appeased.

'I'm glad somebody is happy.' Adam Farquhar was not as delighted as Alfie hoped. He pulled open the drawer of his desk and reached inside, disrupting papers before drawing out a pile of bills, which he waved in the air. 'The organ pipes were ordered from the Continent, I believe? Toy organ pipes for a toy organ. Couldn't someone local make them?'

His implication was that they could have been cobbled together from children's whistles in someone's shed. Alfie sucked in his cheeks, but said nothing.

'It would have been nice to have been consulted about the extra cost before they were ordered,' Farquhar continued.

That was Templeman's responsibility. He was the one who

promised to square things with the 'boss.'

The American was keen to shift the blame. 'Peters assured me the Continental pipes are better quality.'

Farquhar shifted his gaze from Giles to Alfie.

He's the one with his name in the newspaper, not me.

'Skimping on the quality of materials is a false economy,' Alfie said. 'Once the clock is in situ, repairs would cost significantly more.'

'Repairs?'

'If we use cheaper components, there will undoubtedly be repairs. As it is, there will be maintenance costs. You want the clock to last, surely?'

'What is the point of talking about it lasting when the construction hasn't even been started? You promised it would be ready by Easter.'

They hadn't promised, but Templeman stepped in to allay Farquhar's doubts. 'Ready it will be, sir. Alfie, show Mr Farquhar the manikin.'

Mr Peters to you. He wasn't some shop boy.

'This is the basic prototype,' Alfie said, reaching in his bag for the working model of a cooper mending a whisky barrel. As he let go of the ends of the plan, the paper curled back, knocking over a photograph of Mrs Farquhar. Farquhar reached over to grab it at the same time as Templeman. Several items on the desk were displaced, including an open ink bottle that was knocked over. The red ink seeped towards the plans. While the jostling was going on, Alfie looked for somewhere to put his model. Giles grabbed the drawings before they were destroyed by the ink. Farquhar replaced the picture of his wife and Alfie placed the model on the desk beside it. Before Farquhar could object, he wound up the clockwork. The wooden cooper began beating the lid of his barrel with a miniature hammer. Farquhar raised an eyebrow the way Alfie's old headmaster had done before administering a caning.

'The puppet needs to be painted, of course,' Templeman explained. 'The facial expression will be exaggerated for comic effect.'

'At an exaggerated cost, no doubt.' Farquhar's face was growing purple. Giles looked to Alfie for support.

'My wife has a steady hand and a good eye for detail,' Alfie said.

'You are suggesting your wife should paint the town cooper?'

'It won't be the actual cooper.' Alfie re-assured the hotel owner. 'We wouldn't want to offend anyone.'

103

'You had better not, or you will be responsible for the court fees.' Farquhar looked from Alfie to Giles then back at the model. 'I am disappointed gentlemen, especially with you, Peters. I expected more, considering the amount of money the hotel is paying.'

'More?' Giles' voice was half an octave higher than Alfie's, but the words came out in unison.

'Don't take me for a fool. I have done my research. It isn't uncommon for public clocks to show not only the time in situ, but also in the main cities of Europe and America. In addition, in the better clocks, the phases of the moon and the tides are also displayed.'

'That wouldn't be a problem from a clock making point of view,' Alfie controlled his temper, 'but where would I put the dials? Mr Templeman's design for the face has already been approved. Whether it is artistically sublime,' Alfie remembered the phrase from the newspaper, 'or otherwise, is not for me to say, but it allows no leeway for astronomical recordings.'

'What is he talking about?' Farquhar turned to Giles.

'I intend the face of the clock to depict a scene from the Garden of Eden, painted in oils,' Giles replied. 'A place before time.'

'I thought we had agreed on the city's coat of arms?'

'Heraldry is so out of style. I discussed the alterations with Walker. He was thrilled with the sketches.'

'Was he? Then perhaps he can honour this bill for exotic pigments.' Farquhar slammed another paper on the desk.

'I would hardly call vermilion exotic,' Giles protested.

There was a silence disturbed only by the ticking of the wall clock as Alfie clenched and unclenched his fists to its rhythm. Giles pretended to peruse the bill until Farquhar's temper cooled.

'I have had another idea,' Templeman said.

'Yes?' Alfie's response was a fraction of a second ahead of Farquhar's.

'A model railway.'

'You already have that,' Farquhar said.

'We have an engine that puffs smoke, but what I envisage is a complete train, with carriages and cargo wagons. It will ride on a track round the inside of the clock, stopping at stations in different parts of the clock. You can do that, can't you Alfie?'

'Perhaps you'd like the guard to have a pop up sign demonstrating the time in Perth, Australia?' Alfie answered.

'Farquhar stuck out his bottom lip. 'I like that, Peters,' he said, 'but not only Perth, what about Peking, Buenos Aires, Calcutta…?'

'Kathmandu?' Alfie suggested.

'This is a big project, gentlemen. There is no place for mediocrity,' Farquhar answered.

'I couldn't agree more,' Templeman gave a smile, showing a mouthful of well-developed incisors that made him look like a rabbit.

'And who is going to get the credit for this?' Alfie asked.

Farquhar and Templeman stared at him as if he had suggested burning babies.

'I read only Templeman's name in the paper this morning.'

'I can't imagine you read my name either, or that of Squires,' Farquhar replied. 'It was our idea and we are the ones paying for it, but do you hear us complain?'

Both their names had been cited, in two separate paragraphs, but Alfie didn't waste his breath arguing. He made a show of packing up his sketches.

'I'll keep this, if you don't mind.' Templeman lifted the model. 'I can work on the face. Your wife has other things to think about.'

Alfie let him take it. He would need it back later, but for the moment he could work on the clock workings without dolls getting in the way.

'Your wife is expecting, is she not?' Farquhar said as Alfie walked to the door.

'The baby is due at the beginning of February.'

Farquhar looked like he wanted to make a clever comment, but nothing came into his head. He chose instead to give a laugh before consulting his diary. 'I have business in London in a fortnight, so we'll meet again in three weeks. He rose. 'Thank you, gentlemen.'

'I need a drink. Are you with me?' Giles invited Alfie to the bar when they left Farquhar's office.

Alfie would have preferred one of the less expensive inns in town, but Templeman led the way to the cosier of the hotel bars with long strides. By the time Alfie got there, Giles was perched on a stool at the counter. Alfie made a point of sitting at a table in the corner and Giles was forced to come over.

'What's your tipple?'

'Whisky. I'll have a malt, if you are paying.' There was no point being circumspect with Templeman. It was early, but Alfie felt he deserved a drink. Giles made his way to the bar, stepping in front of an older gentleman. He returned a few minutes later.

'I'm sorry you're unhappy about the newspaper article, but there's no need to get in a twist about it,' Giles said. He set the glasses on the table and sat opposite Alfie. 'Once this clock is finished, we'll both have our pictures in more prestigious journals than that local rag. There are important people in the States keeping a watch on what we are doing.' Alfie gave a grunt at the pun. 'Oh, I get it, "a watch",' Giles chuckled. 'What I mean is, this clock will be the making of both our careers.'

'Once it's finished,' Alfie qualified. 'It hasn't even been started yet, as Farquhar pointed out, and it won't be until I receive your final plan.'

'You'll have it by Christmas. I need to add in the new railway and that little stream that runs through the city.'

'You mean the Tay?'

'Sure. Say! That fits with the name of the hotel. We can have a reservoir at the top. The water can flow round the whisky workers and a pumping device can take it back up.'

'Nothing simpler.' Alfie hoped Giles didn't have any more brilliant ideas before Christmas. He would have said something of this nature to Templeman, but he didn't imagine the American understood sarcasm. Templeman's attention had flitted elsewhere. He rose in his seat and tilted his head to see past the two tweed clad gentlemen with golf bags.

'Did you see her?' he asked Alfie.

'See who?'

'The gal.'

Alfie shook his head. 'What gal?'

'The maid. The cute, blonde one. She has a thing for me. Slipped a letter under my door inviting me for you know what.' Giles winked in an un-American manner.

'You mean...? Surely not. The gall. What is the world coming to?'

'Nothing wrong with a bit of amusement on the side, as long as Emily or her father don't find out. I intend proposing to Emily on Christmas day. I've been invited to the house for dinner.'

'Marriage? You hardly know the girl.'

'I've known her long enough to know she's the gal for me.'

'Do you intend settling here in Britain, or is Miss Squires happy to move with you to New York?'

'Once we're married, Emily will support me in my work. If the big commissions are in the States, that's where we'll go.'

'She may not accept your offer.'

'She isn't likely to get a better one.'

'Not even with her father's money?' Alfie enjoyed the abashed look on Giles' face. 'I imagine that will come in useful until you are established. As long as nobody finds out about the maid.'

'What do you mean by that? Damn it man, I haven't touched

the gal.'

Alfie gave a wink, similar to the one Templeman used a few moments earlier. He downed the remains of his whisky and rose. 'If you could let me have the finished drawings at your convenience. The sooner the clock is hanging from the ceiling out there, the sooner you'll be on your way to better things.'

'No wait, there's something else I want to speak to you about,' Giles put a hand on Alfie's elbow and gave a furtive look round. 'That other clock you were working on.'

'The astronomical clock?' Alfie sat back down and signalled the barman to bring another drink. 'You wish to purchase one as a gift for Miss Squires, perhaps?'

'I'm not bothered about the clock, it's time I'm interested in. Time travel to be precise. I've been reading up about it.'

'In the science journals or the fantastic story collections written by writers with too much time on their hands and opium in their heads?'

'I'm an American. I'm not taken in by castles in the air, but we are living in an age when miracles become reality every month, every week. Bridges span gaps never before imagined. Railways connect great cities. Steel-framed buildings are rising to the sky. You do believe time travel is possible, theoretically?'

'Anything is possible, theoretically,' Alfie answered. He thought to add '*even your damn clock design*', but held his tongue, intrigued to hear more of Templeman's outrageous idea.

'I believe a modified steam engine could be attached to magnetised springs, generating the power to…' Alfie interrupted him with a loud guffaw that drew the attention of the golfing gentlemen. 'You have a better idea?' Templeman asked.

Alfie ran his tongue round the inside of his mouth, but didn't answer.

'I see, keeping your thoughts to yourself. Wise man.'

'A time machine?' Alfie pondered. 'It may be possible.'

He paused while the barman served their drinks and loitered at the table until Giles slipped him a coin. The waiter left. Alfie took his time, swallowing the whisky and wiping his lips before continuing.

'It would take more than a steam engine to generate the power needed to travel faster than light and who knows what such power would do to a man's constitution.'

'What would it need?' Giles leaned towards him.

'A better man than me.' Alfie finished his drink. He banged into the table as he stood up and held the edge to steady himself.

'But in material terms?' Giles persisted.

'Cogs and wheels, pistons and pendulums.' He let go of the table and staggered towards the door. The golfers had departed and Alfie stopped when he reached the table nearest the exit and laughed. 'Of course it would need a large casing to house them in,' he said, as if to himself, but loud enough for Templeman to overhear. 'A very large casing. Where would a man find one of those?'

Chapter 7

Templeman was an American, but even so, Alfie hadn't expected him to be quite so gullible, or persistent. It was an amusement at first to lead the young man on with rough sketches showing elaborate time travelling machines with inset diagrams of impossible mechanisms, but the continued questioning became tedious. Giles scrutinised his fantastical suggestions in detail and at the same time his designs for the clock became ever more complicated. Alfie didn't doubt there was a connection between the two, which made Templeman's references to the clock as 'his' invention harder to swallow.

Scribbled additions were added to the plans on a daily basis such that – his clock or their clock - it seemed unlikely there would be a clock at all. This fact didn't slip Farquhar's attention. An extraordinary meeting was called, with the hotelier threatening to close the book on the project.

'Now I've had time to contemplate the matter, I realise we were wrong to commission such a vanity,' Farquhar declared.

'The decision was a joint one.' Squires felt he should put down his mark. 'For my part, I am happy for Mr Templeman and Mr Peters to continue with the work.'

'Work? Ha, I don't see much of that. Only bills.'

113

'I will honour the bills, for now. Imagine the faces of our rivals when they see such a centrepiece,' Squires tried to convince his partner.

'It would be good if we could see it first,' Farquhar countered.

'The plans will be ready by the New Year, won't they, Giles?' Squires asked.

'They will be ready by Christmas Eve,' Giles asserted.

'Then I propose we have another meeting then,' Farquhar dismissed them.

'Christmas Eve? I'm afraid that is impossible,' Alfie answered. 'I have business in Edinburgh on Christmas Eve that cannot be cancelled or postponed.'

'Waiting a few days until after the celebrations will make little difference,' Squires mollified. Farquhar gave a grunt.

'If that is settled, I'll wish you Good Day.' Alfie didn't wait for Farquhar to object. He replaced his hat and made for the door. Templeman and Squires followed him out.

'Drinks, gentlemen?' Squires enquired.

There was a general muttering of agreement and the three men retired to the hotel bar.

'Don't mind Adam,' Squires said. 'He's having domestic problems. His son has taken up with an unsavoury group of artistic drop-outs in Paris.'

'We all have our worries,' Alfie said.

'He's concerned it will interfere with our business plans on the Continent. However, if your wife is to be alone on Christmas Eve while you are in Edinburgh, perhaps she would accept an invitation to our house party.'

'Thank you,' Alfie said. That would stop her wanting to accompany him to the capital again.

'Good. Now I'm sorry I can't stay, gentlemen. Have what you want on the house.' Squires spoke with the bar attendant before he left and the man brought over a neat whisky for Alfie and a bourbon and soda for Giles.

'What's your business in Edinburgh?' Giles asked.

Alfie assumed Giles was only making polite conversation, but he had no wish to answer.

'I understand, you are keeping it secret,' Giles tapped his nose. 'Are you visiting clock makers?'

'Aye, indeed,' Alfie laughed. Visiting clockmakers was the code he invented to tease Giles. Whenever he spoke about a time travelling machine, he would say he was visiting clock makers for ideas or parts. 'A rather grand one at that,' he added.

It wasn't a lie. Dotty had learned from her father and digested the professional journals like a ravenous hippopotamus.

Alfie had begun the tradition of visiting Dotty the first Christmas Eve after her admission to the asylum and he liked to think she looked forward to the occasion. Nancy had boiled up toffee to a stronger recipe, and he felt sure the doctor would permit Dotty a seasonal treat. He wondered how she would receive him. She had been different at the last visit; younger, more alive, more like the Dotty he'd married. There had been no further word of her progress from Dr Matthews, which could be taken in several ways.

'Anybody at home?' Giles interrupted his thoughts.

'I was thinking, the sooner the workmen finish the bridge over the Forth the better. I'm not looking forward to the icy river crossing at this time of year.'

'I'm from New York, I'm used to several feet of snow.'

Alfie had a feeling Templeman would say something of that nature. He hadn't known more than two Americans in his life, but it was common knowledge they were insecure about their country and compensated by exaggeration. Not that inclement weather was something to boast about.

'I wish you good luck with Miss Emily Squires. You did say it is Miss Emily you propose to propose to?' Alfie chuckled.

'Emily, yes. Her sister Lucy is fairer looking, I grant you, but her tongue is sharp to match. Emily has more the temperament for a wife.'

'And she is her father's favourite,' Alfie said. He rose to leave before Giles could reply. It was gratifying to have the last word.

Winnie was delighted with the Squires' invitation to visit on Christmas Eve, but not so happy that Alfie wouldn't be accompanying her.

'You need to socialise with these people,' she reminded him. 'If you want to raise your profile in town. Walker Squires could get you onto the council.'

'I've no desire to be beholden to anyone.'

'I wouldn't call it that. Payment, more like. Think what you are doing for the reputation of his hotel.'

So far he had taken Squires' money and done little work for it, but Alfie didn't explain this to Winnie.

His wallet was barely allowed to rest in his pocket on the days leading up to Christmas Eve. The normally thrifty Winnie let her standards lapse to decorate the house and provide ample food, drink and gifts for all and sundry. On Christmas Eve she was up early, preparing him a mug of cocoa and toasted muffins before he left for Edinburgh.

'I've no time for breakfast.' Alfie struggled with his tie. Winnie knotted it for him.

'You need to keep your strength up.'

She forced a muffin into his hand. He swallowed it in three bites and took a gulp of the cocoa to please her. The drink was hot and burnt his throat. Winnie leaned over to give him a kiss on the cheek. Her belly bumped against his.

'It won't be long now. Isn't it exciting?'

Children were no more than hungry vermin until they were at least three. Alfie pictured Teddy and amended that to five. He prayed Winnie's son would be more suited to clock making.

'I'm excited,' he said to please Winnie. 'I'll try to be back before supper.'

'I could stay overnight with the Squires,' Winnie said.

'That is an excellent idea.'

Alfie thought about Nancy. The hotel would be full over the festive period, meaning Maggie would not be allowed to go home for Christmas. Nancy would be alone, apart from Teddy. Hopefully she would be glad to see him.

The weather was mild for the season and the journey to the capital uneventful. Work had stopped on the bridge, which pleased the ferry crew according to the gossip he overheard.

'With luck the New Year will bring an end to such nonsense.'
'It's progress, man.'

The ferry's horn blasted and Alfie didn't hear the boathand's reply. It started to rain as Alfie waited for the coach and he hoped the temperature would not drop enough for snow. The walk to the hospital was bad enough, without that. Luckily he was spared snow, but the rain continued. The building looked a washed out grey, as he approached, but he could see lights burning inside. There was a new man at the reception desk, a young man wearing a clean uniform and a name badge.

'Where is Warden Thomson tonight, Philip?' Alfie asked, peering at the man's badge. 'Enjoying a Christmas drink in the local hostelry?'

'I'm sorry to say the warden has taken ill,' the man answered.

'Nothing serious, I hope.'

'Mr. Thomson has taken fits. Quite frightful to behold, according to matron. During the last one he bit the tip of his tongue clean off. Dr Matthews had to have him restrained before he did himself a mischief.'

'Gracious, it wasn't anything he caught from one of the patients?'

'I shouldn't be discussing it,' the young man said, 'Dr Matthews thinks it is because he eats too many sweets.'

'Dr Matthews thinks sugar is the cause of every ill in the world,' Alfie said with a frown. 'I had better see my wife. How is she?'

'She's with Dr Matthews,' the young man replied. It wasn't an answer to Alfie's question, or perhaps it was.

'Where will I find them?'

'It's Christmas Eve.'

Alfie began to think the young man was actually one of the patients who had taken over for the evening. 'Should I wait on Nurse Horton?' he asked.

'I wouldn't do that, sir.'

'Why not?'

'She was dismissed last month. Dr Matthews found her shearing the patients' hair to sell to the wigmaker.'

'I thought that was normal procedure. There's no accounting for what Dr Matthews will think to do next,' Alfie said. 'Can you tell me, in plain English, where I can find my wife?'

'She is in the music room. That's where the party is.'

'The party?'

'It's Christmas Eve, sir.'

'So you said.'

The young man's answers were worse than riddles. Alfie decided to make his own way along the corridor. If there was a party, especially in a hospital for the mentally unsound, there was bound to be noise. He headed left along the first corridor, surprised to find the floor had been swept and the walls washed down. Instead of the odour of boiled cod liver, which Dr Matthews prescribed as a diet for all his patients, there was the pleasant aroma of roasting goose. Cheered by this, Alfie stopped below the clock, intending to remove it from the wall to inspect the workings. Contrary to his expectation the hands on the clock were ticking rhythmically.

'Why, this is wrong,' he said aloud, not realising the young man from reception had followed him along the corridor.

'Can I help you?' the man asked.

'Do you think I can't walk along a corridor on my own?'

'I'm just taking a message to the cook,' the man said, waving a sheet of paper.

'What has happened to this clock?'

'It looks to be at the right time, sir.' The young man checked his pocket watch.

'I realise that. I learned to tell the time when I was four,' Alfie blustered. 'But this clock has been at five to two for at least five years.'

'I wouldn't know, sir. I've only been working here a month. I imagine Dr Matthews must have had it fixed. He likes fixing things.'

'Which is why he is a doctor,' Alfie replied.

'My dad likes fixing things. He's a cobbler.'

'I couldn't care less if your father was a circus clown, which well he may have been, judging by his son,' Alfie scoffed.

'I believe it was your wife who fixed the clock.'

Mending clocks? A person needed a steady hand and patience for that.

A bell rang in reception. The young man rubbed his chin with the hand holding the paper, dithering over whether to answer it or continue to the kitchen. He excused himself and walked a few steps then stopped and turned round.

'Dr Matthews is talking about getting one of these new telephones installed,' the young man said. 'They say you can hear people speaking from miles away.'

'Not always a good thing,' Alfie said. 'Hearing what a wife says is the start of many a domestic argument. In my case, at least.'

Alfie immediately realised mentioning arguments with Winnie was a mistake, but the words were out. Fortunately the young man was hurrying back along the corridor and if he had heard, he hadn't engaged his brain to digest what was said.

Alfie continued along the corridor. He reached the end wall without finding the party and turned down the passageway on his right. The receptionist's words stuck in his head.

Telephones and sound travel.

He spoke the words aloud and the sound of his voice bounced off the polished floor tiles. There was a staircase at the end of the corridor. Hearing the strident notes of an out-of-tune piano, Alfie made his way up. He stopped to get his breath on the landing and noticed coloured ribbons tied onto the handle of the door in front of him. He paused outside to listen. The music was coming from within. He waited until the tune finished before opening the door.

The room was bursting with mirth. Happy faces, laughter, smiles and applauding. For a second Alfie feared he had walked into a Dickens novel. The hospital staff mingled with the patients. He recognised one of the nurses although the woman was not in uniform, but it was impossible to tell the others apart. His eyes moved to the upright piano in the corner. Dotty was seated on a stool, balancing her fingers on the keys and studying the music sheet. She was wearing a delightful blue dress. Beside her, close beside her playing a duet, was Dr John Matthews. The laughter died as the people in the room spotted Alfie. Dr Matthews rose.

'Mr Peters, do come in. We weren't expecting you. You should have told us you were coming.'

'I come every Christmas Eve,' Alfie replied. 'Perhaps you should have informed me of this social gathering.'

He spoke to the doctor, but looked at Dotty. She had her face half turned away from him, but he saw she was blushing.

'Dr Lutheral forgot to inform me. Please, have a seat. Dorothy was about to perform a piece from Handel.'

'I'm sorry, I can't.' Dotty rose from the piano stool.

The patient sitting nearest the window began barking and the woman next to her baa-d like a sheep. This set off a medley of animal noises. Instead of trying to calm the room, Dr Matthews allowed the farmyard chorus to continue. Alfie was standing in the doorway, but he moved into the room and took hold of Dotty's arm.

'Come, we'll talk away from this bunch of lunatics.'

'I'd rather you didn't use that word,' Dr Matthews said.

'What else can you call a grown woman acting like a rabid dog and another crawling on the floor like a snake?' Alfie didn't wait for a medical answer from the doctor. He manoeuvred Dotty to the door and into the corridor. Dr Matthews made his way past the revellers and followed them out.

'You can speak here,' Dr Matthews said, opening the door to the neighbouring room. It was sparsely furnished, but clean and bright.

'Thank you,' Dotty spoke softly.

Dr Matthews glanced at Alfie, who still had hold of Dotty's arm. He let go and the doctor left to return to his patients.

'I didn't know you played the piano,' Alfie said when they were alone.

'John has been teaching me.'

'John?'

'Dr Matthews.'

'I know his name. I was questioning your intimacy. The man is your physician, not your brother.'

'Dr Matthews likes us to use first names. He says it makes the atmosphere more relaxed.' Dotty moved to the window to look out. The weak sun poked a ray through the clouds.

'This is a hospital, not a play park,' Alfie argued. Dotty didn't answer and he walked across to stand next to her. She took a step away from him.

'You like Dr Matthews, don't you?' he accused.

'He is kind. He cares for his patients. He is a good doctor.'

'So good he's forced to work here.'

'Nobody forced him. What is wrong with working here?' Dotty asked. Alfie made a face, but didn't explain. 'We shouldn't talk about Dr Matthews on Christmas Eve, Alfie,' Dotty said.

'What should we talk about?'

'Us. You could tell me what you are doing. Are you keeping well? How is the work on your clock?' She clapped her hands. 'I'd love to hear about that.'

'There is nothing to tell.'

'Please, Alfie.'

'I would if I could, but Templeman hasn't produced the final plans yet. Now he wants the Tay running through the casing.'

'A water clock? Why, that sounds wonderful,' Dotty's face brightened. 'Think of the intricacies. You could use an escapement with springs and epicyclical gears.'

Alfie stared at her then laughed. 'As long as we don't spring a leak and soak the hotel guests.'

'I wish I had a pencil and paper so I could draw it for you.' Dotty looked around the room, but there was nothing available.

'I saw you mended the clock on the wall,' Alfie said.

'That was simple. One of the cogs was stuck. A dead spider was blocking the works.'

'A spider?' Alfie's laugh was genuine.

They spoke about clocks and repairs. Dotty's face glowed and her breast seemed to swell beneath her dress. Alfie was drawn to the pale, smooth skin. He felt hot and felt a rush of blood. Ridiculous, he thought. This is Dotty. He reached out a hand, but the door of the room opened and he drew it back.

'I'm not disturbing you, am I?' Dr Matthews asked. 'It is getting late. The other patients are desperate to hear you sing, Dorothy. They won't settle until you do. Would you mind if I borrowed your wife, Mr Peters?'

'We are having a discussion,' Alfie said. 'Can't it wait?'

'Not if all the windows are to remain intact.'

'I have to go,' Dotty said. 'I promised I would sing. I shall ask for paper and a pencil and have the drawings we spoke of ready for your next visit.' She walked to the door and turned to Alfie. 'Did you bring me any toffee? I'm sure Dr Matthews will let me have some, since it is Christmas.'

'Well, perhaps one,' Dr Matthews relented.

Alfie felt in his pocket. His fingers touched the bag of toffees. Dotty was smiling at him. The fringe of her hair covered most of her defect. 'I'm sorry I must have left them on the dressing table at home.' Dotty's face fell.

'Don't be sad,' Dr Matthews said. 'Cook has something sweet planned for pudding tomorrow.'

Dotty clapped her hands, gave Alfie a curtsey and bobbed out of the room.

'Will you join us?' Dr Matthews asked Alfie.

'No, I should be getting back to Perth. Dotty is looking well.' He paused and chewed the inside of his gum. 'I think perhaps my wife's constitution may be able to stand the necessary anaesthetic and surgery to improve her face.'

'Am I to understand then that you give permission for your wife to have an operation?' Dr Matthews asked.

'That is what I said,' Alfie answered. 'When will the procedure be performed?'

'I shall speak with my surgeon friend and let you know as soon as I can. Thank you. Dorothy will be delighted. Once she recovers, there will be no impediment to her leaving the hospital.'

'There are risks involved with the surgery, I imagine,' Alfie said. 'Your friend will be cutting near the facial nerves.'

'Dorothy is willing to take the risk and I am glad you support her.'

Alfie nodded to the doctor and left before his better judgement cautioned him to change his mind. The piano was playing and he could hear the faint hum of 'O Holy Night.'

'You are missing the concert,' he said to the young man at reception.

'I have the day off tomorrow. I'll have enough singing from my grandmother to last until Easter.'

'Give my best wishes to the warden for a speedy recovery.'

'I'll do that sir, but I wouldn't be too hopeful. They had to use the straight-jacket this morning.'

'I see. How is Dr Lutheral? Faring better, I hope.'

'Indeed sir, he has retired to a nursing home in the Swiss Alps.'

Out of the way of inquiries. We won't be seeing him again, Alfie thought.

'He sent a card.' The young man reached over to pick up a card with a picture of a snow covered mountain. 'The Jungfrau, I believe.'

'Apt,' Alfie said. He glanced at the card, but didn't read the greeting. It was no doubt written by the doctor's wife. 'Merry Christmas,' he said to the young man, touching his hat.

Outside he deposited the bag of toffees in the nearest litter bin. He doubted the city council would thank him for the dead rats the following morning.

Chapter 8

Snow crystals clung to the train windows as Alfie boarded. He had dallied to buy Christmas gifts in Edinburgh and now Fife was invisible in a flurry of white. By the time he came to alight there was a thick covering on the ground and it was doubtful the train would complete its journey to Perth that evening. Nancy was waiting for him on the platform, wrapped in a woollen shawl.

'I thought with this weather you might not come,' she said, grabbing hold of his arm to link it to hers.

'It was braw in Edinburgh when I left,' Alfie said. He spotted Teddy throwing snowballs at one of the village dogs. A chunk of ice caught the animal's ear and it let out a shriek. Ted laughed.

'See mum, I hit it.'

'Good boy, now come to your father.'

'Have you brought me a present?' the boy demanded.

For a wicked second Alfie wished he hadn't thrown the toffee away. 'Yes, but you have to be good.'

'I'm always good, ain't I mum? I'm her angel.'

The angel picked up more snow and threw it at a small girl on the platform, dressed in a pretty pink dress and red coat. Ted hid behind Nancy's legs when the mother looked round.

'Let's get home,' Alfie said.

'That's the first time you've called my cottage home,' Nancy said with a beam.

'That can't be true,' Alfie answered. He thought of Winnie and her house in Perth. That wasn't his home. Neither was old Charlie's empty apartment above the shop. An image of Dotty busy in her father's workshop flashed in his head. A happy, whole Dotty.

'How is Dotty?' Nancy asked, as if reading his thoughts.

'Remarkably well,' Alfie said. 'You might almost think she was in sound mind.'

Nancy stopped walking and let go of his arm. 'You gave her the toffees, didn't you?'

'No, I threw them away.'

'Why?' Nancy's voice was harsh.

'Because the warden has been eating them.'

'Oh. Is he well?'

'He has taken fits. Bad ones. He must have a very sweet tooth.'

'Oh,' Nancy said again. She brushed the snow from her coat.

'Don't worry about Dotty. I have agreed for her to have surgery on her face. The risks are severe. If she survives the operation, it is likely the butcher will have made her repulsive even to the good doctor. The distress will be too much for her to bear.'

Nancy pouted for a second. Alfie put his arms around her waist. 'The sooner we are indoors, the sooner we can take our clothes off.'

She pushed him away. 'You only come here for one thing.'

'You enjoy my company, don't you?'

'Yes, but I wish we could talk more too.'

'What would you like to talk about?'

'I don't know.'

'Women always want to talk, but when they are given the chance, they have no opinions on anything but domestic matters.'

'Tell me about Perth? Maggie says the city is looking bonny for Christmas, with the shop windows decorated. I'd love to see them and buy roasted chestnuts from street sellers. So would Teddy, wouldn't you?'

Teddy had run off to slide in the snow.

'He'll ruin his trousers doing that,' Alfie moaned.

'He's just a boy.'

'And I'm the one paying for the trousers.'

'Maggie sends us money too,' Nancy said. Alfie took this as a reproach.

'Don't I give you enough?'

'You are in a strange mood today, Alfred Peters,' Nancy said.

She increased her pace and Alfie puffed as he kept up. 'Maggie has left the hotel,' she informed him as they reached the cottage.

'Dismissed?'

'Why do you say that? No, she has found a place in a respectable household. The money is a deal better.'

'There is no such thing as a respectable household,' Alfie grumbled. At least if the girl was away from the hotel she would be out of his hair. They went inside. Teddy was reluctant to stop his play, but a look from Alfie made him drop the snowball he was about to throw at the neighbour's window and go inside. Nancy filled the kettle and put it on the stove.

'We'll have a nice cup of tea,' she said.

'If you've nothing stronger to warm the bones,' Alfie said. He hung up his coat, hat and bag before taking the best seat beside the fire.

'Where's my present?' Teddy demanded. Alfie gestured towards his bag. Teddy ran across, but couldn't reach it. He swung on the stand, intent on knocking it over. Luckily Nancy saw him and steadied the wooden pole before it fell on top of the boy. She lifted the bag down, rummaged inside and handed Ted the toy train Alfie had bought in Edinburgh. The boy grabbed it and ran off without thanks.

'Why, what is this?' Nancy removed a pink box with a yellow ribbon and bow from the bag.

'No,' Alfie leapt up. Nancy's hand shook and she dropped the gift. Alfie bent to pick it up. 'It was meant as a surprise,' he softened his voice.

A surprise for Winnie. An expensive one at that.

Nancy opened the box to reveal a glass jar of French perfume. 'You shouldn't have.' She moved to kiss his cheek. 'I haven't had anything like this before.' She took the lid off the bottle and splashed the liquid on her neck and arms. The smell of flowers was overpowering.

'A little at a time, dear,' Alfie said. 'That's how the ladies in Perth use it.'

'What would you know of the ladies in Perth?' Nancy teased.

'I am going up in the world,' Alfie boasted. 'I may be elected to the city council.'

'Wonderful,' Nancy paused. She hopped from one leg to the other. 'Alfie, I was thinking, do we really need to wait until Dotty has…you know… before we set up home together? We could buy a nice house in Perth, beside the river.'

'You are talking nonsense, woman. Haven't I just told you I wish to get onto the council? There can be no impropriety'

'People would understand. It's a pity Dr Lutheral has retired. I believe he would have obliged with a false death certificate for Dotty, if you'd asked him.'

Alfie felt his cheeks redden. 'Paid him, you mean.'

'It would have been worth it.'

'Dr Matthews is in charge now. I can't see him agreeing to anything illegal.'

'We'll put our hopes on the surgery, then,' Nancy said. 'I'd better go and see to Teddy.'

'You are always running after that imbecile boy.' Alfie reached out and prevented Nancy from leaving. 'It's time you looked after me.'

'Don't worry you'll get your present. Let me see to Teddy, first.'

Nancy was not as accommodating in bed as usual. Alfie left before the sun rose the following morning. Nancy was sleeping, despite the whooping noises from Teddy in the next room. He spotted the perfume bottle in the living room as he gathered his hat and coat. He had promised Winnie a gift from Edinburgh, and hell would break loose if he didn't bring her something. Making sure the bottle was well stoppered, he slipped the perfume into his bag, confident that Nancy would blame Teddy for its disappearance. He would have to top up the bottle with water to

135

placate Winnie, or she would wonder why it was a quarter empty.

The snow was clearing to leave ice and sludge. The walk to the station in the dark was unpleasant and precarious. The railway timetable was disrupted and he had to wait a good half hour for the train. He blew on his hands and took a seat in the waiting room. He didn't have a newspaper, so there was time to think. In a week it would be the start of a new year and only a few months until his birthday. He didn't lay much store by celebrations, but he would be fifty, half a century, a milestone in any man's life. The thought of marking the occasion was rumbling in his brain. It would coincide with the unveiling of the clock – if things went to Farquhar's plan.

'Do you intend travelling, sir?'

Alfie was preoccupied with his thoughts and hadn't seen or heard the train draw up. The guard had raised his flag, preparing to signal for its departure. Alfie jumped up and rushed for the nearest door. He found a seat at the window and as the train pulled out he spotted his bag sitting on the station bench.

Winnie was fussing around arranging decorations on a tree while she waited for his arrival. She rushed at him with a sprig of mistletoe the second he closed the front door.

'How was Edinburgh?' she asked.

'Grey,' Alfie answered.

'That can't be true,' Winnie was in a playful mood, cavorting about like a mountain goat on heat.

'I left your present at the station.'

'In Perth?'

'No, in... I've reported the situation to the gentleman at the lost property office,' Alfie moved to the tree and adjusted the star on the top.

'What did you get me?' Winnie asked.

'Perfume.'

'What kind?'

'French. I can't remember the name. It had a floral aroma.' Alfie could smell the particles remaining up his nostril from Nancy's over-enthusiastic application. 'How did you get on at the Squires'?'

'It was so thrilling. Mr. Templeman proposed to young Emily Squires.'

'Did she accept?'

'She took her time, teasing him over dinner, but when the carol singers were singing O Holy Night she said "yes".'

'More fool her,' Alfie grumbled.

'You are such an old cynic,' Winnie said. 'Lucy Squires gave her sister an evil look when Mr. Templeman proposed. She complained of a headache and had to retire. The poor girl missed the brandy pudding. Jealous, no doubt. She is a good two years older than Miss Emily, and still unmarried.'

'I fancy Miss Lucy isn't keen on marriage,' Alfie said.

'I fancy she had an eye on Mr. Templeman herself,' Winnie said.

'Really?' Alfie considered the point and gave a laugh. 'So, when is the wedding?'

'In March.'

'Why so soon?' Alfie raised an eyebrow.

'It's nothing like that,' Winnie said, assuming he was suggesting a baby might be involved. 'Giles wants it to fall in with the inauguration of the West Tay clock.'

'If the clock breaks, so does the marriage,' Alfie pondered. 'There is always Miss Lucy to fall back on.'

'Don't be horrid.'

'Who said the clock was going to break? I'm responsible for the workings, remember.'

'I know,' Winnie said. She repositioned a candle on the table before relaying her next piece of news. 'The Squires have got a new house maid.'

'That doesn't mean we have to get one.'

'No?' Winnie twirled her skirt.

'What is she like?' Alfie asked.

'The maid? A strange sort of girl, pleasant to the eye although a little too attractive for her position. She can't have been in service long. Her manners left much to be desired. She kept looking at me as if I had three heads. When she spilled the coffee on my blouse, I'm sure it was no accident.'

'You are imagining things, dear.'

'I got the feeling we had met before.'

'All maids look the same. I need to freshen up before lunch.'

Alfie took his time washing and changing. When he returned downstairs Winnie was at the door talking to somebody. She shut it as he approached.

'Who was that?' Alfie asked.

'A boy from the railway company. He brought your bag.'

'Excellent.' Alfie held out his hand. Winnie clung onto the bag.

'Funny,' she said. 'You didn't leave it in Edinburgh.'

'I didn't say that I did,' Alfie said.

'No, but how did it get to a village over five miles from here?' Winnie opened the bag and lifted out the bottle of perfume. 'And why is this half empty?'

Chapter 9

Winnie accepted his excuse of returning a repaired watch to a housebound client and she didn't make a fuss when he explained he had spilt the perfume when sampling it.

'You and your clockmaker hands,' she scolded, giving him a kiss.

Nevertheless, Alfie knew it wouldn't be wise to visit Nancy again in the near future. The thought didn't bother him. He barely thought of her or Teddy when he was in Perth and he certainly didn't expect another visit from Maggie quite so soon. The city was recovering from the New Year celebrations when she breezed into his shop, bringing with her an icy wind.

'Shut the door,' Alfie called from behind the back shelf. He heard the latch click and set aside the watch he was working on.

'Happy New Year, da'.'

Alfie grunted. He wrapped the broken watch in a linen cloth before venturing out to face Maggie. 'What are you doing here?'

'I brought this.' She waved a rolled up parchment in front of her like a colliery band master's baton.

'Am I supposed to be concerned or excited?'

'You could at least be interested.' Maggie dropped her hand to her side.

'I have better things to do than play childish games. Are you going to tell me what it is, or not?'

'If you're going to be like that, I'll take it back to Mr Templeman and tell him you couldn't be arsed to look at it. I'll tell Mr Squires as well.'

'Mind your language, girl. What have you to do with gentlemen like Mr Templeman and Mr Squires?' Alfie squinted to look for clues on the parchment.

'I work for Mr Squires, don't I? Mr Templeman is never away from the house, courting his petted daughter.'

'Your mother told me you had left the hotel,' Alfie recalled. He could see the edge of a pencil sketch and took it to be Templeman's plans for the clock. The man must be out of his mind entrusting the delivery of a document as valuable as that to a serving girl.

'That's right. I'm the personal maid to Miss Lucy Squires and her sister Emily, although I spend more time running after their mother. She asks me to read to her. Says she likes my voice. It's mell...mellu...something.'

'Mellifluous,' Alfie suggested, 'although that isn't the word I would use.'

'Think what you want. I have a room to myself in their fancy

141

house overlooking the river. Mr Templeman got me the job. Put in a good word. The sort of thing a father might have done.'

'I offered to find you a place in Edinburgh, if you remember, but you thought going into service was beneath you. What made you change your mind?'

'Mr Templeman. He's a real gent. So is Mr Squires. He lets me have the dresses Lucy and Emily have finished with.'

'Anyone would think you were a beggar.' Alfie tapped his fingers on the counter. 'Enough of this, give me the diagram.'

Maggie held the paper out, but drew it back when Alfie tried to take it. 'I met Mrs Peters at Christmas. Expecting a baby, she was. At least, she was introduced as Mrs Peters, the clockmaker's wife, but that can't be right can it? Your wife is still alive, in a hospital in Edinburgh.'

Alfie lunged forwards and grabbed Maggie's coat, lifting her off the ground.

'Let go of me.' She struggled, but when she couldn't free herself she spat in his face.

'Any more of that and I'll call the police,' Alfie threatened.

'What will they charge me with?'

'Troublemaking, for a start. And slander, to boot.'

'It isn't slander if it's true.'

'You will find telling the truth can be very dangerous,' Alfie said. 'Nobody will believe a guttersnipe like you.'

'We'll see. Call the police,' Maggie dared.

'I shall accuse you of stealing.'

'I haven't touched anything of yours.'

'Maybe not of mine, but I imagine you have been lifting little trinkets from the Squires' household? The scent you are reeking of, perhaps? Is that why you left the hotel? Frightened you might get caught nicking trinkets from the guests' bedrooms?'

'I haven't taken anything,' Maggie's voice was too high to be convincing.

'That parchment was given to you by Giles Templeman to be delivered to me. You have refused to do so. I shall say you demanded money before you would hand it over. The police will not look kindly on that.'

'Here, take the paper.' Maggie dropped the document on the floor.

'I don't want it now,' Alfie said, letting Maggie go with a thrust of his hand. 'I shall tell Templeman that you wouldn't give it to me unless I gave you a guinea. I'll make sure Mr Squires knows about it too.'

'Really? What if I were to tell mum that even if your wife died tomorrow – your real wife – she won't be going down the aisle as the next Mrs Peters? Aah, I've got you there.'

Alfie chewed his lip. Maggie bent to pick up the parchment and wiped dust from it before setting it on his counter. She stood opposite him, gloating.

'What do you want?' he said.

'Like you just said, I don't want to spend my life in service.'

'That's what you don't want. I asked what you did want.'

'You're not listening to me. You never do.'

'You are not still harping on about going to school to be a doctor?' Alfie feigned a laugh.

'What's so funny about that? If Teddy wanted to be a doctor you'd give him the money.'

'I can't see Teddy being anything more than a clown, but that isn't the point. Teddy is my son.'

'And I am your daughter. Why can't you admit it?'

'You are not my daughter. Your father was a drunken soldier who got himself killed fighting somebody else's war. Or hasn't your mother told you that? Now get out of here.'

Alfie snatched the diagram and turned towards the upstairs apartment. Maggie didn't move. He couldn't have her standing there. There was no telling what she might say to his customers.

He stopped at the door and turned back. 'Do you intend standing there all day, wasting your employer's time?'

'What's that to you? I can stand here if I want.' She ran a finger along the top of the counter.

'Very well, the next time I am in Edinburgh I shall speak to Dr Matthews and find out what the possibilities and requirements are for a woman to study medicine in the city.'

'Promise?'

'Promise,' he replied.

Maggie jumped towards him and for a moment he thought she might try to kiss him. He stepped back and opened the door to the apartment. 'Now go.'

'I'll hold you to it. I'll tell mum about you and Mrs Peters if you don't.'

'Blackmail is not a nice trait in a young woman.'

'It comes in handy.' She reached the door and opened it. 'Mum says I've got your nose,' she volleyed before leaving and slamming the door.

Alfie waited a moment before returning to the counter. He cleared it of various watch parts in order to spread out the diagram, setting a carriage clock on top of the paper to prevent it rolling back. Templeman might be a decent designer, but he had no training in draughtsmanship. The proportions didn't make sense and the markings were fanciful fabrications. The outcome was a mish-mash of styles, cobbled together in the manner of a second rate shoemaker. The plan wasn't even complete. In one corner he had simply written *'insert working model to represent the seasons'*. Alfie assumed Templeman had put in the note to remind himself, rather than expecting the clockmaker to come up with an idea.

'Preposterous,' Alfie grunted. The casing was a Gothic nightmare, not at all suited to a progressive establishment like the West Tay Hotel. The owners were looking forward to the twentieth century, not back to the thirteenth. Squires talked about having the place powered by electricity with lifts taking guests and their luggage to the upper floors.

His first impulse was to crumple the paper up and toss it on his fire. Perhaps the plan was one of Giles' jokes, which would explain why he gave it to Maggie. The real plans would be sent by a more official method. They had better come soon. Farquhar had called a meeting for the following day.

The afternoon came and went, tailing into the evening. There was no messenger boy with new plans. The shop was empty, which Alfie blamed on the icy pavements, and he decided to take

146

a brisk walk to the hotel to see if Templeman was there. Reason told him the American was more likely to be at the Squires' house with his fiancé, but he had no desire to go there and be greeted by Maggie.

The girl on the hotel reception informed him that Mr. Templeman had gone out, as Alfie expected. He decided to have a drink to warm his bones before heading home. The West Tay wasn't his usual tippling hole - Farquhar had a nerve to complain about *his* bill with the prices he charged – but since he was there he stepped into the lounge. He was about to order the cheapest drink on the list when he spotted Walker Squires scrutinising one of the pictures on the back wall. A quick wave and he was drinking a malt whisky at the hotel owner's expense.

'What do you think of the painting?' Squires asked.

'I'm not partial to these modern geometric designs,' Alfie admitted. 'Give me a good old-fashioned landscape any day.'

'Ah, but the hotel is moving forwards. Did you get the plans for the clock?' Squires asked.

Alfie had taken a sip of whisky and swirled it in his mouth. He intended to savour the spirit before responding.

'Giles had the girl take them over. Don't tell me she didn't find you?' Squires continued.

'Those were the actual plans?' Alfie choked on his drink.

'What do you mean?'

'I assumed it was his American humour. What I saw was a cartoon strip of preposterous ideas.'

'What have you done with them? Don't tell me you've destroyed them. The only other copy is at the printers and we won't get it back before the meeting tomorrow.'

'I have them here,' Alfie tapped his bag, 'They are completely unworkable. For a start, I don't believe the ceiling will have the strength to hold the weight. I'm no builder, but looking at the beams now, I would say it is impossible.'

Squires glanced towards the decorative plasterwork of the ceiling. 'I imagine we can get it reinforced.'

'That will involve architects and builders. Do you think Mr Farquhar will agree to the cost? I think we shall have to go back to the original idea of a free-standing clock.'

Walker Squires spluttered out his drink. 'A "suspended masterpiece" has been advertised on all the hotel's promotional pamphlets. Leaflets have been distributed on the Continent and in the United States. Advanced bookings have been made on the strength of it. Journalists have written articles. There are more waiting to be published. I believe the design has been nominated for prestigious awards.'

Alfie took his time finishing his drink.

'It will be down to Mr Farquhar and yourself, of course. I am simply stating the facts. Thank you for the whisky, but I must be off. Give my congratulations to your daughter Emily on her engagement. I imagine the wedding will be a grand affair.'

He meant an expensive one. Squires' face wasn't visible as he left the lounge, but he imagined it was a deep red.

Winnie was feeling off colour that evening and retired to bed after dinner. Alfie stoked the fire, made a pot of tea and decided to examine the clock plans in greater detail. Templeman would bluster his way around explaining the components, leaving the floor open for him to come up with practical solutions that would impress Farquhar. Hopefully enough for him to agree to the extra cost needed to complete the job. The main problem was how to devise a mechanism to circulate water through the clock the way Templeman outlined. Alfie scribbled diagrams of interlocking wheels and pneumatic pistons on the side of the paper. What was called for was a series of locks, similar to those used by canal builders. Ideally, he would like an opinion from someone experienced in such matters, but he doubted Farquhar would pay for that.

He rolled the plans up and ventured upstairs. From the fifth step he could hear Winnie snoring and decided not to disturb her. The house had spare rooms, but they were covered in sheets awaiting joiners and decorators. He settled for a night on the sofa, tossing the cushions around as fantastic ideas jumped in his head. When he remembered Dotty's suggestion, he fell off onto the carpet. He rubbed his back and sat back on the sofa, propped against a cushion Winnie had embroidered. If only he could remember the details. He hadn't really been listening. A further visit to the asylum was out of the question. He wouldn't be able to justify it to Winnie. She was already asking pertinent questions.

The thought came to him that he could write to Dotty. He hadn't written in the past because there was nothing to say, and Dr Lutheral would not have allowed her to read letters. Dr Matthews was different. He stood up and walked to the sideboard to light a lamp. It was four in the morning, night birds flew in silence. The only sound was his own breathing. Having lit the lamp, he moved across to his desk. Winnie hadn't liked the idea of a desk in her lounge, the walnut was out of keeping with the flimsy furniture his wife preferred, but there was nowhere else to put it.

Sitting down and shuffling the chair nearer the bureau, he took out a sheet of paper, a pen, ink and a blotter. He twiddled the pen between his fingers then wrote 'Dear Dotty' at the top of the page. The first, and only, sentence instructed her to send him the drawings of the water lift they had talked about. That would do. He closed with a simple 'Alfie' and folded the paper into an envelope. He wondered whether he should have asked about her upcoming surgery, but he had sealed the envelope before the thought came. He addressed the envelope, stuck on a stamp and laid it aside, ready to take to the post box in the morning. There was one on the street a few yards from his shop.

With his head clear, he settled back on the sofa and was soon dreaming. He woke to the sound of Winnie nagging. She had pulled back the cushions he had used as covers and he felt a chill on his toes.

'What are you doing sleeping here, ruining my sofa? Do you know what time it is? I could have invited friends for morning tea. Imagine the disgrace if they'd seen you like this. You haven't even shaved.'

The words ran into one another. Alfie rubbed his eyes. He had slept in his work clothes. He fumbled for his pocket watch.

'It is half past eight,' Winnie told him, pointing at the clock on the mantelpiece. 'The shop should have opened half an hour ago. Do you expect the customers to serve themselves?'

'There are never any customers this early,' Alfie answered.

Winnie looked for something else to chastise him. Her eyes caught the letter on his desk. She picked it up. 'What is this?'

'It is a private letter. I would ask you to put it down.'

'It is addressed to Mrs Dotty Peters at the hospital in Edinburgh.' Winnie looked confused. 'Dotty is dead. You aren't writing to a corpse, are you?'

'Of course not.' Alfie eased himself from the sofa as he thought up a reply. 'It's some business with her things.'

'She died three years ago. What business can there still be?'

Alfie couldn't think of a reasonable response. He held his hand out for the letter.

Winnie puckered her lips. 'I don't see why it is addressed to Mrs Dotty Peters. It's gruesome.'

Alfie took the letter from her. 'Calm yourself, woman. Stress isn't good for the baby.'

Winnie felt her abdomen and smiled. 'It's kicking,' she said. 'Here and here.'

Alfie moved to put a hand on her tummy to please her. Apart from her greasy skin, he felt nothing. 'It must have legs for ears to kick in both places at once,' he remarked.

'It must be a boy,' Winnie said.

'Really. In my opinion, girls are far more trouble than boys.'

He was forced to listen to five minutes of baby talk, but it distracted Winnie from delving too deeply into his affairs.

'There doesn't seem any point opening the shop this morning,' he said, when Winnie paused and he managed to get a word in. 'There's a meeting about the clock in the hotel at ten.'

'Another meeting? All you do is talk about this clock. When will you get round to building it?'

'The plans are complete,' Alfie said. 'At least I hope they are.' It would be easier explaining the deficiencies of the plans to a brainless sheep than to Winnie, so he didn't bother.

'Where will you build it?' Winnie asked. 'There won't be room in the workshop and you can hardly mess up the hotel with your bits and pieces.'

For once, that was a sensible question. Alfie hadn't given it any thought. With Templeman humming and hawing about the casing, the thought of building it seemed as far off as the completion of the Forth Bridge. 'I imagine Mr Squires will find a suitable space. There are warehouses to lease on the river.'

'That is too far from the shop,' Winnie objected.

'I won't have time for the shop once the work starts.'

'Don't think I will be able to help out, not with the baby due.

You will need to employ an assistant.'

'That is easier said than done. Finding a suitable young man will take time.'

'What about a young lady?' Winnie asked. 'I've heard gentlemen buy more from young ladies.'

'So have I,' Alfie leered.

'I didn't mean that.' She gave him a gentle punch on the arm.

'I have business to attend to before the meeting,' Alfie said. 'And I shall have to wash and shave.'

Winnie didn't take the hint. She moved around the room, busying herself adjusting the cushions and straightening ornaments. Alfie gave up any chance of working at his desk and retired upstairs, taking the letter to Dotty with him.

He walked past two mailboxes on his way to the hotel. When he opened his bag in the hotel reception hall, he spotted the letter nestling at the bottom.

'Damn,' he swore.

'Is there a problem, Mr Peters?' Squires was standing behind him.

'I've forgotten to post a letter, that's all.'

'I can have one of the hotel boys see to it for you.'

Alfie was about to hand the letter over, but a picture of Winnie flashed in his head. He didn't want Squires noticing the name and address too. 'It's not urgent, thank you.'

'Shall we go in then?'

Squires' tone was curt and Alfie sensed it wasn't going to be an easy meeting. Lines had been drawn. Farquhar sat behind his desk. To his right were two gentlemen; one in a well-cut suit, the other in a jacket that didn't match his trousers. His arms dangled a foot below the cuffs. Alfie recognised the smarter gentleman as Menzies McLean, a local surveyor. He had sold him a grandmother clock. A decent gentleman, he hadn't squabbled about the price, but insisted on having the casing carved from ebony. Winnie had joked that perhaps he had a calling as an undertaker. Looking at him standing there, cracking his fingers, Alfie thought she might be right. He didn't know the second man, but guessed he was a builder from the roughness of his hands. Giles was on Farquhar's left, his backside balanced on the work surface with his legs straddling the corner. Alfie took his place beside Giles. Walker Squires stood uncomfortably at the door, preventing anyone from leaving before they were dismissed.

'Now we are all here, I think we should begin,' Farquhar announced. 'I have examined the plans and so have Mr McLean and Mr Davidson. I am reliably informed the ceiling would need to be strengthened by twenty pounds per square foot.'

'It will mean inserting reinforced iron beams,' Davidson said.

'I won't have anything as ugly as that on show,' Giles slapped his thigh.

'Perhaps if Mr Templeman didn't require as much gold plating in his design…' Alfie began, but Farquhar cut him off.

'We won't stand for any shoddy fool's gold. It is the amount of lead in your workings that is causing the problem.'

'Have you considered using lighter alloys?' Squires pretended to know what he was talking about.

'That would add to the expense. If there weren't so many complicated applications, with pipes and water reservoirs…'

'There will be no extra funding,' Farquhar declared. 'Mr McLean and Mr Davidson have been paid their consultation fees. Any new building work must come out of the original price we agreed upon.'

It took a moment for Alfie to gauge the extent of the implication. Templeman would make sure he got his salary and wouldn't skimp on the materials for the external casing. That left only the cost of his experience and workings to cut back on. It was time to play his hand.

'If that is the case, gentlemen, I can no longer be associated with the project. I shall submit a final bill for my inconvenience, which will be with you by the end of the week.' He walked to the door, but Squires didn't move aside.

'You're pulling out?' Squires said.

'I say, that is a bit steep, Peters,' Templeman removed his leg from the desk and stood like a cavalryman about to strike his sabre.

'I'm afraid there is no alternative. I am an artisan, unaccustomed to working with second rate materials. I do not intend lowering my standards and I take it as a personal insult that you should ask me to.'

'Nobody is asking you to compromise your standards,' Squires appeased him. 'That is not what Adam meant.' Squires gestured to Farquhar.

'Leave if you wish,' Farquhar answered. 'There are other clockmakers. If not here in Perth, we can send for one from Edinburgh.'

'At double the cost,' Alfie reminded him.

'Alfie has invested a great deal of his time and knowledge already,' Templeman spoke up. 'It would be a shame to start again with someone new.'

It was Squires, as always, who broke the impasse. 'If it is

merely a matter of money, I will be prepared to fund the difference in price between the original quote and the actual cost.' He looked to Alfie and Giles. 'Within reason, of course. Is that acceptable to you, Adam?'

Farquhar opened and closed his nostrils three times, giving the effect of a snorting bull. 'When can we expect the work to begin?'

'As soon as we have a workshop,' Alfie said.

'I've thought about that,' Templeman said. 'I've negotiated a good price for the lease of a warehouse, which can be fitted out by the end of the month.'

'The *end* of the month?'

'More as like the middle, Mr Farquhar,' Templeman appeased.

'My men won't be able to start on the ceiling until mid-March,' Davidson said. 'It'll take a good two or three weeks.'

'That will disrupt the activities of our spring guests,' Squires said.

'I could get extra men in, on short term contracts, but that would cost more.'

Squires was stuck in a hole of his own making. Before anyone could speak the door was thrust open, sending Squires tumbling across the room into Templeman. A messenger boy looked round at the faces gaping at him. It wasn't one of the hotel boys or he would have been instantly dismissed.

'Is there a Mr Peters here?' the boy asked.

'I am Peters.' Alfie stepped towards him.

'You'd better come quick, sir. Your wife has had a fall. She's gone into labour.'

Chapter 10

Squires offered Alfie the use of his carriage and insisted on travelling with him. Alfie couldn't see him mucking in with the delivery, but accepted the ride. When they stepped from the carriage outside the house, they were greeted by a tussle-haired woman holding a white Persian cat.

'My neighbour, Mrs Allendale,' Alfie introduced her to Squires.

'And this is Puss,' Mrs Allendale stroked the cat's ear. 'He was the clever boy who found your wife. I came out looking for him and there she was, collapsed among the rose bushes.'

'I can guess what Puss was doing in the rose bed,' Alfie grumbled.

'Thank you, Mrs Allendale,' Squires was more appreciative than Alfie. 'Has a doctor been called?'

'Yes, and the midwife. Mrs Peters told me she wasn't due until the end of the month. The shock of the fall must have started something.'

Alfie abandoned Squires to Mrs Allendale's words of wisdom and rushed indoors. There was screaming from upstairs. A young girl in a blood-stained apron climbed the stairs carrying a bowl of water close to her chest. Alfie followed her up, but was stopped at the top of the steps by the doctor.

'May I have a word, Mr Peters?' It wasn't a request. The doctor directed Alfie back down the stairs and into the lounge.

'How is Winnie?' Alfie said, taking off his hat and coat.

'She's had a fall. The midwife is with her.'

'Will she die?'

'You needn't be quite so blunt, Mr Peters.' The doctor glared at him.

'Sorry, it's the shock.' Alfie moved to the drinks cabinet and set out two glasses. His hand shook as he poured the whisky.

'Not for me,' the doctor said.

Alfie drank his whisky, replaced the glass on the cabinet top and lifted the drink he had poured for the doctor. He held tight to the glass, without drinking.

'Your wife will be incapacitated for several weeks,' the doctor continued. 'I can recommend a nurse to tend her and the baby, if it survives. Is there anyone who can look after the household for you?'

Winnie had a cousin, but they weren't close. He couldn't remember her name - Jean, Joan or Jane. The conversation was interrupted by the sound of a baby crying.

'My son.' Alfie slammed down the whisky glass.

161

'I would wait a moment, until the baby has been cleaned and swaddled,' the doctor advised.

'I want to see my son.'

'Or daughter,' the doctor said. He walked to the door to delay Alfie. 'Remember your wife is weak. Don't upset her.'

They heard footsteps clomp down the stairs and the doctor opened the door. The young girl with the stained apron was standing there, with her hand out ready to knock and her mouth agape.

'What is it?' Alfie asked.

'Ma Stanton says you can gae up noo,' the girl said. She wiped her hands on her apron and looked as if she wanted to say more, but a yell from the midwife made her turn on her heels and scamper back upstairs.

'If the baby is well, the midwife will deal with matters. I shall take my leave,' the doctor said. 'I have other urgent calls, but I shall return this evening to check on your wife.'

The doctor showed himself out. Alfie took the stairs two at a time. His heart was ticking down like a stopwatch. His throat was dry. The sensation was unexpected. He hadn't felt like this when Teddy was born, but he had the business with Dotty to sort out then.

He stopped outside the bedroom. The door was closed and he felt obliged to knock. The door opened slightly and the head of the young girl appeared.

'It's Mr Peters.' The girl turned her head to inform the others in the room.

'Who else would it be?' Alfie stuck his foot between the gap in the door and tried to edge in.

'Tell him he will have to wait,' a severe voice answered, loud enough for Alfie to hear without the girl repeating it.

'You are the one who said I could come up.'

'Alfie?' Winnie's voice was weak.

'This is no place for a man. There is a complication. Tell him to come back in ten minutes.'

'You've tae come back in…' the girl began.

'I heard,' Alfie grumbled. 'The whole street probably did. What is the complication? Is it serious? I want to see my wife.' He thought about barging past the girl, but decided against it.

'Is everything all right?' He heard Squires' voice echoing up from the hallway.

'I've been shut out of my own bedroom by some slip of a lass,' Alfie said as he made his way down the stairs.

'Best to do what the women say, when it comes to these

matters,' Squires recommended.

'Will you take a dram with me?' Alfie asked.

'Thank you, but I had better get back. Give my regards to Mrs Peters, when she is feeling better.'

Squires left and Alfie went into the living room to finish his whisky. There may be complications, as the midwife put it, but he had heard a baby cry. The child was alive. He had a son. Of course it was a boy. A girl wouldn't cry in such a hearty manner.

Complications, though.

He poured another measure of whisky. After a sip he thought better of downing it. What would the midwife think if he toppled onto the child's crib? He sat on the sofa, crossed and uncrossed his legs and waited. It was quiet upstairs. Too quiet. He jumped up and walked to the window. Mrs Allendale was still outside. He counted three cats with her. She spotted him looking at her and he gave a wave. Her hands were too full of fur to wave back.

'You can come up noo, sir.' The young girl poked her head round the door.

'Are you sure this time?'

She didn't answer, but he followed her up the stairs. The bedroom door was open, which was a good sign. He could see Winnie in bed. Her face was pale, but she was sitting up, nursing a baby. Alfie tried to smile as he walked in, but the stench of blood, soap and something acrid made him retch. The windows were closed and the curtains drawn. There was a pile of stained sheets in the corner. No wonder his wife was ill. If he stayed there long he would be sick too.

'Let me see my son,' he said.

Winnie smiled and drew part of the cover from the babe so he could see its face. It was ugly, as most babies were to Alfie.

'He's rather small, is he not?'

'He wasn't expected for two weeks,' Winnie said.

'Of course. Why, he's a fine chap,' Alfie said. 'Excellently proportioned. I shall make sure he has only the best in life.' He leaned over to poke a finger at the bundle. The baby cried and Winnie rocked him. Alfie took a step back and banged into the midwife who was bending over the cot. She righted herself and glared at Alfie.

'Now you have admired your son,' the midwife said, 'Perhaps you would like to see your daughter?'

She moved aside to show another baby, wrapped in blankets and sleeping in the cot.

'A girl?' Alfie looked from the tiny blob of pink in the cot to the one in his wife's arms.

'You have twins, Mr Peters. A boy and a girl. The girl is the older of the two, by a matter of minutes.'

'Isn't it wonderful?' Winnie said, before a gobbet of phlegm rose in her throat to choke her words. The midwife moved to take the baby as Winnie struggled to get her breath. She handed the boy to Alfie while she attended to Winnie. The baby bawled and Alfie felt a trickle of fluid on his hand. The young assistant was standing next to him, gabbling nonsense at the baby.

'Here.' He thrust the child into her arms. 'I need a cup of tea.'

'We could all do with one,' the midwife said. 'I take a goodly splash of milk and two sugar cubes.'

Alfie was dispensed to make the tea. It took him time to find the kettle, which had been used for boiling water for the birth. The sides were stained with blood. He wiped them with a dish towel then tossed the cloth in the corner. After five minutes the young girl came down to ask what was keeping him. She completed the task of making tea. Alfie took his cup and collapsed on the sofa.

He had admired the babes, as a father should. It was time to return to work, but how was he supposed to concentrate with all the commotion in the house? He finished his tea and placed the cup on the table. His work case was sitting beside his desk.

Squires must have brought it from the hotel. He had forgotten it in the kafuffle. He found paper and pencils in the desk and stuffed them in the bag, then picked up his coat and hat. The thought crossed his mind to call up the stairs to say he was going out, but he shooed it away. The devil could find work for idle hands, but it took a woman to find work for hands already over-stretched – and there were three women in his house.

Mrs Allendale watched him stride down the garden path.

'A little boy or a girl?' she asked.

'Both,' he answered briskly and turned the corner out of her sight. He made his way to his shop, but he couldn't settle to work. His new domestic situation dominated his thoughts. The doctor was right, he would need somebody in to help, but he was against having a stranger meddling in his affairs.

Winnie came up with a solution that evening. The room had been sanitised. The pile of dirty linen had been dispatched to the wash house, the curtains were open and the midwife was gone, leaving the young girl to sit with the babies. Alfie had eaten in a local inn and Winnie had no appetite, but the girl looked hungry. Her stomach rumbled and Alfie thought he should offer her some bread and cheese at least.

'What took you so long?' Winnie asked when he finally

brought up a crust of stale bread and a chunk of mouldy cheese.

'Finding anything in your kitchen cupboards is trickier than mending a broken cog,' Alfie complained. 'There is no method to your arrangement.'

'You aren't used to cooking. We should invite my mother to stay and run the household while I am bed-bound,' Winnie suggested.

'What?' Alfie dropped the plate. The young girl managed to catch it before the crockery smashed, but the bread and cheese landed on the rug. She scooped them up and began eating.

'We could have the spare room prepared for her. The babes can stay with me here.'

'Where should I sleep? The basement is flooded and the attic is filled with junk. You can't expect me to sleep there.'

'The basement is merely a little damp, but there is the sofa, if you prefer. It won't be for long. Mum will love to help with Freddy and Sylvia.'

The thought of his mother-in-law organising the daily routine made Alfie feel nauseous, but he could think of no other answer. 'I can sleep in the apartment above the shop, if needs must. I'll send your mother a message,' he allowed.

'No, I'll write,' Winnie said. 'It would be better coming from me.'

He fetched her paper and a pen. Winnie was weak and her handwriting was illegible.

'Even your mother won't understand that,' Alfie took the letter from her. 'Tell me what to write.'

Winnie dictated the message. When she finished Alfie folded the page into an envelope and sealed it.

'Wid you like me tae post it for you?' the girl asked. 'I shid be getting home noo. There's a post box on ma way.'

Alfie handed her the letter. 'Where do you live?'

She mentioned a run-down area of the city.

'It is too late for you to be walking the streets there alone.' Winnie was concerned.

'She can stay here tonight,' Alfie suggested.

'Thank you sir, but I hae tae get back. I ken the streets weel enough. Ma father is expecting me. He's housebound and I maun tak care o' him. Besides, he worries aboot me when I'm oot.'

'So he should,' Alfie agreed. 'How old are you?'

'Sixteen, sir.'

'I can't allow you to walk home on your own. I shall accompany you,' Alfie decided. 'Let me fetch my coat and hat.'

Alfie waited at the door while the girl arranged Winnie's

pillows and collected her shawl. He watched her move down the stairs, with her breasts bobbing beneath her blouse. She was a pretty thing, with a trim figure and her hazel hair tied back as it should be. Her skin was fair and soft, fit to be stroked liked one of Mrs Allendale's felines. He held the door open, ogling her backside.

There was a chill wind, but the snow stayed away. They walked in silence along the road that hugged the river. The girl kept a steady pace and Alfie struggled to keep up. She stopped at the letter box and slipped the letter through the slot. Alfie rested to catch his breath, remembering the letter to Dotty, still in his bag.

'I'll be fine frae here sir, thank you,' the girl said.

'Hold on a moment, I don't even know your name.'

'Lisa, sir. Lisa Mulligan.'

'Will we see you tomorrow?'

'No, sir. I hae tae help Ma Stanton.'

'The midwife?'

'Aye sir. The doctor will send a nurse tae help your wife. A hae tae go.'

Alfie reached out a hand and held onto her shoulder. He drew her towards him until he felt her sweet breath against his cheeks.

'How about a kiss before you go?'

'No sir, you mustna…'

Alfie smothered her words with his lips, pressing them hard against the girl's mouth. She felt soft and warm. He reached beneath her shawl for her breasts and felt a sharp pain in his face. She pushed him away with more strength than he expected from a young girl. He stumbled, tasting blood from his lips. His hat toppled from his head and blew along the street.

'You bit me, you bitch.'

'Get awa frae me or I'll call the police.' Lisa stood shaking for a moment then turned and ran down the narrow vennel behind her.

'You are the one who has assaulted me, you impudent whipper-snapper,' Alfie called after her. He wiped his mouth with the back of his hand. His hat was dancing towards the river at the speed of an eightsome reel. He trundled after it, only to watch as a gust sent it spinning down the bank to rest on the waters of the Tay.

'Damn,' he swore, as it drifted downstream towards Dundee.

The wind blew round his ears on his way home. It was an old hat, but a good one and he regretted losing it. Inside his house, he stopped in the hallway to flatten his hair in front of the mirror and examine his lower lip. It was turning a blue colour and had started to swell. The tooth mark was obvious. He would have to think of a suitable excuse for Winnie. He removed his jacket and made for the stairs, but decided against going to see his wife. One of the babies was crying – the girl most likely. Winnie would be feeding her and she might need her coverings changed. He had no wish to be involved with that sort of thing. He settled on the sofa and despite the lack of blankets and prickly horsehair, managed to fall asleep within minutes.

He woke to the doorbell ringing. It rang and rang until he opened the door, bleary-eyed.

'Mr Peters?' The woman held out her hand.

'You must be the nurse,' he said, opening the door wider to let her in. 'My wife is upstairs.'

'And top o' the morning to you too. O'Reilly's the name. Kathleen O' Reilly. Mrs.'

The woman took her time, bustling around, removing her coat and shifting things around in her over-sized carpet bag.

'I'll leave you to it,' Alfie said. He was relieved to be out of the house, even without breakfast or a kiss from Winnie. He made his way to the safety of his shop, posting the letter to Dotty on the way. In his workshop at the back of the retail area, he fussed around making enough work to justify staying late. Supper was cold meat and cabbage in the same inn as before and he lingered over his ale, putting off going home.

'Landlord, another whisky please.'

He left the inn when his money ran out and dawdled towards the river. There was a light on downstairs when he reached his house. He struggled to find his key, but the door was opened before he found it. A short, but stout woman with ginger hair and a mole on her cheek stood with her arms folded. Alfie wondered how she could possibly be Winnie's mother, but indeed she was.

'What kept you?' She greeted him.

'Work. Someone has to pay the household bills.'

She narrowed her eyes and screwed her nose, but couldn't think of a reproof. 'Winnie has been asking for you.'

'I'll go up and see her, if I can get in.'

'Winnie can wait. I have questions for you.' Winnie's mother turned and strode to the living room like a war bound Amazon. Alfie closed the front door behind him, noticing that the nurse's coat was hanging from the stand. What had he done to deserve a house full of nagging women?

His mother-in-law stood at his desk, waving papers at him when he entered the living room.

'What may I ask are these?' she demanded.

'If you stopped fanning the air and allowed me to see them, I might be able to answer. Have you been nosing in my private papers?' He stepped towards Norma, but she moved away.

'This is a bill for an asylum in Edinburgh.'

'My first wife, Dorothy, unfortunately was a patient there,' Alfie said.

'Your wife died three years ago. This bill has last month's date on it.'

'Let me see.'

Norma handed him the invoice. There was no mention of the service provided.

'While you are thinking about that, you can explain this. It is a birth certificate for a young boy.'

Alfie ran his tongue round the inside of his mouth. He took Teddy's birth certificate from Norma before she could examine it in detail. He opened his desk and slipped it and the hospital bill in one of the compartments.

'I'm waiting,' Norma said.

'The explanation is simple, if tragic. I have kept it from Winnie, as from everyone else. In her state of confusion, my first wife was seduced by a travelling salesman and a child was born. It will help nobody to go into detail. The father made himself scarce and to avoid a scandal I claimed the baby as my own. Suffice to say that the boy wasn't a healthy one. He suffered from severe attacks, which endangered others as well as himself. The doctors did what they could, but the condition worsened,' Alfie was growing into his tale. He paused and cleared his throat.

'If the doctors did everything they could, they would have put the wretch out of its misery,' Norma said. Alfie pretended to be shocked.

'I continue to pay the boy's hospital fees, but there is little hope for him. The last time I saw him he was little more than a vegetable.'

Norma was silent for a moment. Alfie couldn't tell if she believed him or not. She gave a 'humph' and walked to the door of the room. 'You were right to keep this from Winnie,' she said. 'I would lock your desk in future.'

Alfie took a small key from his waistcoat pocket and did just that.

Despite her habit of interfering with his affairs, Alfie had to agree that Norma kept the household running as well as it could with two screaming babes, an invalid wife and a demanding nurse. Nevertheless, he spent the greater part of his time either in his shop or in the warehouse Templeman had leased to construct the clock. Farquhar had sent one of his own men to supervise and catalogue the arrival and storage of equipment and parts. Jonas Weir was a dour, kirk elder, but he was efficient and had a knack for making sure there was no slacking.

'Have you seen Mr Templeman?' Weir asked as Alfie examined the main pendulum one morning a fortnight after the births.

Alfie looked at his watch. 'It's a little early for our American friend,' he answered.

'He hasn't been here for the last eight days.'

'I imagine he is working on his own. You know what the artistic temperament is like.'

'Mmm,' Weir didn't approve of the artistic temperament. Alfie saw him take out his notebook and scribble notes.

'Is there anything I can help you with?' Alfie asked.

'I need to know how many men I shall require for the construction of the clock. I take it you and Mr Templeman do not intend hauling the wheels and beams into place on your own. Then there is the transportation to the hotel.'

That was something Alfie hadn't given thought to. He was used to working in miniature, with fiddly parts. He did a rapid calculation. 'A score, at least, I should think.'

Jonas Weir logged the numbers in his notebook and chewed

the end of his pencil. 'I can't see our expenses stretching to more than four.'

Then why did you ask?

Alfie forced a smile. 'You will need to speak with Mr Squires about it.'

Weir didn't rely. From his demeanour it was clear he considered Alfie impudent to suggest the idea. He stomped around, clattering against boxes, for the rest of the morning. It was impossible to work with the commotion and after lunch Alfie returned to his shop. It was raining and puddles carpeted the pavement. He made a note that when he was elected to the council he would have something done about the city drainage.

'Thank goodness ye're here at last. I've been waiting for o'er an hour. I'm soaked tae ma skin.'

Alfie had the key in the lock of his shop door. He turned to see a young girl step out from the doorway of the neighbouring shop. Her dress was soaking and her sodden hair fell over her face, dripping water onto her worn shoes. She had on a woollen shawl, but she wasn't wearing a coat.

'It's me, Lisa,' the girl said. 'The midwife's dogsbody.'

'What has happened? Is there a problem with my son? Did my mother-in-law send you?'

'No sir, I havenae been tae your hoose. Can a come inside?'

Alfie looked down the street. There was no-one about. He opened the door and put an arm round Lisa's shoulder to guide her in.

'What do you want?' he asked.

'For a start, I widnae mind something tae dry masel' wi',' Lisa said. 'An then maybes a drink.'

'I meant, why are you here?'

'Ma dad sent me.'

'If you have been telling tales…'

'Ma dad said, if you want to kiss me and touch me, you hae tae pay for it.' She stood back and undid the top button of her dress, sending droplets of water splashing onto the nearby watches.

'Watch what you're doing. These are delicate instruments.' Alfie shoved her away from his goods.

'Dae you want me or no?'

'You've done this before, haven't you, you little whore?'

'Ma dad cannae work. We need to mak a living and with your wife sick in bed…'

'How much?'

'That depends on whit you want, sir.'

Alfie moved past her to lock the door. He put the key in his jacket pocket. 'You'd better go upstairs and take your clothes off. If you hang them by the fire they should be dry by the time you need them again.'

Chapter 11

It was the beginning of February and although Winnie felt well enough to rise from her bed, she spent the day resting on the sofa drinking tea, with her mother running after her and the twins. Alfie hadn't realised month old babes made more noise than a flock of wild geese, and twice as much mess. With the excuse of working on the hotel clock, he had taken to staying in the flat above the shop - with Lisa. Her housebound excuse for a father had taken up with a local washerwoman and there wasn't space in the one-roomed flat for the three of them and her wash tub. To avoid tittle tattle, Alfie put her on the books as his shop assistant, although she couldn't write more than her name or count beyond the number of her fingers. Still, she had a cheery way with the clients and his sales were rising.

The first Tuesday of the month was frosty. Alfie had sent Lisa upstairs to make tea, when the shop door banged open. Alfie groaned. There was only one person who made an entrance like that.

'Off work again, or here on official business?' he asked before Maggie could greet him.

'I do more work than you,' she snapped back. 'You haven't spoken to the doctor yet, have you?'

'I've been busy working on the hotel clock. You can ask your friend Mr Templeman if you don't believe me.'

'When will you visit the hospital?'

'I don't know. I can hardly leave Perth with the clock at a crucial stage and two babies in the house.'

'I forgot to congratulate you on your bastards. I heard I had a new brother and sister.' Maggie lifted one of the ladies' pocket watches from the shelf. 'Nice.'

'Put that back.'

'You didn't give me a birthday present. I turned sixteen last week, or don't you remember?'

'Put it back or I'll call the constable.'

Maggie shoved it on the shelf.

'You can't tell the time anyway,' Alfie sneered.

'Can so. I learnt at school. I was good there, before I had to leave. Your twins don't stop you coming here, so why should they prevent you taking a trip to Edinburgh?'

'My wife is ill. I need to get home early in the evenings.'

'Your *wife* is ill. That's why you need to visit her in Edinburgh. That slut who lives in your house is as capable as you or me. She just enjoys being treated like a baby.'

'Don't speak about Winnie like that.'

'I'll speak about her as I like,' Maggie answered. 'Until you do what you promised to do.'

Alfie tried to stare her out, but she had the glare of Medusa. The door to the apartment opened and Lisa's back appeared. She manoeuvred into the shop carrying a tea tray. 'Gi' me a hand, Alfie,' she said before spotting Maggie. 'Whit are you gaping at?'

Maggie turned to Alfie. 'Didn't take you long.'

'Wha is she?' Lisa asked.

Alfie took the tea tray and set it on the counter before there was an unfortunate incident. Introductions were in order. 'Maggie is the daughter of an old friend,' he said to Lisa. Maggie gave a hoarse laugh. 'Lisa is my new shop assistant. She looks after things while I am working at the warehouse.'

'I bet she does,' Maggie said.

'An old friend?' Lisa's words over-rode Maggie's.

'Since there are only two cups, I will leave you girls to make friends while I attend to more pressing business.' Alfie said. He walked to the door, collected his coat and marched out.

There was work to do at the warehouse, but it involved careful measurements and he couldn't concentrate. Templeman was back and banging at his casing with a hammer, clearly without metalwork skills. Weir couldn't work either and had gone home an hour before with the flimsy excuse that he had left his drawing room window open. He hadn't returned. The design looked ugly on paper, but in reality it was an affront to even a farmyard pig's senses. Alfie said as much to Giles.

'You are behind the times, Alfie. This is modern. It's exciting,' Giles assured him. 'People don't want columns of angels nowadays.'

'I'm not sure they ever did. They want clean lines, uncluttered by...whatever these monstrosities are. The whole thing looks too... too...American.'

'What exactly do you mean by that?'

'It's more like a cross between fantasies of Edgar Allan Poe and Washington Irving, with Davy Crockett poking out of the side.'

Templeman scratched his head while he pictured the image. 'The States are where things happen. You are looking at the future of clock design. A clock built for the twentieth century.'

'Or the House of Usher,' Alfie argued. He disliked Templeman's air of superiority. It was time to tease him again. He stopped what he was working on to pace round the half-finished casing, mumbling clipped phrases. 'Rip van Winkle...the wrong time period...the dimensions won't do.' He snapped his fingers three times as if trying to come up with an answer, then shook his head. 'No, it isn't suitable at all. I can't see it working, or just maybes....'

'Hold on, Peters, it's a little late to complain. You will have to make your clock workings fit the space available. You assured Farquhar they would.'

'And they will, plus your miniature organ, river, railway and mechanical models. That is not what I am talking about. I am referring to - as I thought you were – a clock built for the twentieth century. And the twenty first. Perhaps even the twenty second, if fate allows. Time travel, my friend.'

Templeman leapt to his feet. 'You know how to do it?'

Alfie tapped the side of his nose. He knocked on the casing. 'Adaptations could be made.'

'Such as?' Giles moved to stand beside Alfie and peered at the casing as if for the first time.

'There has to be a control centre,' Alfie said. 'Big enough for a man to crouch in.'

'How tall a man?'

Alfie looked Giles up and down.

'I see, of course, but what about the rest of the workings?'

'They can be incorporated into the design, with extra pedals and gumplestroff.' Alfie made the word up on the spur of the moment. He felt time travel should have its own jargon and gumplestroff sounded suitably technical.

'Gumplestroff? Do we have that?'

'Not yet. It's expensive, but I can get some,' Alfie answered.

'Better not charge it to the clock accounts. We don't want Weir asking questions,' Templeman said.

'Then I don't see how…' Alfie tailed off, allowing Templeman to suggest the hoped for solution.

'How much money will you need?'

Large figures bandied about Alfie's head, but he settled for a hundred guineas. That would get him membership of the golf club, the proper dress for the game and a good set of clubs. There might be a little left over to buy Winnie a new dress for the babies' christening. Templeman puckered his lip.

'A hundred guineas you shall have. The clock has to be ready for Easter. Do you think you can do it by then?'

Alfie puckered his lips the way Giles had and took another walk around the casing. He cocked his head and muttered some numbers.

'Well?' Templeman was as excited as Teddy was with his new train.

'Aye, it could be done.'

'Good man,' Templeman gave him a thud on the shoulder. 'Order your gumple stuff and I'll have the money for you by the end of the week.'

Alfie grinned as he returned to his work bench. All he had to do was produce some weird piece of equipment and Templeman would be fooled.

Jonas Weir returned as Alfie and Templeman were finishing for the day. He was carrying an evening paper and made a show of unfolding it.

'What have you there, Jonas?' Giles asked.

'An article on page four that I think you will appreciate Mr Templeman. I'll read it to you.' Weir removed his spectacles from his top pocket and positioned them on his nose, shuffling them up before he began.

'***Work is well underway on the new clock to be displayed in the entrance hallway of the West Tay Hotel in Perth. It is understood that the brilliant young artist, Giles Templeman, has pushed clock design to the limits and the construction is fast gaining the nickname of the "Wonder of the North". Details of the plans have been leaked to several art critics and they are straining at the bit to be the first to review it.***'

Weir folded the paper and handed it to Templeman. 'Straining at the bit, no less,' he repeated.

'Art critics? What do they know about clocks?' Alfie grumbled.

'I like the brilliant, young artist label.' Giles took the paper and Jonas pointed to the relevant paragraph.

'I shall wish you both a good night,' Alfie said.

It was tempting to go back to the flat and discover how Lisa and Maggie got on together. No doubt hair would have flown before they settled down to the tea and biscuits. The account would have to wait until the morning, when Lisa had time to embellish it. Norma was complaining that he was never at home and there were plans to be made for the upcoming Christening of the twins. Winnie was feeling brighter and she wanted a large do to show off the children. He had refused at first, but Winnie had worked on the Squires' ladies. Walker Squires had taken him aside after a meeting to advise him that a social gathering of the sort was what was needed for forging civic connections, if the right people were invited and the catering was more than generous.

'Do you think we should invite Mr Farquhar?' Winnie asked after dinner that evening.

'I suppose we shall have to,' Alfie answered.

'Mr Farquhar is a fine gentleman,' Norma put in.

'But he is very severe,' Winnie said. 'I don't think he ever smiles, and he's always talking about money and how not to spend it. I'm not surprised his son has run off. Lucy Squires told me he has married a travelling girl and rides horses in a circus in Poland.'

'She probably made that up,' Norma answered.

'Lucy Squires isn't the sort of girl to make up fanciful stories,' Winnie said. 'Miss Emily, perhaps…'

'Don't worry about Farquhar,' Alfie said before the ladies could digress. 'We can invite him, but he will come up with an excuse not to attend.'

'He may still send the children a gift,' Norma was hopeful.

'I doubt that,' Winnie and Alfie said in unison and laughed.

'How many invitations are we sending?' Alfie asked. 'The sitting room won't hold more than ten people in comfort.'

'There's no need to worry about space,' Winnie said. 'Mr Squires has offered us a room at the hotel.'

'With special rates, I hope.'

'He is charging nothing. It is his Christening gift,' Winnie answered.

'I can't see Farquhar being happy with that.'

'They should both be happy with all the work you are doing on their clock,' Norma said. 'Why, you are never at home.'

'I'm here now and I'll get started on the invitations tonight.' Alfie appeased her.

The conversation was brought to an end by crying from the nursery. Winnie got up to attend to the babies and Alfie and Norma finished their dinner in silence. As he expected, there was little for him to do in regard to the invitations. Norma and Winnie had arranged everything and he spent the evening signing cards for Norma to fit into envelopes.

'We'll get these off in the morning.' Norma was satisfied with the work. 'Good night.'

'No you don't,' Alfie jumped up, twisting his back. 'It's my turn to have the bathroom.'

Alfie posted the invitations the following morning. He thought little more of them until two days later when he was busy in his shop. Lisa had gone to the market for fruit and vegetables. He wasn't anticipating customers and imagined it was her returning when the door opened.

'Did you get what you wanted?' he called.

'You have a nerve to ask that,' Maggie's strident voice shook the shelves.

Alfie swore under his breath. 'I told you, I shall speak with Dr Matthews when I can. In fact, I shall be visiting Edinburgh within the next three weeks.'

'I'll believe that when I see it, but yon's no why I'm here.'

She slammed a card on the counter. Alfie recognised it as one of the Christening invitations. It was addressed to the Squires.

'Don't I get an invitation?' she said.

'Don't be ridiculous. I don't invite serving girls to my parties.'

'Just toffs? Whit aboot Lisa? Are you inviting her?'

'Whit aboot Lisa?' Lisa pushed her way into the shop, her hands full of bags.

'Nothing,' Alfie said. 'Maggie is leaving.'

'I'll leave if you tell me, but don't think because I huvnae got a proper card I'll be keeping awa. I'm family. I'm your dochter, whether you like it or no.'

She lifted the invitation and barged past Lisa on her way out.

'Quite a handful,' Lisa said. 'Is she your dochter?'

'No.'

'I dinnae mind if she is. She's guid company.'

'She is not my daughter, she is not good company and it is time something was done about her.'

Chapter 12

Maggie fingered the letters on the page, sounding aloud the syllables of the unfamiliar word - vac..ci…nation, vacci…nation.

'It's vaccination,' Miss Lucy's voice caught her by surprise and she dropped the book. Engrossed in her reading, Maggie had not heard Lucy enter the back parlour. The ladies of the Squires family usually took a stroll through the park at that time of day and Maggie had not expected to be disturbed.

The shock of being caught reading caused Maggie, momentarily, to freeze. Lucy bent to pick up the book. She read out the title.

'The Popular Cyclopaedia of Modern Domestic Medicine.'

'It's a library book, Miss,' Maggie said.

'So I see,' Lucy answered, having flicked open the cover to spot the stamp.

'I have finished all my morning tasks,' Maggie explained.

'I'm sure you have. What interests you about modern domestic medicine? Wouldn't you rather read a romance?'

'Oh no Miss. I dinnae care for made-up stories. I'm nae jist reading aboot common diseases, there's a guid deal more I maun ken. I want tae be a doctor, ye see.' Maggie felt her face redden. Miss Lucy would either think she was insolently aiming beyond her station in life or that she was simply deluded.

'Do you?'

'Begging your pardon, that is. Not that there is ocht wrong wi' being a maid, and yer family hae been guid tae me, but..'

'I understand,' Lucy cut her off. 'There's no need to explain. I wish more women would aspire to a life beyond the domestic. We need women in the law courts, in the church and certainly in hospitals. We need the vote and then we need women standing for parliament themselves. How do you intend taking matters further?'

'I don't really know, Miss.' It was on the tip of Maggie's tongue to tell Lucy about Alfie's promise to speak with the doctor in Edinburgh, but a voice in her head warned her that if she said too much to Lucy, Alfie would find out and use it as an excuse to renege on his word. As it was, she had little faith that he would carry out his promise.

Lucy tapped the closed book against her palm, as if pondering over what to say. Eventually she spoke. 'There are people in our society who may be able to help you. You would need to be able to demonstrate your desire and commitment to them.'

She gave no indication of who these people were or what society she was referring to. Maggie suspected there was something secretive about the group and didn't respond.

'More than just reading library books,' Lucy added. She handed the book back to Maggie. 'Mother would like some tea in the drawing room, with one of Cook's currant buns, if there are any left.'

'Yes, Miss.' Maggie curtseyed. Not quite believing what had just passed between them, Maggie stood rooted to the spot.

'Now please, if you don't mind,' Lucy said.

Maggie curtseyed again and left, with thoughts not of tea and buns, but of proving her determination to go to medical school.

****

Alfie had told Maggie he intended to visit Dotty in the near future, but in truth he had had other matters to worry about. Maggie's visit brought Dotty and her upcoming surgery back to mind. Had she already gone under the knife? He hadn't heard from Dr Matthews, but that was no indication of anything. He should indeed visit and find out, but it wasn't a good time. The Christening celebrations were only a week away and before then he anticipated a trip to Glasgow. It was a city he had visited once as an apprentice and after getting involved in a scrap with local youths and spending a night in the police cells, he preferred to avoid it. Unfortunately the Society of Watch and Clockmakers was holding its annual meeting there and he was keen to attend. There were still a few glitches with the clock workings and he hoped his colleagues at the assembly would help with a way of solving them.

'I'll be able to get a vial of gumplestroff oil there,' he told Templeman.

'Gumplestroff oil?'

'Lubrication. It's vital the intricate parts don't wear down with friction. I wouldn't want anyone to be stuck in the future because a dribble of oil was lacking.'

'Gracious, no. How much does that cost?'

Alfie hadn't thought of charging Templeman any more for his imaginary time machine, but a figure of five guineas sprang from his lips. Templeman slipped him the money the following day and he prepared a mixture of linseed oil and liquid paraffin, which he tinted red with beetroot juice. He funnelled it into a glass jar and stuck a label reading *glstroff oil* written in green ink on the side.

He hid it under the counter of his shop, ready to produce it when Templeman asked.

Norma was unhappy about his trip to Glasgow, but Norma was unhappy about everything he did. On the day, she packed him bread, cheese and pickle for the journey.

'I'm going to Glasgow, not the South Pole,' he protested.

'Might as well be the same thing,' Norma huffed.

'You have never been there, mother,' Winnie said, linking arms with Alfie and giving him a kiss on the cheek. 'It can't be as bad as you imagine.'

'Are you sure you have to stay the night in that city?' Norma hadn't finished having her say.

'The talks finish late and there is a dinner afterwards,' Alfie said. 'I hope to be elected to one of the sub-committees. I need to make my presence visible.'

The mention of an office, however small, placated Norma. He was forced to look in on the twins before he left.

'Daddy won't be away long,' Winnie crooned to them.

'They don't understand you,' Alfie reminded her.

His son was a weakling babe, always coughing and bringing up milk. The girl was healthier, but she was forever bawling. Why did it take so long for children to grow? If he could invent a time travel machine he would jump forwards at least five years.

Lisa saw him off at the station. 'Why cannae I come tae Glesga wi' ye?'

'I need someone to look after the shop.'

'There willnae be ony customers,' Lisa argued.

It was tempting to have Lisa with him, despite the inevitable comments about their age difference, but it was impossible. He hadn't been honest with Winnie and Norma. He could have done everything that needed to be done in Glasgow and made it home for supper, but he intended taking a detour to Edinburgh on his way back.

'Please Alfie.' Lisa worked on his hesitation. She pressed her breasts against his chest.

'You would be on your own for a good deal of the time,' he said. 'Women aren't allowed to attend the dinner.'

'Yon's no fair. Dinnae you hae women clockmakers?'

'Not in our society.'

That was something Dotty objected to. Granted she was cleverer with her hands than most of his colleagues, but when it came to the science behind the art, there was no place for female intellect.

'I dinnae mind being on ma own. I can dae some shopping. I'll hae you tae cosy up tae in ma bed at night.'

Lisa expanded on what she meant by "cosying up" and in the end Alfie gave in. There was time to buy her a ticket before the train departed. When he returned to the platform she was stuffing her face with one of his sandwiches.

'Wha made this pickle?' She spat it onto her handkerchief.

'My mother-in-law.' Alfie frowned and sat on the bench beside her. 'Did nobody teach you manners?'

'It tastes like... like... gumplestroff oil.'

'What?' Alfie jumped up. 'You haven't…?'

'Naw, I've nae really tasted it, silly,' Lisa laughed. 'I like the name and you must admit, it smells disgusting, like your mother-in-law's pickle.'

'I should leave the gumplestroff oil well alone,' Alfie said. 'If you spill it on your skin, it has been known to cause serious burns.'

'Oh, I didnae touch it,' Lisa said, rubbing her nose. 'Look, here's oor train noo.'

The train journey was uneventful. Lisa looked out the window as the verdant pastures changed to industrial grey. Alfie read a professional journal. It was a quiet period for British clock making and there wasn't much new to read about.

'I don't believe it.' He slammed the journal on the table in front of him, waking the elderly lady who was sharing the compartment. She had nodded off with her head on Lisa's shoulder.

'Oh dear, is there a problem with the train?' the lady asked.

'No. Go back to sleep, I'll wake you when we arrive in Glasgow,' Alfie told her.

'I'm getting off before then.'

'He's being nasty,' Lisa said. She turned to Alfie. 'Whit is getting your gander up noo?'

'Have you seen this?'

Lisa was sitting opposite Alfie. She picked up the journal, but the words made no sense. 'Whit's it aboot?'

'It is about Mr Templeman and his fabulous new clock.'

'Is that nae braw?' Lisa turned to the lady. 'Ma Alfie here is helping Mr Templeman mak it.'

The woman smiled across at Alfie.

'I am not "helping him make it". I *am* making it, not that anybody would know. This is supposed to be a clock making journal, not an artists' catalogue. It details nothing of the intricate processes involved.'

'That's because you havenae telt anyone,' Lisa said.

198

'I am not some common commercial salesman.'

'Neither is Mr Templeman, but he kens hoo tae boost himsel'.'

'He is an American.'

'My husband knew an American once.' The lady caught the tail end of the conversation. 'A gentleman from Washington.'

'Your husband has my condolences,' Alfie answered.

'Oh, but they were great friends.'

'That says nothing for your husband, madam.'

The lady smarted and said no more until her station. After she alighted, the train trundled on towards the city. The clockmakers' convention was in a hotel near the station. For the sake of propriety, Alfie arranged a separate room for Lisa.

'On the same floor, if possible,' he requested.

'Would you like me to take the lady's luggage to her room?' the porter quipped.

'It is following on,' Alfie said to avoid Lisa's embarrassment.

There was no unpacking to do, but he left Lisa in her room and went downstairs to meet up with his colleagues and register for the conference. A group of attendees were talking in the smoking room. He recognised two of them and went to join them.

'That wasn't your wife I saw you with on the way in?' one of them, Forbes McGregor, was quick to notice.

'My niece,' Alfie answered. 'She has business in the city.'

'You're Peters from Perth, aren't you?'

Alfie didn't recognise the man who asked.

'The fair city,' Alfie agreed.

'You must know about this ground-breaking clock,' a third man said. 'They say the casing is the size of a small room, is that true?'

Alfie looked around the reception hall they were in. 'Aye, about quarter the size of this room.'

'Can you imagine what any clockmaker worth his salt could do with that?' McGregor gave a low whistle.

'Aye,' Alfie answered.

'I haven't read who the clockmaker is, but somebody here must know him,' the man next to Alfie said.

'I imagine it will be some genius whisked up from London,' another man replied. The company mumbled in agreement with the statement and unanimous disapproval of the fact. Alfie waited for interest in the topic to wane.

'I was hoping to meet you, Forbes,' he turned to his friend. 'Last year you were talking about developing a mechanism for keeping an accurate track of the time in New York and linking it to the phases of the moon. Have you patented your idea?'

'Nothing came of that, I'm afraid. I'm working in miniature

now - a watch that can be worn like a ring.'

'Sounds intriguing. It's a pity you have given up on your lunar calculations though. I was hoping you could help me with the workings for the West Tay clock.'

It took a moment before the implication of what he had said reached the brains of the gathered clockmakers.

'You are working on the West Tay clock?' the man on McGregor's right asked. 'Allow me to introduce myself, William Drury. My workshop is in Stirling.'

Alfie shook hands with him.

'I thought it was some American dude,' the man across from Alfie said in a poor New York accent.

'Giles Templeman, the casing designer, is indeed from New York, but his Thanksgiving turkey has a better idea of horology than he does. Left to him, the clock would be nothing more than an empty shell, a decorative one, granted, but utterly useless.'

Alfie enjoyed the conversation for ten minutes before excusing himself, thus giving the clockmakers time to talk about him. Lisa had made an important point. If he didn't want Templeman to steal the credit, he had to advertise his own role. It was more than satisfying to hear his name bandied about over dinner and he had no trouble in being nominated and seconded as chairman to the sub-committee. The position brought with it a chain of office, which Winnie would have him display in the shop to impress his customers. He showed it to Lisa that evening and she insisted that he order champagne to celebrate.

Champagne! He should have charged Templeman more for his gumplestroff oil.

Over breakfast the following morning he managed to talk with McGregor and teased out the information he wanted regarding international time systems. The mechanism was ungainly and would take up space. The casing wasn't as large as he had boasted and he needed to set aside a reasonable area to convince Templeman of the time machine element. There had to be a way of bringing everything together in a tidy manner, a simple formula. He couldn't put his finger on it and the thought lingered as he finished his kippers. Alfie felt pensive as he made his way to Lisa's room.

'Will you hae breakfast wi' me?' Lisa asked.

'I've already eaten.'

'I'm nae hungert ony roads. Dae we hae time tae go shopping? I need tae git wool and threads for a frock.'

'Can't you get that in Perth?'

'The shops there dinnae hae whit I'm looking for.'

202

Alfie hesitated and Lisa gave him a wet kiss on the lips to press her point. She wiped her mouth to rid them of the taste of the fish.

'Of course you had better go shopping,' Alfie moved to give her backside a playful slap. 'But not here.'

'Whar then?'

'Edinburgh. I have business in the city before going home.'

'But I'm nae dressed for Edinburgh. You shid hae telt me.'

'I didn't know you were coming until we were at the station. Besides, what is good enough for Perth should be more than suitable for Edinburgh. We aren't guests at Holyrood Palace. Not today.'

They caught a train to Edinburgh. Alfie left Lisa at Haymarket with enough money to keep her amused until they met for lunch. He took a coach to the hospital. It wasn't officially spring, but the weather was mild. A weak sun shone through the clouds. Alfie noted that repair work had begun on the hospital windows and the roof boasted new slates. Leaves were sprouting from flower bulbs planted along the entrance drive. The cheerful young man greeted him at reception.

'You're early Mr Peters. We weren't expecting you until this afternoon.'

'You weren't expecting me at all,' Alfie answered. 'This is an impromptu visit.'

The young man consulted the diary in front of him and scratched his head. Alfie struggled to read the upside-down writing, but he made out the name "Peters" scrawled on the page. The receptionist had confused him with another patient's visitor.

'Your wife is in the music room with Dr Matthews.'

'Doesn't he have any other patients?'

Dr Matthews seemed always to be with Dotty, but Alfie didn't expect the young man to answer. He made his way along the familiar corridor. There were new pictures on the walls, bright, modern pieces in vibrant colours. Enough to send any man demented, Alfie thought. He heard the piano playing as he reached the room. It had been tuned and a Beethoven piece was sounding from it.

Alfie waited outside for a moment, listening to the notes. There was laughter from inside the room followed by a discord. Alfie pictured the good doctor leaning over to distract Dotty and pushed the door open without knocking. Dr Matthews was at the piano, helping an older woman with her fingering. Dotty was at the window looking out to the back garden. She looked round. Her face was covered in linen bandages, with holes for her mouth, eyes and nose. Alfie was reminded of a museum exhibit from the ancient Egyptian section. She must have seen him gaping, because she turned back to the window.

'The garden will be beautiful when all the flowers come out,' she said.

'Indeed,' Dr Matthews answered. 'Why don't you take a walk and show your husband the garden?' He turned to Alfie. 'We have land at the back where we have planted shrubs, bushes and a vegetable plot.'

'A walk, in this weather?' Alfie objected.

'It is a lovely morning,' Dotty said. 'I shall get my coat and hat.' She walked past Alfie and out the door.

'You are allowing your patients to come and go as they please,' Alfie turned on the doctor.

'Not all of them, but as you can see, your wife is cured.'

'Cured? Why, it seems to me the lunatics are running the asylum.'

The lady at the piano gasped and held a hand over her mouth.

'Really Mr Peters, I must ask you to modify your language,' Dr Matthews said. 'This is a hospital.'

'My wife may appear cured, but I know more of her history than you. Any minor upset could set the fits off again. And what of her face?'

'Dorothy took the chloroform well. My friend is happy with the surgery. It is too early to say what the final outcome will be. We must wait for the swelling to go down and for the stitches to be removed.'

'The scar will be as bad as the blemish.'

'I don't think so, but it could be covered by a lock of hair.'

The older lady thumped her hands on the keyboard and Alfie jumped back. Dorothy was behind him, dressed for the outdoors. Her bonnet was low over her face and she wore a scarf high round her neck to cover her chin and mouth. She took Alfie by the hand and led him out. They didn't speak until they reached the back door, where Dotty lowered her scarf to ask one of the nurses to open it. The woman obliged. The garden was a manageable size and laid out in even rows. The bushes were drab, still in their winter foliage, but there was evidence of new growth. Dorothy stopped to lean against a wooden arch.

'You really shouldn't be out,' Alfie said.

Dotty began to answer, but he couldn't make out a word from behind her scarf and bandages. She lowered her scarf.

'Dr Matthews took me to the botanic gardens last week. He promised to take me to the seaside when the weather improves.'

'Did he now?'

'He thinks I need cheering up, after my surgery and the sea air will clear the chloroform from my lungs.'

'Does your face hurt?' Alfie asked.

'Not so much now. The nurse applies cream three times a day and changes the bandages.'

'Have you seen…'

'No. Dr Matthews won't let me near a mirror. Not until the stitches are out.'

'Wise, I suppose.'

Dotty didn't want to speak about her surgery. Either that or she had been instructed not to.

'I have been in Glasgow, at the Society Convention. I met Forbes McGregor, from Forfar. Do you remember him?'

'Of course.'

He couldn't see any of Dotty's face, but from her exaggerated tone he imagined she was smiling.

'Is he still trying to perfect his lunar measurements?'

'No, he has admitted defeat on that. He is making a watch that will fit on a ring.'

'Knowing Forbes, it won't be a miniature watch, rather a gigantic ring.'

Alfie gave a chuckle. 'I was hoping he could help me with the West Tay clock. I still haven't worked out where everything will fit in the casing.'

'That is because you are thinking in three dimensions, Alfie. Odd, considering you spend your life working with time.'

'Time?'

'It is a clock, after all.'

'Time is fixed. It is only the other three dimensions we can alter and Templeman is loath to change his casing.'

'I'm not talking about time, but of timing. You have a train running round the casing. Once it has moved on from a particular spot, the space is free to be reused. The river could flow along the same track a few seconds later, or one of your planetary models could be lowered or raised into the space.'

Alfie clicked his fingers. 'Dotty, you are a genius.'

He leaned forwards as if to kiss her. She drew back. He took hold of her hand and shook it instead.

'Thank you Dotty. Thank you very much. Now, we'd better get you in before you catch a cold.'

Dotty made to raise her scarf up, but hesitated. 'There is something I would like to talk to you about, Alfie.'

'Yes, yes, but not now.' Alfie checked his pocket watch. 'I have to be off. I'll be back as soon as I can.'

For a moment Dotty looked as if she had something further to say, but she replaced her scarf and walked ahead of him towards the building.

Dr Matthews was at the door to meet them. He took hold of Dotty's hand and she gave a small shake of the head. 'Your hand is freezing,' Dr Matthews said.

'I warned against going outside,' Alfie said.

'So you did. Do you have time to talk?'

'Not today. I have business in Perth with the chri...with the hotel clock. I can't see me managing back until after Easter.'

Dotty gave a gasp and looked to the doctor.

'No sooner? Then I shall write to you beforehand,' Dr Matthews said. 'To keep you informed of Dorothy's progress.'

'Aye. I'll show myself out.'

Alfie was in a hurry to get home to work on Dotty's idea. The coach reached South Queensferry before he remembered Lisa. He was supposed to be meeting her for lunch in Princes' Street. He looked at his watch. There was a train into the centre of Edinburgh in ten minutes. If there were no delays he might manage it.

Lisa was not happy at being kept waiting. She was bored

hanging around when there were streets of enticing shops to look at. She had spent the money he gave her long since.

'Can we visit the castle after lunch?' she asked.

'I need to get back to Perth.'

'You wouldn't want me to tell your wife what we got up to last night.'

'Very well, but just the castle.'

After a tour of the castle and a stroll down the Royal Mile to view Holyrood Palace, with Lisa painting a picture of living there, she was ready for afternoon tea.

'Anyone would think you were a lady,' Alfie moaned as Lisa poured the tea. 'Don't think we'll be making a habit of this.'

'You like your scones, don't you? You've had three already.'

They finally made it across the Forth and onto the train for Perth. The coaches were full and they had to walk down the carriage to find seats. They settled beside a corpulent couple. The man's breath smelt of garlic and the woman had the habit of passing wind. Alfie put up with it for longer than he would have if Lisa wasn't beside him, but eventually he stood up and walked out of the compartment. Lisa followed him.

'Why, isn't that Maggie?' Lisa waved to somebody at the far end of the carriage. Alfie struggled to see past a man in a fur collared coat.

'You must be mistaken. Why would she be on this train?'

'She told me her family lives outside Perth,' Lisa answered. 'She may have been visiting them.'

They hadn't reached Nancy's station, but Alfie didn't correct Lisa. The girl, whoever she was, had vanished. A number of passengers got off at the next stop, allowing Alfie and Lisa to find seats in a vacated compartment. Lisa closed her eyes and the movement of the train sent her head drooping onto Alfie's shoulder. When she started to drool he pushed her away, but she didn't stir. Alfie had a hard job shaking her awake as the train drew into Perth.

'Are we here?' Lisa yawned.

'We've been here ten minutes. If you don't get off your backside, we'll be heading to the sidings.'

It was an exaggeration, but it succeeded in rousing Lisa.

'Is that the time?' She spotted the station clock as they got off.

'You are the one who wanted to stay in Edinburgh for afternoon tea,' Alfie chided.

'You said the train got to Perth before nine.'

'There was a delay on the line.'

The unscheduled stop, about five miles from the city, lasted over twenty minutes. Alfie had left Lisa sleeping and ventured along the corridor to ask a guard what the problem was, but had returned to his seat no wiser.

It was a slow walk back to the flat, with Lisa leaning her head on his shoulder for most of the way. It would have been quicker to thrust her over his shoulder and carry her like a shepherd with a lamb, but he didn't want his honest neighbours to report him for inappropriate conduct.

'Are you ready for bed, Alfie?' Lisa asked, undoing his tie before they reached the stairs. 'I have a surprise for you.' She patted one of the bags she brought from her shopping trip and gave a giggle.

'I shall have to call in on Winnie,' Alfie said. 'She will want to know that I'm home and how things went, but I'll be back as soon as I can.'

'I bought this for you to give her.' Lisa put her hand in the smaller bag and brought out a pair of ladies' gloves. 'I knew you wouldn't remember.'

'You're a good girl, Lisa.' Alfie took the gloves and gave her a kiss. 'Keep the bed warm for me.'

It was a chilly evening and Alfie wished the gloves fitted him. His fingers were too cold to fit his key in the lock, but Norma opened the door. Winnie had retired to bed, but her mother had stayed up to wait for him. Her mood was sour.

'The train was delayed,' he said.

'From ten in the morning? That's when your conference ended.'

'I had to go to Edinburgh.' Alfie couldn't think of a suitable lie.

'Why?'

'Clock business.'

'I heard there was an accident on the line outside Perth.'

Norma grumbled, but accepted his excuse. She made tea and between gulps he convinced Norma his days away had been spent missing Winnie and the twins. The proceedings of the convention gave him an excuse to return to the shop.

'Do you really need to work so late?' Norma asked.

'The ideas are fresh in my head. I want to sort out the details before I forget. The West Tay clock has to be ready for Easter.'

He wasn't thinking about the West Tay clock as he made his way back to the apartment. Lisa's 'surprise' must be something she bought to arouse him. Lace lingerie perhaps. The door to the shop was open and the lights downstairs were lit. It set Alfie on his guard as he approached and he knelt to pick up a stone from the road. He stuck his hand with the stone in his coat pocket, feeling the weight on his fingers, then stepped into the shop. There was no evidence of a disruption. The shelves appeared undamaged and he scanned them to check if anything was missing. A police officer was standing at the back of the shop, with his elbow resting on the counter. Lisa was beside him. The man turned when he heard Alfie enter.

'Are you Mr Alfred Peters?' He consulted his notebook for the name.

'Yes, this is my shop,' Alfie answered. 'How can I help you?'

'There was an incident on the railway earlier today,' the policeman said, stepping towards Alfie.

'So I heard,' Alfie said. 'What was the problem?'

'A young girl was attacked and thrown off the train.'

'Goodness, I hope she wasn't seriously hurt,' Alfie said.

'I'm afraid, sir, she is dead.'

Chapter 13

Lisa gasped and fell towards the policeman. He caught her before she hit the floor, but struggled with the weight. Alfie stepped in to revive her.

'A young woman? Was it someone we knew?' Alfie asked, putting his arm around Lisa's shoulder. She was shivering under a thin lace nightdress and he took his coat off to wrap round her.

'That is what I am here to ascertain,' the policeman said. 'I'm sorry to disturb you and the young lady, but we are treating this as murder.'

'Murder? Surely you are mistaken? What was the girl's name?'

'We have been unable to identify her. From appearances we would say she was a serving girl, but we found this among her possessions.'

The policeman reached in his tunic pocket to bring out a lady's pocket watch. 'It seems rather an expensive item for a maid. It has your name on the back.' The man turned the watch over and demonstrated the maker's mark. 'My sergeant sent me to ask if you kept a record of who you sold your watches to.'

Alfie set Lisa down on a chair next to the counter and handed her his pocket handkerchief before taking the watch from the officer. He recognised it at once. It was the watch Maggie had been admiring on her visit. He walked to the shelf, but wasn't surprised to find the space empty. Had she pretended to put it back and slipped it up her sleeve? There was no other explanation. The officer was waiting for an answer.

'What did the girl look like?' Alfie asked.

The man read from his notes. 'About sixteen, blonde hair, pretty in a plain sort of way. Her dress was quality material, but patched.'

'Did she have a birthmark on her neck?'

Alfie didn't need to hear the officer's affirmation. Maggie was dead. Should he tell the man the truth, the watch was stolen by the Squires' maid? Hearing her dead daughter was a thief would kill Nancy.

'Yes, I remember this timepiece. One of my regular clients was interested in the fine detail. I entrusted it to her maid to show to the young lady.'

'And who might this client be?'

'Miss Emily Squires. She is the daughter of Walker Squires who owns the West Tay Hotel.' Alfie hoped the name would mean something, but the policeman seemed unimpressed.

'I see. You gave the watch to the maid,' the policeman repeated. 'When was this?'

'I'm not sure. Do you remember when Maggie was here last, Lisa?'

'Maggie?' She took a sharp intake of breath. 'Why… you don't mean? Constable, you can't…?'

'The young lady's name was Maggie.' The policeman wrote in his notebook. 'Do you know her surname?'

'I'm sorry, I only knew her as Maggie. Mr Squires will be able to supply the details you require regarding her family.'

Alfie saw Lisa glaring at him, but she had the sense not to open her mouth.

'Thank you for your help, Mr Peters, Miss…'

'Mulligan,' Lisa said. 'Wi' two "Ls". Are you nae gan tae write that doon?'

'I don't think that will be necessary,' the policeman answered.

'What about the watch?' Alfie asked.

'We shall need to keep that as evidence for the moment, sir.'

'Of course, but afterwards?'

'We'll make sure it gets returned.'

'Thank you.'

The officer tapped his hat and strode out. He was hardly off the premises when Lisa turned on Alfie. 'Your dochter is deid and a' you can think aboot is a watch.'

'She wasn't my daughter and it is an expensive timepiece,' Alfie remarked, locking the shop door.

'You dinnae care aboot the poor lass, attacked and murdered,' Lisa paused then gasped. 'She wis on the same train as oorsels. We need tae tell the police laddie that. We micht hae seen something, withoot kenning it.'

'Really, Lisa, this isn't some fanciful crime novel. We saw nothing. We don't know that the girl you saw was Maggie.'

'A ken whit a saw.'

Alfie moved across to put his arms round her.

'Of course, but you know what the law is like, always interested in everybody's affairs, criminal or not. If we told the police we were on the train, they would want to know what my business was in Edinburgh and I need to keep that private.'

'It's horrible thinking aboot it. She was gye near the same age as me.'

'Don't think about it then. Come to bed. I've got a sleeping tonic you should drink.'

The police were at the hotel the next morning. A plain clothed detective was speaking to Walker Squires, with his sergeant taking notes, when Alfie dropped by. Squires didn't notice his arrival and Alfie decided it was better not to interrupt police proceedings. His business at the hotel could wait. He had the choice of working on the clock or going to see Winnie. The situation with Maggie had stolen the excitement of the clock design and he found himself walking towards his house.

Norma was in the garden, beating a rug. She had a strong right arm and dust obliterated Alfie's view of her face, but he had little doubt it wasn't the carpet she imagined she was beating. One of Mrs Allendale's cats watched from the bushes. Norma stopped when she spotted Alfie.

'About time. I need you to pay the baker for the Christening cake and you have to speak with the minister. Winnie and I have chosen suitable hymns. You need to know the order of service and what responses are required.'

'I'll do it later,' Alfie said.

'You said that yesterday evening. There won't be time later. Did you see Mr Squires about the hotel suite?'

'He was busy this morning.'

Alfie sensed his lack of enthusiasm was not appreciated and gave Norma a wide berth, avoiding her stick, as he made his way to the house. Winnie was in bed, resting, while Mrs Allendale was in charge of the twins.

'I'm glad you are here, Mr Peters. Children are not as easy to look after as kittens.'

'I imagine not,' Alfie agreed. If his mother-in-law hadn't been blocking his escape, he would have turned round and headed back out the door.

The following day may well have been chaotic as far as Norma was concerned, but Alfie spent it in the warehouse smoothing out the final problems with the clock design. He only had mice for company for most of the day, but as he prepared to leave, Templeman appeared. He was less boisterous than usual and Alfie assumed his demeanour was due to news of Maggie's death. The American strode around the warehouse until a piece of scrap metal caught his eye. He rubbed his fingers down it before spotting Alfie.

'Ah, I see you are still here, Peters. Is this the gumplestroff?'

'No, no, that's...part of the cross dimension safety mechanism,' Alfie invented.

'Of course.' Templeman paused and rubbed his chin. 'I was in Edinburgh yesterday and happened to meet an American friend there. We talked about time travel and she suggested special suits would be needed.'

'She? What do women know about time travel? She was probably worried about fashion and appearances,' Alfie scoffed.

'I believe, like you, she was thinking of safety considerations. She feels with the rush of time, there would be an increase of pressure on the body?'

'On the weaker female frame, perhaps,' Alfie said. 'I imagine it would be safer to wear period costumes when going back in time. You wouldn't want to be arrested as a wizard and burnt alive.'

Templeman's laugh wasn't convincing. 'It is safe, though?' he asked.

'It is untested,' Alfie admitted.

'The pioneering spirit. That's how the west was won and that's what's needed here.'

Alfie collected his coat while Giles examined the piece of metal.

'There is another matter I wanted to speak with you about,' Templeman said before Alfie could leave. 'My American friend told me the New York train line is being extended to reach Manhattan, with a new station in the centre of the island. The station planners want a clock and it's almost certain I will be invited to make the casing. It won't be as spectacular as this one, but I would need someone to fit in the workings. What would you say to a trip to the United States?'

'That would certainly be worth considering,' Alfie agreed. It

221

was difficult to hold back his excitement at the prospect, but he managed a dour smile.

'Well, I won't keep you, I'm sure you have plenty to do. I shall see you in church tomorrow.'

It hadn't been his idea, but Winnie had asked Emily Squires to be the twins' godmother. She was delighted with the role, but insisted Templeman should be their godfather. With their upcoming nuptials, Alfie couldn't think of a reason to object.

Norma and Winnie were busy dressing the babies in different costumes, deciding which they preferred. Fred didn't mind, but Sylvia was kicking like a March hare.

'Trust girls,' Alfie grumbled.

'What will you wear?' Norma was keen to make sure nothing went awry.

'You could wear your new chain,' Winnie said.

'I don't think that would be appropriate.'

'Oh, please do,' Winnie wheedled.

'You want people to notice you, don't you?' Norma added her tuppence worth.

'I'm not a doll for you to dress up.' Alfie stamped out of the room.

'Trust men,' he heard Norma grumble.

Winnie had purchased a double pram and Alfie had the job of pushing it to the church the following morning. Thankfully the weather was mild and the clouds drifted over without dropping rain. Winnie was feeling off colour. Her mother brushed her symptoms away as signs of stress, but Alfie insisted she and her mother took a cab to the church.

'What about the babes?' Norma fretted. 'Surely you will need help with them?'

She meant a woman's hand.

'I'm not a fool, I can push a pram.'

There was more of a knack to controlling the vehicle than he imagined. The axle was stiff and he had to force the handle. Every time there was a bump in the road one or other of the babes would start to bawl. On one occasion he was tempted to smother the blanket over their faces, but the pavement was busy with folks heading to the kirk and he was compelled to smile and exchange pleasantries.

The service was long-winded and Fred regurgitated his milk over the minister. Winnie had a cough, which she made worse by trying to suppress. Giles Templeman spent the time flirting with Emily Squires, which seemed unnecessary since they were engaged. Alfie couldn't concentrate on the sermon, thinking of

Dotty. What if her surgery had been a success? He pictured a fresh-faced Dotty sitting beside him instead of Winnie, smiling at their son.

The organ began for the final hymn. Winnie had chosen 'When Mothers of Salem, Their children brought to Jesus,' which was rather a dirge to Alfie's mind. The organist struggled with the timing and the congregation floundered. Sylvia was crying. It was just as well Alfie was sitting between Winnie and Emily Squires, or he would have fled out of the church. The music ended and the minister raised his right hand to give the benediction. Alfie took the opportunity to look round, hoping Lisa was in the church.

There was a young girl playing with her hair at the end of a pew in the centre of church. She looked up and Alfie jumped. Maggie? It couldn't be. He blinked and looked again. The woman was older and her hair was too dark, but for a moment he remembered Maggie's warning of being there. His heart was racing when he felt a tug on his jacket. Everyone had sat down and the minister was waiting for him to do the same. It was a relief to finally get out of the building. On the church steps Alfie found he was expected to shake hands with everyone in the congregation before he could escape. His palms were sweaty and he rubbed them down the side of his trousers.

'You must be so proud.'

'Aren't they sweet.'

'He's a fine lad and the lass looks just like you.'

The bobbing of his hand had a clock-like rhythm and he pictured the movement of the drunken cooper in the West Tay clock.

Lisa had been sitting at the back and she appeared to help Norma with the babies while Alfie and Winnie went on ahead to the hotel. The manager had things in order. The room was decorated, the food was ready to be served and hotel employees were on hand to direct the guests. Alfie helped himself to a ham sandwich.

'Can't you wait?' Winnie scolded.

'Not if you don't want my stomach rumbling louder than Sylvia's screaming.'

He lifted two more sandwiches to make a point. One was salmon, which he didn't like. He forced it down then reached for a glass of wine.

The guests arrived and after congratulating the parents headed for the buffet. The party was well underway when Alfie saw Squires signalling to him from the door. He excused himself from a conversation with Mrs Allendale about whether cats had second sight and went over.

'I'm sorry to bring the matter up here, but it's about my daughters' maid,' Squires began.

'The girl who died?'

'You've heard, of course. The business with the watch, I suppose. Terrible, truly terrible. I've spoken with her mother. She lives in one of the villages not far from the city. The poor girl didn't have a father. The funeral is arranged for Wednesday, here in Perth. I feel I should attend, so the next meeting will have to be postponed.'

'Yes, I understand. We must get our priorities right, but isn't that rather soon for the funeral? I wouldn't have thought the police would release the body until they finished their investigations.'

'They've got their man,' Squires said. 'A number of the passengers reported seeing a sailor showing her unwanted attention.'

'And none of them stepped in to help her?' Alfie remarked.

'Nobody admits to seeing the actual deed, but the police believe this sailor threw her from the train.'

'A waste of a young life.' Alfie shook his head.

'Two lives,' Squires corrected him. 'Maggie was expecting a baby.'

Alfie was holding a glass of wine. His hand shook and the contents spilt down his trouser leg. Squires offered him his handkerchief.

'Do you know who the father was?' Alfie scanned the room while he wiped his trousers. Templeman was sharing a joke with Emily and Lucy Squires.

'No, she didn't mention a fiancé to us.' Squires' voice was light, but when Alfie looked at him, the hotel owner's eyes were hard fixed on the American.

Chapter 14

Alfie knew he should speak with Nancy before the funeral, but it wasn't a task he looked forward to and he put off making the journey. He had received a message from Farquhar re-scheduling the clock meeting for the following day and had barely finished organising his diary before Templeman was in his shop.

'We need to have something to show him.' Giles slammed a fist on the counter, sending the cogs Alfie had placed there hopping towards the edge.

'Careful, man.' Alfie grabbed the cogs in time to prevent a scramble to retrieve them from the spiders' webs below the serving desk. He would have to remind Lisa to be more attentive with her sweeping.

Templeman ignored the chastisement. 'I have an idea, but we will need something substantial to show Farquhar by tomorrow.'

'Another new idea?' Alfie opened a drawer and slipped the cogs in.

'You will be amazed. Why, I bet you a new hat this has never been done before.'

Alfie stared at Templeman, forgetting to close the drawer.

'Wait until you see the plan.'

'Another plan?'

'An addendum.'

Templeman did not have the drawing with him and it was necessary to accompany Giles to the warehouse. The river was high after a winter of snow and rain and it was pushing up waves round the island in the centre.

'Watch your feet,' Alfie warned as Templeman slipped on some mud. He regained his balance by grabbing Alfie's arm.

'Wouldn't want to fall to my death there,' Templeman agreed.

'Where would you want to fall to your death?' Alfie asked.

Templeman stared at him. 'Falling must be the worst part,' Alfie pondered. 'For those few seconds, knowing there is nothing you can do to save yourself. They say time slows down when you are about to die.'

'You sound mighty despondent.'

'I was thinking of that poor girl, the one who was thrown from the train.' Alfie tried to judge Templeman's expression. 'You knew her, didn't you? She was Miss Emily's maid.'

'I don't remember individual maids. They are all just pretty faces in uniforms.'

'She used to work at the hotel,' Alfie persisted.

'Did she?'

You know damn well she did.

If Alfie had been twenty years younger he would have lifted Templeman by the lapels and thrown him into the Tay. As it was, he decided to let the matter rest – for the moment. 'So, when is your big day?' he asked.

'My big day?'

Alfie hummed a wedding march.

'Oh, you mean my marriage to Miss Emily? That's a tricky one.' Templeman rubbed behind his right ear. 'It was supposed to be a late spring ceremony, scheduled for the beginning of May, but I shall have to go to New York quite soon. I told you about the commission for the station clock.'

'A station clock, as yet, without a station,' Alfie reminded him.

'It will go ahead, I have no doubts. I would be there now, if it wasn't for my commitment here. I don't suppose there is any way of getting this damn clock working before Easter?'

'I doubt it. We're lucky Easter is late this year.'

'The 25th of April, as Farquhar will remind us tomorrow.'

'We have eight weeks, give or take a few days. I shall hold no quarter with cutting corners.'

'If you could sort out the problems we're having with the parts manufacturers, and if Squires pays promptly for the labour, it could be ready to hang by the middle of April,' Templeman argued. 'A full week or more in advance.'

'Have the builders started on the ceiling reinforcement yet?' Alfie asked.

'I've spoken with Davidson. He can spare the men from next week. He assures me the ceiling will be ready by the end of March, beginning of April at the latest.'

'We could aim to have the clock finished by the middle of April,' Alfie conceded.

Templeman blew a raspberry.

'What is your problem with that?' Alfie said.

'The clock may be ready, but there's still the transportation and hanging of it. That will take two days at the least.'

Alfie put a hand on Templeman's shoulder. 'You are forgetting that once our special features are in place, you can set the clock to go back a month or two. For all we know, you could be talking to your New York colleagues in Manhattan as we are speaking now.'

Templeman scratched his head. 'Gee, I hadn't thought of that. I could be...while we're standing here... gee.'

'I don't see why not. The gear level arrived a few days ago. I saw Weir marking it in his notebook.'

'The gear level? Jonas didn't ask any questions about it?'

'He doesn't have the gumption.'

'Wait, wouldn't there need to be two of me. One here and one in New York?' Giles scratched his head.

Two Templemans, heaven forfend!

They had reached the warehouse, saving Alfie from responding. Weir was inside, talking to the foreman of the labourers. They heard his voice as they entered.

'Gentlemen, I am glad you have arrived. Mr Johnstone needs precise instructions for his men.'

'I'll leave the nitty gritty to you, Peters,' Templeman said.

Alfie spent forty minutes explaining the clock layout to Johnstone and his men. Finally the foreman snapped his fingers, showing he understood. Alfie made him repeat back the instructions, but it seemed the man had indeed grasped the complexities and was able to organise working groups to assemble the parts in order. Alfie was about to leave when he remembered his reason for being there. Templeman was doodling sketches of trains in his notepad when Alfie approached him.

'Is that your new idea?' He pointed at the sketches and Templeman snapped the notebook shut.

'No, over here.' Templeman directed him out of sight of Weir.

'Why the secrecy?'

'Weir reports everything we do to old Farquhar, haven't you

noticed? I want this to be a surprise.'

Templeman retrieved a scrap of paper from his jacket pocket and unfolded it. There were some scribbles in pencil with the words 'travel through time' in bold capitals. 'Brilliant, if I say so myself.'

Alfie took a pair of reading glasses from his pocket and put them on to examine the paper. The glasses weren't his and the drawings appeared blurred. He had collected them from the jewellery and eye glass shop for Winnie. The expense was eye watering, but he had been given the blame for breaking them. They had fallen from the table, which had been knocked over as he shooed the neighbour's cat out of the house.

'Astounding,' he said, removing the glasses. 'One little matter, though.'

'Yes?'

'Perhaps it's me, but what exactly does this mean?' He pointed indiscriminately at the paper.

'Can't you see it? It's meant as a joke. The clock will depict people travelling back and forwards in time and only we will know the truth of it.'

'You have changed the entire design,' Alfie spluttered.

'I have added to it, that's all.'

'Everything will need to be rearranged. Do you want it finished in a month?'

'There's no rush, not now that you've explained I can simply go back in time to fill in the gaps.' Templeman laughed in a superior manner.

'Farquhar will not see things that way,' Alfie reminded him. 'What is this?'

'A hot air balloon. It can travel back in time to ancient Egypt or the founding fathers. In the future, here, I have people travelling in their own personal mini trains. What do you think?'

'I think it will be complicated and expensive.'

Templeman snapped his fingers. 'I knew you would say that. You're hung up on Farquhar's response. I've pre-empted it by leaking this new design feature to the local paper. They are running a story about it this evening. Farquhar won't have the nerve to veto it.'

'I imagine it will be Squires who pays,' Alfie surmised.

'He'll get his money back tenfold with the people coming to the hotel to see it, even if they only stop for one drink in the lounge.'

'Farquhar will benefit from that too, and he hasn't signed a single cheque. Walker Squires is getting a poor deal from his partner.'

'They can sort the money out between them. There's no reason for us to worry about it. Are you up for making the balloon or not?'

'Hot air will interfere with the clock mechanisms, but it could be raised by a hoist and invisible wires. It will be a matter of re-adjusting the balance. I shall have to see Weir about ordering new weights.'

'Don't tell him about this new plan.'

'Your secrets are safe with me.' Alfie emphasised the use of the plural, but Templeman didn't rise to it.

'Good man.'

Alfie purchased a newspaper on his way to the flat and spread it across his table to read it. The editor had given over the centre pages to the story, with a photograph of Templeman grinning at the camera. Alfie crumpled the newspaper into a ball and tossed it onto the floor.

'I have a good mind to write to the paper and put matters straight.'

Lisa gathered the paper and folded the pages. 'Can I hae this for the fire, if you dinnae want it?'

'Burning is too good for that swine.'

'Language, Alfie.'

'Did you see him in church yesterday, crawling all over Emily Squires?'

'They are engaged.'

'I didn't tell you that Maggie was expecting a baby when she was killed. His baby.'

Lisa gasped. 'Hoo dae you ken that?'

'I just do. The funeral is on Wednesday. I should go to support her mother. Have you seen my black tie?'

Alfie could think of nothing but the newspaper article until the clock meeting. It pleased him that Farquhar was as delighted by the feature as he was. His naturally crimson face had turned deep purple. Squires tried to placate his partner.

'It is publicity, Adam. You can't be displeased about that.'

'I would have liked to have been informed before it went to the press. What is this about a hot air balloon and travelling back in time? We are supposed to be looking to the future.'

'I have included a futuristic town in the design,' Templeman explained.

'Miniature trains are hardly the future,' Farquhar scoffed. 'I want to see a bigger and brighter tomorrow. If your clock could really travel through time, that would be something.'

Templeman gave a nervous laugh. Alfie rolled his eyes.

'What have you to say, Peters? Are you happy with this?'

'I can fit the workings in, as long as Mr Templeman doesn't come up with any other surprises.'

'Well said,' Squires muttered.

'I expect this to be our final meeting before the clock is ready for the grand unveiling. If there are problems, Mr Weir will deal with them. Squires and I are travelling to Paris in regard to opening a hotel in the Champs-Elysées. Depending on how things go, we may wish to have a clock in the entrance hall there.'

'I told you it would be fine.' Templeman slapped Alfie on the shoulders as they headed for the bar.

'Indeed,' Alfie said. 'By the way, you owe me a new hat. You bet a hat that your idea of a balloon in a clock was unique, but I discovered in one of my journals that in 1820, Mr William Kirk, a clockmaker in Nottingham, made a wall clock with the hands following the flight of a balloon.'

'Mine will be much superior,' Templeman grumbled. 'But a wager is a wager and I won't be accused of defaulting on one. You shall have your hat, Peters.'

'The hat maker in town has my measurements. I'm told I have an odd-shaped crown, but I believe that is a sign of distinction.'

'Sure thing. Can we get started on the new section tomorrow?'

'It's Maggie's funeral tomorrow,' Alfie reminded him.

'Maggie? Ah, Maggie, yes, but why should that bother you?'

'I know her mother, a little. What about you?'

'Walker is going. Emily wanted to, but I have advised her against it. We hardly knew the gal, after all. My turn to buy the drinks, I think. What will yours be?'

'Bitter.'

Chapter 15

There was a fresh turn of snow the following morning, covering the ground and blowing the good citizens of Perth along the pavements like skaters. Alfie hoped there wouldn't be too much standing around in the kirkyard or his toes would be numb. He met Nancy at the railway station in Perth. Teddy was being looked after by a neighbour while she was away. Her eyes were puffy and an unattractive red colour. She gripped her sodden handkerchief as if wringing it out would drain away her grief.

'Oh Alfie,' she collapsed into his arms. 'My poor baby.'

Her behaviour was melodramatic and attracting attention. He hoped she would be revived by tea. If it didn't help her, it would at least steady his own nerves. There was time for refreshments before the service and Alfie escorted her to a tearoom in town. The waitress recognised him.

'How is your wife, Mr Peters?' she asked. 'My aunt told me she wasn't well. She heard it from a lady at the guild who is a neighbour of yours.'

'Improving,' Alfie answered, helping Nancy to her seat.

'And the babies?'

'Doing well, if you could bring us tea and scones, we don't have much time.' He hurried the girl away.

239

'What was that about babies?' Nancy asked.

'Cavies,' Alfie answered. 'I keep a pair of guinea pigs for showing.'

'I wouldn't have thought that of you,' Nancy said. 'Perhaps I should get one for Teddy, as a pet. Now that Maggie has gone…' She wiped her eyes with one of the table napkins.

'Now, now. Pull yourself together. We are in a public place.'

'I don't know what she was doing on that train,' Nancy sniffed. 'She hadn't been to see me and Ted.'

Alfie had been wondering that too. 'Most likely meeting a lad,' he answered.

'Maggie was a good girl.'

'You know what girls are like at that age. They are easily led astray.'

If Nancy had been told of her daughter's condition, which no doubt she had been, she was in denial. The waitress brought the tea things and laid them out. Alfie hoped she wasn't about to make any further comments about his family life in Perth as she poured. He stared out the window to avoid eye contact.

Nancy sipped her drink, allowing it to go cold. She didn't touch her scone, but Alfie had room for two. The church clock struck the hour and it was time to go. Alfie left the money on the table and they made their way out.

The service was short and as cold as the church building. The minister clearly felt uneasy about extending a Christian burial to an unmarried girl carrying a child, but the fact that she came to her end in such a violent manner swayed him. Either that or it was the implication by Squires that he would look sympathetically on appeals for church funding. The sermon was based on the qualities of a virtuous woman being worth more than rubies. There were few mourners at the grave. Walker Squires was there with Lucy. A maid Maggie befriended at the hotel brought a bunch of wildflowers. Alfie held Nancy's hand and a police officer made up the numbers.

'There would have been more people if we'd had the funeral in the village,' Nancy said.

'I imagine so. A sad way to go,' Alfie remarked. 'Born by a drunken soldier and killed by a drunken sailor.' He knew it was a cruel thing to say, but he couldn't control the surge of anger he felt as he watched the coffin being lowered into the ground.

'There was no drunken soldier, Alfie,' Nancy said. 'You were the only man for me. Maggie was your daughter. I didn't tell you at the time, because we would have had to marry. Dotty was still a child, but I knew her father had you marked out as her husband

and his successor. If you had married me, you wouldn't have inherited the business. I couldn't let that happen. I thought you understood, Alfie.'

He let go of her hand. The minister sprinkled a handful of earth into the hole in the ground. The thud echoed in his ears.

'I have to go. Mr Squires will see you get back to the station in time for your train.'

'Alfie?'

He didn't look back, but lengthened his strides, squelching his foot in a puddle of melted snow. Norma and Winnie were nattering in the kitchen when he arrived at the house. He didn't look in to see them, but went upstairs two at a time and into the bedroom. The babies were both asleep. It was hard to tell them apart, but Winnie dressed the little girl in yellow and the boy in blue. Sylvia had a fatter face and rosier cheeks. Her brother was pale and drawn, as if he didn't get enough milk. Alfie reached to pick Sylvia up, wrapped in her blanket. She was awkward in his arms and she woke up. He rocked her to stop the crying and walked to the window. The room was stuffy and he cradled Sylvia in his left arm while he jerked the window up with his right. One of Mrs Allendale's cats was in the garden, digging up the rose bed. He would have thrown something at it, but that would have disturbed the baby. He moved the blanket from around her head. She had fair hair, like his own mother's.

'You are my daughter, Sylvia,' he said. 'And I shall make sure that no man ever harms you.'

He turned to see Norma and Winnie staring at him.

'What are you doing with the child?' Norma asked, reaching out to take the baby from him. 'Come away from the window.'

Chapter 16

Templeman had less faith in the viability of the time machine than he pretended and it came as no surprise to Alfie when on the 4th of March Jonas Weir handed him a letter from Giles. The handwriting added credence to Alfie's belief that schools in the United States were of a primitive order. From what he understood of it, Giles was on his way to Liverpool to join the RMS Etruria to New York, confident that Alfie could complete the work on the clock in his absence. He would be back in four weeks, five at the most, which would give him ample time to apply the finishing panache before the clock was hung in the hotel.

'Seems a long way to go to get out of buying me a new hat,' Alfie grumbled to Weir.

'I wouldn't fancy a long sea voyage at this time of year,' Weir answered.

Twelve words. Alfie counted them. It was the most he had heard Weir string together in one sentence. The man was clearly ill.

'These liners are luxury,' Alfie said. 'It's not like the crossing to Queensferry. I wonder who is paying for his passage.'

'Mr Squires,' Weir answered with an unexpected hint of gall. 'Young Miss Emily, Mrs Templeman to be, has gone with him.

With an aunt as a chaperone.'

'Port out, starboard home.' Alfie imagined the restaurants, lounge bars and dancing girls on board. He pictured champagne parties in New York. If Templeman won the new commission, he could enjoy such a lifestyle too.

Jonas Weir was in an overly talkative mood that day. When Alfie stopped for lunch, Weir cornered him to ask if he had seen the newspaper headline. The sailor accused of murdering Maggie had escaped on his way from the prison to the courtroom.

'How could that happen?' Alfie snatched the paper and read the piece. The police hadn't released details, but warned residents to be on their guard.

'It will have been an inside job,' Weir said. 'Someone will have bribed the officers. He'll find a ship in Dundee to take him abroad.'

'The authorities should be able to find him.'

'If they have a mind to.'

'What do you mean?'

'Perhaps the police had the wrong man, and knew it.'

'Escaping is no way to prove your innocence,' Alfie grumbled.

'No easier with a rope around your neck.'

'That would be for a judge and jury to decide.'

'We may never know.'

That was Weir's answer to most things. It didn't satisfy Alfie.

His mind was distracted during the afternoon, such that he instructed the workmen to assemble one of the larger wheels in the wrong place. The mistake didn't come to light until late in the day and the men were kept back to sort things out.

'Mr Squires won't be happy paying overtime,' Weir informed him.

'Mr Squires won't be happy with a clock that runs backwards,' Alfie snapped. The curtness of his reply silenced Weir.

If only he could go backwards in time. He was on the same train as Maggie. Lisa had pointed her out although he hadn't believed her. Not at first, but later when he saw her with his own eyes...Why hadn't he gone to speak with her? But he had, hadn't he? While Lisa was sleeping. He asked her what business she had that took her out of Perth and she had laughed in his face. If he hadn't walked off... if he had invited her to sit with them...if he'd known she was his daughter...

Weir was staring at him, expecting an answer to whatever question Alfie had failed to hear.

'Mr Squires need not fear, I'll make the time up tomorrow,' he said. 'Good evening.'

He had promised Lisa he would stay the night at the flat, but the thought of her boiled cabbage and potato stew with macerated turnip made him feel sick. It was the smell of boiled cabbage. It was still too cold to leave the window open and the odour lingered round the enclosed space for days. Winnie and Norma would be having beef with pudding and gravy. Sweet suet dumpling to follow, washed down with good ale. That was a great deal more appetising and he was half way to his house without realising. He could take Lisa flowers the next day to make up. Fragrant ones, to mask the residual stink of cabbage.

'We weren't expecting you,' Norma greeted him. 'What happened to your important meeting?'

'It was cancelled.'

'Couldn't have been that important.'

'Never mind,' Winnie interrupted her mother's flow. 'It's good to see Alfie. There is plenty of stew for three.'

'Mrs O' Reilly isn't here?' Alfie queried. The nurse usually ate with them when she was around.

'She stopped coming weeks ago, dear,' Winnie said, taking his coat and hat. He followed Norma into the dining room.

'The stew smells good enough to open a bottle of wine,' Alfie decided. He kept three bottles of French wine in a cabinet that was seldom opened. The key was kept in his waistcoat pocket. He enjoyed making a show of unlocking the cabinet, selecting the wine, uncorking the bottle and pouring the liquid. He allowed himself a generous measure, but allotted Norma and Winnie smaller portions.

'Are we celebrating? Should we raise a toast?' Norma asked. 'It isn't your birthday.'

'I shall still be young, daring and handsome for another month.'

'Fifty isn't that old,' Winnie said, but her voice wasn't convincing.

'Twice your age,' her mother reminded them.

Winnie brought the stew, still bubbling in the pot, to the table. They sat down, Alfie taking his seat first. Norma listened to make sure the babies were settled before serving. Winnie waited until Alfie took a mouthful before eating.

'I am thinking of having a party to mark my birthday,' Alfie said as he leaned over to help himself to extra stew. Winnie gave a titter. Norma had taken a gulp of wine. She choked at the news and a dribble of wine filtered down her nose.

'A party? After your complaints about the Christening do, are you feeling well?' Norma said, once she had recovered.

'If you are put out by the idea, you do not need to come,' Alfie said.

'We don't have room here,' Winnie looked around the room, as if it would grow in size if she stared long enough. 'We don't have enough chairs for more than five.'

'Who needs chairs when there will be dancing,' Alfie answered mischievously. 'I shall have it in the West Tay,' he explained. 'I shall invite everyone associated with the clock and some of my clock making friends, as well as the city councillors and members of the golf club.'

'What golf club?' Norma asked.

'The one I joined last week. Walter McLeod, the secretary, is advising me on the best clubs to buy - a niblick, some reasonably priced brassies and a damned straight cleek.'

'You are spending money as if the heavens are about to open and the world ends,' Norma said.

'Not like poor Mr Squires,' Winnie added.

'There's nothing poor about Walker Squires,' Alfie said.

'That's where you are wrong.'

Winnie had some gossip to tell, but she was making sure they teased it out of her sinew by sinew.

'He has one less female in the house to contend with.' Alfie chewed a tough piece of beef. 'That can only be a good thing for

249

any man. Young Emily has gone with Templeman to the United States.'

'I hope the voyage is a calm one, or the relationship may be tested. There is nothing a man likes less than his fiancée being seasick,' Norma put in.

'There's a lot a man likes less,' Alfie corrected her, ' But I agree having your stomach contents gurgle up to meet what's in your mouth doesn't lend itself to a romantic tryst.'

'Really Alfie, not while we're eating,' Winnie chided.

'Your mother started it.'

'I didn't bring up the business of Emily going to New York,' Norma countered.

'We were talking about the Squires having to make cutbacks to their household,' Winnie said. 'They have let one of their gardeners go and they haven't replaced the maid who died.'

'Surely they haven't allowed Miss Emily to travel to New York without a maid?' Norma was horrified.

'No, the tubby girl, Betsy, has gone with her, but it means they are short in the kitchen. And that isn't the only thing. The last time I went to visit they had plain biscuits instead of cake.'

'Hardly worth going for that,' Alfie chuckled.

'Maude was actually darning a sock. She said keeping her

250

fingers busy stopped them from getting stiff, but no one believed her. She could play the piano if she wanted to wiggle her joints.' Winnie paused and put her hand to her mouth as if trying not to tell a secret. 'They are selling the grand piano too, and replacing it with an upright one.'

'I don't see what the problem is,' Alfie said. 'The hotel is doing well. There is talk of them opening a new one in Paris, indeed they have visited the site. I can't see Squires as a gambling man. Has he invested unwisely?'

'I wouldn't know about these things,' Winnie said. 'Now, have you both room for apple suet pudding?'

'Give me a minute, woman,' Alfie undid his waistcoat buttons and rubbed his stomach.

'I'll take these plates away and attend to Fred and Sylvia first.' Winnie rose and cleared the dirty dishes.

'It's time you employed a maid,' Norma told Alfie when Winnie was out of the room. 'My daughter may be feeling healthier, but you impose too much and with the nurse gone…'

Alfie thought to reply that if Norma would go home there would be far less work to be done, but he wasn't in the mood for an evening with two huffing women.

'You may be right,' he conceded. He got up and walked to the mantelpiece where he had left his pipe. Norma knew not to disturb him with her chatter while he performed the ritual of filling and lighting it. Once he had drawn the first satisfying puff, he gave a nod and conversation resumed.

'I can interview potential staff, if you don't have time,' Norma assured him.

Staff? His idea of one maid seemed to have been lost on Norma.

'Now, what of this party you are planning?' Norma added.

The notion had rather oddly entered his head that morning, when thinking about Templeman in New York. He had let it sit there and before he knew it, an idea had taken root.

'I don't know much about celebrations, but it's not every day a man reaches half a century,' Alfie replied. 'I shall need to sleep on it.'

With the thought out in the open, and Winnie talking of music, dancing and inviting long lost cousins, there was no going back. The following day she was already making a list of the material and ribbons she needed for a new dress. The week after, during a quiet period, Alfie took a stroll to the hotel to speak with the manager about arranging a suitable day and a reasonable price. The man was in a meeting with Farquhar and Alfie decided to wait in the lounge bar. He ordered tea, took the seat beside the fire and read the newspaper until his drink was served.

'There's a piece about the clock on page five,' the waiter said as he set the tea things on the table in front of Alfie. Alfie looked up, about to make a sarcastic comment, when he realised it was Squires himself. There was no sign from his demeanour that he was floundering in the financial sea.

'May I join you?' he asked, sitting down before Alfie could reply. Alfie set the newspaper aside.

'I was waiting to speak with your manager,' Alfie said, implying he didn't make a habit of drinking tea in grand hotels during office hours.

'About the clock?'

'No, about a party. My fiftieth.'

'A milestone in any man's life. Winifred mentioned it was coming up. Next month, I believe.'

'Yes. I was hoping to have a small party in the hotel. Would that be a problem?'

'On the contrary, I have a suggestion for you. Since it will coincide with the completion of the clock, why don't we combine the two events?'

'I'm not sure I understand.' Alfie had his right hand in his pocket with his fingers crossed. Things might be working to his advantage for once.

'I planned to throw a pre-launch party for local bigwigs and those involved in the project.'

'One party is certainly more than enough for any man,' Alfie agreed before Squires could go into detail about the funding.

'Good, we'll talk about it later,' Squires rose.

'How are Giles and Miss Emily getting on? Have they arrived in New York yet?'

'I imagine they will have, although I haven't heard from them,' Squires said. 'Damned inconvenient, Templeman rushing off like that.'

'The sooner they arrive there, the sooner they will be back,' Alfie said. It was plain Squires wasn't happy about Giles' absence. He gave a grunt before he left. Alfie finished his drink, ignoring the article on page five of the newspaper. When he heard the manager's raised voice, he turned his chair to look out into the reception hall. The builder had arrived and was instructing his men on where to erect the scaffold. The manager was keen to keep any disruption to a minimum.

'You'd better speak with Mr Squires or Mr Farquhar,' Alfie heard Davidson say in his calm Highland accent. 'If they want their clock suspended from the ceiling, they will need the scaffolding.'

Alfie was thinking about adding his voice to the argument when a stranger entered the lounge. He wasn't one of the usual clientele and Alfie imagined he was part of Davidson's workforce. The room was empty and the man fixed his gaze on Alfie. He hobbled over before Alfie could rise to leave. From a few feet away, Alfie could tell his assumption was wrong about the man. His hands were not builders' hands and his dress was more suited for lighter work. The material was not high quality and the man paid little attention to its cleaning or repair. A thread hung loose from the sleeve of his jacket and it gave off an unpleasant musty odour. Indeed most things about the man, including his unshaven chin and unwashed hair, were odious. Alfie avoided eye contact, but it was too late.

'Where is he?' the man demanded.

'Where is who?' Alfie asked.

'What?' the man leaned towards Alfie, exhaling tobacco breath over him. 'You're his mate, ain't you? I've seen you with him in the street. You know where he is. He can't hide from me.'

'I really have no idea who you mean,' Alfie said.

'I don't know his name. The one he gave me was false - Davy

255

Jones. He takes me for a fool, but I'll not be had.'

The man slipped his jacket open to reveal the horn handle of a hunting knife jutting from his belt.

'I wish I could help you,' Alfie rose and tried to edge past the man. The stranger was smaller than he was and of a wiry nature, but nimble. He managed to block Alfie's way.

'The American. I would say the American gentleman, but he ain't that. A gentleman wouldn't default on a debt.'

Alfie knew several men who called themselves gentlemen, who considered that to be their duty. It wasn't the time to explain.

'You mean the clock designer? Mr Templeman? Tall, wavy hair, clean shaven, prominent chin?'

'Aye, that's him.'

'Am I to take it, he owes you money?' Alfie asked.

The man was becoming calmer. He closed his jacket to conceal the knife. Alfie was keen to leave, but he was curious to learn what the stranger's business was with Templeman. It couldn't be a card debt. He didn't take the American for a gambling man.

'Aye,' the man answered. 'Ten pounds.'

'He owes me a new hat,' Alfie said, 'I'm not expecting it for at least a month. He left for New York over a week ago.'

'New York?' The man puffed out his cheeks and released the

air with a sharp whistle. 'A week ago?'

'He isn't due back for another month,' Alfie said.

'I can't wait that long.'

The man lunged at Alfie and grabbed his collar. He shook it hard. His eyes bulged and for a ghastly second Alfie feared they would pop from their sockets. Just as suddenly he let go and dropped into the nearest chair.

'He promised me the money,' he wailed, like a dog with toothache.

'Can I ask what for?' Alfie said. The man narrowed his eyes. 'I believe Mr Squires may be able to advance you money on Templeman's behalf, if he knew why you needed it.'

'I can't tell nobody that. It's my business alone, and a strange one at that,' the man said. He fidgeted with his coat buttons, fastening and unfastening them. 'I don't know this Mr Squires.'

'He is a true gentleman,' Alfie emphasised. 'It is clear you are in dire need of the money.'

'Aye. My family can't live on goodwill and promises, sir. Three weeks' rent is owing and the bairns are always hungry.'

Alfie sat beside the man and signalled to the bartender to come over. 'Can I get you tea, or something stronger?'

'A whisky, if you're offering.'

The attendant looked to Alfie and he gave a nod. The man returned to the bar, selected a glass from the shelf and clanked it on the counter. A minute later he brought a watery drink to the table and set it before the stranger.

'Will that be all?'

'For the moment. You can charge it to Mr Squires,' Alfie told him.

'Thank you sir.' The stranger raised the glass to Alfie and downed the drink in one gulp. He burped and wiped his lips with his sleeve before looking from his empty glass to the waiter. 'Call that whisky?'

The waiter returned to the bar without answering.

'You were about to tell me how you were of service to my colleague, Mr Templeman,' Alfie said.

'Your colleague?' The man picked up on the phrase and Alfie regretted the admission. 'That makes a difference. I let him in to see the prisoner, didn't I?' The man spluttered purulent saliva over Alfie's jacket. 'No weapon search and no questions asked.'

'That isn't routine procedure,' Alfie said.

'Not in my prison. Not in the fifteen years I've been there. Followed all the rules, I did, and what good did it do me? Barely a decent wage and now tossed out without a farthing.'

'Which prisoner are we talking about?' The whisky had loosened the man's tongue and Alfie thought it wiser to get to the point before the prison officer's mood changed.

'Why the sailor, who else? The one accused of killing that wench on the train.'

'The man who escaped,' Alfie said in a mildly accusing voice. The man sat up and reached inside his jacket towards his knife. 'Not that anyone is blaming you,' Alfie added.

'That is the problem, sir,' the man said, returning his hand to the table and nudging his glass. 'People are blaming me, though I was told to let him through by the top brass. It wasn't going to be one of them that was held to account. A scapegoat, that's what I am. Only following orders. It is always the poor folk at the bottom of the heap who carry the brunt of things. Out on my ear, I was. They said I was lucky not to be charged with aiding and abetting.'

'The gentleman who visited the prisoner…?'

'The American, sir. Told me he would give me ten pounds for my cooperation.'

'Did Mr Templeman tell you why he wished to speak with the prisoner?' Alfie asked.

'He didn't say and I didn't ask. I should have demanded to see

259

the money before I did the deed, more fool me. If the American doesn't pay up I shall go to the prison governor and tell him everything I saw. They thought I was having tea, but I was watching them, you see. You can tell your friend that from me, James Bailey.'

'As I said, Mr Templeman is in New York. I won't be in contact with him until his return,' Alfie explained.

'I need the money now.'

Bailey was growing more irrational. 'You could give me it.'

His voice was menacing. Alfie rose and stepped away from the man and his knife.

'It is of no consequence to me whether you report the matter or not,' Alfie said.

The man held onto the arms of the chair to ease himself up. He pointed a knobbly finger at Alfie. 'You say you are a colleague, maybe you were the colleague on the train.'

'What do you mean?' Alfie's voice shook.

'I heard the American tell the prisoner that he saw a colleague arguing with the girl on the train. He described you down to the last button on your waistcoat. He went across after, to see if she were needing help.'

'She was alive when I left her,' Alfie stammered.

'Can you say the same for your friend? I've been thinking about things. It sharpens the mind, not having an occupation and worrying about not being paid when there is rent to be accounted for. The two of you could have been working as a team.'

'I hardly think so.'

'Two respectable looking gents,' Bailey went on, expounding the story in his mind as he spoke. 'It would be simple to blame a poor sailor lad, and him a foreigner with little of the Queen's English, when things took a nasty turn.'

'You have a fanciful imagination. I wasn't arguing with the girl. I asked her the time, that is all.'

'You a clockmaker, not knowing the time,' the man sneered.

'My watch was stolen.'

'Suspected the girl, did you?'

'I believe there were witnesses on the train who saw the sailor molest the girl.' Alfie swung the conversation away from his own actions.

'He's a scapegoat, just like me. I can see you would have let him swing. Maybe your American friend didn't have the stomach for that.'

'Any more of this slander and I shall call the police and have you arrested. You've already admitted breaking prison rules. What will the authorities think of that?'

'I don't care who killed the girl, I want my ten pounds.' Bailey had one thing on his mind and he wasn't giving ground.

'You think to blackmail me? I am an innocent man. I have nothing to fear from you.'

'All I'm asking for is what is rightly mine.'

Alfie stood glowering at the man. His temper was up, but he needed to think straight. Any accusations against him, however spurious, would ruin his hopes of being appointed as a town councillor. It wouldn't be good for business either.

'Very well,' he said. 'I shall give you five pounds. You will need to wait on Templeman's return for the remainder.'

The man held out a grubby hand.

'I don't have the money on me,' Alfie said.

'I can come to your shop. I know who you are now. Your shop is the one with the big, gold letters.'

'You most certainly won't go anywhere near my shop,' Alfie spluttered. 'I shall meet you in North Inch Park, at the bridge. Tomorrow evening.'

'Can't you spare me any money now? The bairns…'

'Save me your sob stories,' Alfie reached in his pocket and drew out a ten shilling note. He thrust it onto the table and Bailey made a grab for it, knocking his glass to the floor, where it shattered. The bartender looked over at them.

'You can pay for that,' Alfie said to the man and strode out.

He had to clear his head. The man, Bailey, was low life, who deserved to be behind his own prison bars, but he would have to be handled as delicately as an intricate cog. He was a desperate man and desperate men did rash and foolish deeds, like threatening upstanding citizens with knives.

Maggie and Templeman had been on the same train as he and Lisa had been. Coincidence?

The sailor was a foreigner with little English.

Convenient.

James Bailey was a lying rogue, any reasonable man would see that, but where did the truth lie?

Alfie walked towards the river thinking about Templeman's action.

*Why had he gone to see the sailor? If he were the father of Maggie's child – he **was** the father of Maggie's child – he might have wanted to face her killer in the eye. Yet Bailey implied that Giles had helped the sailor escape.*

It made little sense, unless Giles believed the sailor was innocent.

He stopped to watch a fallen branch swirl in the current and become tangled and trapped among some grass at the water's edge.

Templeman claimed to have seen him talking to Maggie. He couldn't have, the corridor was empty, but he had spoken with Maggie. He couldn't remember the conversation. His head was in a daze since the policeman had called... and with the shock at the Christening...

An idea crept into Alfie's mind as the wood bobbed on the surface of the water before being dragged under.

Terminations were illegal, an affront to God and man, yet all it took was money and the right connections. Had arrangements been made and Maggie travelled to Edinburgh to see a doctor, then decided against the procedure? Templeman and Maggie may have quarrelled. It seemed unlikely, but it would be an idea to find out about Templeman's visit to his friend in Edinburgh.

Chapter 17

Alfie had no desire to give Bailey anything other than a bleeding nose and he had no intention of meeting the man in the park as arranged. He read in the newspaper about a spate of burglaries in the north of the city and being a good citizen he informed the police of a ne'er-do-well he had seen loitering in the area. He was able to give them a detailed description of the man, down to the missing buttons on his coat and paint stain on his trousers. In his experience, once the police arrested their man, the courts didn't need evidence to convict him. Mr James Bailey might well find himself on board a ship to Australia, with any luck.

Apart from supervising Weir's workforce, there was little to do on the clock. Business in the shop was slow and Alfie found, for the first time since Christmas, he had time on his hands. He thought about the railway clock in New York. Travel was a young man's game and he was well past his youth, but he felt more adventurous now than he ever did in his twenties. An extended trip across the ocean would free him from the domestic duties of being a husband and father. He could even devise a plan to take Lisa with him.

He might leave her in the States.

Lisa had her attractions, pert breasts and warm lips, but

keeping her secret from Winnie was becoming difficult. Some of his customers opened their mouths wider than their wallets. It would help if Lisa took the trouble to read about clocks and watches, or even pens, but she seemed unable to learn.

Pah, they hadn't laid the first rail yet. There were no foundations. A clock would not be high on the list of priorities, whatever Templeman thought or hoped for.

Nancy was another problem. He hadn't heard from her since the funeral although he assumed she got home safely. He had no wish to visit her while she was in hysterics over Maggie, but neither did he want to leave Teddy with her when her mind was in the clouds. It was possible she could harm the boy by neglect. Teddy was old enough to be sent to school. The discipline would do him good.

Thinking about Nancy brought Alfie back to Maggie. The image of her was rarely from his thoughts. Walking home from the hotel the previous afternoon, looking over the river and thinking of Templeman, he had heard a woman's voice behind him. She had called his name in a mocking manner, which shocked him into looking round. Who should he see, but Maggie cradling a babe in her arms. His senses were playing tricks. The wind was whistling round a lamp post and the gaslight threw eldritch shadows, but it made his heart jump. At home, when Norma informed him that a young woman with a child had called asking to see him, she was concerned about his paleness of face. The woman was from the shop next door complaining about water leaking into her husband's premises - one of Lisa's frequent mishaps with the taps, but enough to give him apoplexy.

It was on his mind to visit Nancy and sort things out about Teddy, when he received a letter from Dr Matthews. Dotty's dressings had been removed and the surgery, it seemed, had gone better than even the doctor had expected. Dorothy was in superb health and excellent spirits and Matthews wished to speak with him about her future. He could attend to affairs with Nancy and Dotty on the same railway journey. It was simply a matter of deciding when.

Things were never straight forward and the afternoon after he decided on a day, he received a message from Nancy telling him that Teddy had chickenpox. Ted was a strong boy and it wasn't a serious case, but the disease was contagious and he had no wish either to contract it or carry it home to the twins. He sent Nancy money to pay for a qualified doctor with a regret that he was too busy to travel. No doubt she would employ some quack and spend the money on a new bonnet, but that was her look out. Dorothy and her doctor would have to wait too.

'I shouldn't imagine the chickenpox epidemic will reach Perth,' he commented to Winnie and Norma.

'Epidemic?' Norma stopped eating with her fork halfway to her mouth.

'That's what it said in the paper.'

'Which paper was that?'

The conversation had the unexpected, but welcome result of convincing Norma it was time to return home. Alfie didn't beg her to stay and by the end of the week the house was empty of her grating voice and constant door banging.

'Do you hear that?' he asked Winnie.

'Hear what, darling?'

'Exactly.'

Alfie had forgotten what a pleasure it was to have the house to himself and Winnie. There were the twins, but they didn't listen in to conversations and make ridiculous comments – not yet. On Sunday, Winnie insisted on going to church with the Squires.

'You're not turning religious on me?'

Alfie was relieved to learn it was merely a social norm. He prepared a pot of tea for her return and they sat by the fire.

'The Squires have received a letter from Miss Emily,' Winnie said, slipping off her shoes to relax her feet.

'Oh? How is she enjoying New York with Giles Templeman?'

'She didn't mention him much. Maude showed me the letter. All the excitement is about a colossal statue that is to be erected in the harbour.'

'Jonas Weir mentioned that to me,' Alfie interrupted. 'It's to be sited on one of the small islands. Apparently it made the trip from France in parts. The workers can't start to reassemble it until they finish building a pedestal.'

'Such a lot of effort and money for a statue,' Winnie sighed.

'The Americans like having structures that are bigger and better than everyone else. It makes up for them lacking in other departments. This statue will be nothing more than a passing fancy until something larger catches their eyes. Then it will be left to fall into disrepair,' Alfie said. 'If it's made of copper, it will turn green.'

'Sounds like it isn't the only thing,' Winnie muttered. Alfie heard her, but refused to be drawn.

'What else does Emily say?' he asked.

'They are staying in a hotel near Central Park. She and Betsy, that's her maid, took an afternoon stroll through the gardens. She writes that there is an imitation castle in the middle of the city.'

'We don't need imitation ones in Scotland,' Alfie said. 'Anything else?'

'That's all. According to Lucy, Emily can't understand the accent of the people in New York. She hates the food and the climate. She doesn't like city life and Giles has been too busy with his meetings and business dinners to take her to the theatre or parties.'

'I can't see that boding well for a happy life together,' Alfie said.

'It takes all sorts, but I got the impression that things weren't working out the way she or Mr Templeman anticipated,' Winnie confided. 'The railway is still several years away.'

'I did tell him that.'

'He may have the opportunity to build a clock for one of the harbour buildings, but the fee won't be the same.'

'He'll design a clock in the shape of a giant boat, no doubt,' Alfie laughed.

'You can ask him about it when he returns,' Winnie said.

'When will that be? Did Emily say in her letter?'

'She told her mother that they had booked tickets to Liverpool, leaving on the last Saturday of the month.'

Alfie checked the calendar. 'That was yesterday.' He calculated the length of the voyage and allowed for travel up from England. 'Templeman should be back by next Monday. Not soon enough. There are finishing touches to be added to the clock and we only have two and a half weeks before the unveiling.'

'And your party,' Winnie reminded him. She raised her teacup to hide her smile.

'Aye, that too.'

Giles and Emily were held up in England for three days, with Giles arranging to meet a hotel proprietor to discuss a piece of artwork. By the time they arrived in Perth it was the eighth of April. Jonas Weir's pencil had been whittled down to a stump. Templeman presented him with a new one, 'direct from the States.'

'If you hadn't been off gallivanting, on West Tay time…'

Templeman sidled away and Weir was left grumbling at the floor. Giles was keen to find out how things had progressed in his absence. He strutted round the clock, prodding the models and shaking levers.

'Are we able to see it working?' he asked Alfie.

'Individual parts, yes, altogether, no,' Alfie said.

'Why not?'

'It needs to be raised from the ground for the train to pass under the casing.'

'That wasn't in my specifications.'

'It was necessary to allow for the movement of the main pendulum. It was either sending the train under the casing or round the back. You weren't here and a decision had to be made. I opted for the former.'

'What other business have you settled on my behalf while I've been away?'

Alfie had a flash of James Bailey and his knife, but decided it wasn't the time to bring it up. He would have his moment soon enough.

'Your trip home has done nothing for your temper,' he remarked.

'The voyage was a difficult one.'

'You suffer from seasickness?' Alfie asked.

'I'm American, my constitution is fine. Emily is the one who suffers on the sea.'

'I'm told ginger can help.'

'A little late now.'

'Can I ask how Miss Emily found New York?' Alfie felt like stirring up trouble.

'You will have to ask her.'

272

Alfie suppressed a chuckle. 'How do you cope with adjusting to the time difference?' he asked.

'It is not a problem.'

'Good.' Alfie gave him a wink. He took his arm and led him out of the hearing range of Jonas Weir. 'There is another reason the train goes underneath. We don't want it getting in the way of the more delicate equipment.'

Giles opened his mouth, but all that came out was a garbled 'Ah.'

'How did you fare with regard to your business in New York? Did you manage to secure any commissions?' Alfie continued.

'I did, actually. Not the railway clock, that is a good way off yet, as I told you, but in the harbour master's building.'

'They are looking for an elaborate clock?'

'A spectacular one, according to the men I spoke to. They want maritime detail, naturally, but otherwise I have free rein. I have left sketches and I believe they are impressed with them. The casing will be in the shape of an enormous ocean liner with working funnels and horns.'

'I've coped with your railway, river and balloon, so funnels and horns should be childs' play,' Alfie said. 'When do they want us to start?'

'Ah. They want it working by Thanksgiving, but they have their own clockmakers to do the mechanical bits and bobs.'

'Mechanical bits and bobs?' Alfie spluttered. 'If that is all they require then I'm sure even American clockmakers can manage it.'

'Don't fret, I did mention your name to several important people,' Templeman said as Alfie walked off.

The two men kept their distance in the warehouse. Templeman dabbled with the paintwork on the clock face and varnished the models. Alfie sat on a bench, thinking up names for Templeman, none of which were fit for the golf club smoking room. Now and then he spat out the phrase 'mechanical bits and bobs', loud enough for Templeman to hear.

'Where would you like the pendulum to go, Mr Peters?' He was roused from his thoughts by the labourers' foreman. He had to prevent himself from giving a rude reply involving Templeman's nether regions.

'Haven't I explained the layout enough times?'

He had done so three times in his reckoning, but there seemed to be a different foreman every week. He blamed Weir for that. Jonas wasn't happy unless he was complaining, and Farquhar used his grumbling as an excuse to deduct charges from the men's wages. It was no surprise half the city refused to work for him.

The current foreman had a west coast accent.

'The main pendulum has to be attached to the hands with the counterbalance…'

Alfie stopped talking. His mouth gaped open. There was someone hiding behind the casing. It wasn't Templeman, because he was talking to Weir. Alfie walked towards the clock. The shadow darted across to the empty crates. It was the shape of a girl. Alfie rushed across and pushed the wooden crates aside.

'What are you doing?' Weir's voice was sharp.

'I saw a …' The light was better from where he stood and there was nobody to be seen. Alfie looked across at Weir and Templeman. 'A rat. I saw a rat.'

'There are bound to be plenty of rats in a warehouse,' Templeman said.

'Aye,' Alfie agreed acidly, 'But we don't want them nibbling away at things they shouldn't.'

'Mr Peters has a point,' Weir brought out his notebook. 'I shall factor in a sum for pest control.'

'A couple of cats should do it,' Alfie said. 'I know a lady who could help us.'

'You can never trust cats,' Weir answered. 'Slippery creatures with too much brain. Poison is much safer.'

'If you say so.'

'So what about the pendulum?' the foreman said.

Alfie put an arm around the man's shoulder and led him away from Weir and Templeman. 'I have realised the current design will require changes. We must leave the pendulum for the moment.'

'Mr Weir wants the work finished here by next Monday.'

'Monday? Why so soon?'

'He needs time to finalise the arrangements for transporting it to the hotel.'

'Of course,' Alfie said. 'Don't worry, it will take a day, at the most, to work out the new plan. The pendulum can wait until tomorrow.'

'Aye, but tomorrow morning at the latest, sir.'

The workmen weren't disappointed with Alfie's decision. It meant more drinking time for them that afternoon. To avoid explaining to Weir, Alfie returned to his shop to work out the details of his new plan. Lisa was talking to a customer when he arrived and he overheard the end of their conversation.

'What does this part do?' the customer asked. Alfie could see the man was twisting a pen between his fingers, trying to get a feel for the lacquered wood.

'It writes?' Lisa helpfully advised him.

'And this compartment?' The man twisted the top of the pen. Alfie thought it better to step in before Lisa's instructions had him cover his white shirt with black ink. He took the pen from the man.

'This is one of our newer models. The ink is stored in the chamber here and is directed to the metal nib giving an even flow, thus.' Alfie demonstrated the writing ability of the pen on a piece of paper. Underneath he wrote a figure in pounds. 'Quality comes at a price, I'm afraid.'

'I shall have to think about it,' the man said and left the shop.

'I was about to make a sale,' Lisa said.

'He couldn't hold the pen, never mind afford it,' Alfie answered. 'What's that smell?'

The stink of burning cabbage was drifting down from the apartment and making its way beneath the door into the shop.

'Crivens, it's your dinner. I was so busy wi' the gent, I forgot aboot the pot. It will be ruined,' Lisa cried, darting to open the door. A rush of smoke gusted out. Lisa waved it away with her hands and hurried up the stairs.

'It would have been ruined anyway,' Alfie mumbled. He wanted to get down to work, but not on an empty stomach. If he made an excuse to return to his house for dinner, Winnie would

277

come up with one job or another that needed urgent attention, ensuring he got no work done all evening. He checked his wallet. There was enough to eat at one of the cheaper hotels. He supposed he would have to take Lisa too. Pity he hadn't made the pen sale, he fancied a bottle of good wine.

'Do you bring your wife here?' Lisa asked as she stared round the gloomy room. They were the only diners in the inn and the proprietor hadn't lit the fire.

'No,' Alfie said.

'Whaur dae ye tak her?'

'Does that matter?'

Lisa was quiet for a minute. Alfie suspected she was sulking. 'What are you having?' she asked, holding the menu upside down.

'I might try the fish today,' Alfie said. Lisa screwed her nose. Alfie knew she didn't like fish. 'I'm told the mutton cutlet is edible,' he said. 'Or you might like the ham.'

Lisa took her time choosing and he ordered a flagon of ale while she made up her mind. By the time the man had brought the jug and tankards, Lisa had decided on the pie. Alfie poured the ale, filling his tankard to the brim while barely covering the bottom of Lisa's. He raised the cup to make a toast.

'To the clock and all who sail in her.'

Lisa laughed, but Alfie knew she didn't understand. He finished his drink while Lisa rabbited on about the gossip she heard in the shop. He didn't recognise the city from the stories she told: wife swapping, deliberate arson, smuggling. The cook was taking his time, considering they were the only customers. Perhaps he was out catching the fish.

'I've a mind to go to the kitchen and see what is keeping the lazy fool. Some of his own ale, no doubt.'

'Sit down, Alfie.' Lisa quietened him. Alfie sat down and emptied the remaining ale from the jug into his tankard. 'Here it comes now,' Lisa said.

A plate of steaming vegetables and a mutton chop was banged on the table in front of Alfie.

'What's this? I ordered the fish.'

'I heard you say you were in for the chop,' the waiter said in a voice too high to be his own. Alfie started and looked up. Maggie was standing behind the man, peering over his left shoulder with a manic grin. Alfie's body shook. The hand holding his tankard wavered. He grabbed at it with his free hand, but instead of steadying the vessel the ale spilt out. It dropped onto the plate of food and splashed up to cover Lisa's blouse and the waiter's shirt. It ran along the table to drip onto Alfie's trousers.

'Wet yourself, have you, you stupid old fool?' Maggie's voice cackled in his ear like a vengeful carlin's.

'Alfie, wit's wrang?' Lisa jumped up, trying to clear the stream of ale with the top of her skirt.

'Get away from me, you godless ghoul,' Alfie swiped at the table.

The waiter removed the plate of food before Alfie could knock it to the floor. He hurried for a towel and returned with the cloth and the manager. Alfie was sitting still, gazing into the empty space ahead of him with wide pupils. Lisa knelt in front of him with her hands on his lap.

'I think you should take him home,' the manager said. 'He needs to see a doctor.'

Lisa shook Alfie's arm, but he didn't respond. The waiter helped her lift him to his feet. He staggered forwards, but kept his balance.

'Would you like me to call for help?' the manager asked.

'He's been working too hard,' Lisa explained. 'He'll be fine after a guid night's kip.' She reached inside his jacket pocket and removed the wallet, without Alfie objecting. After handing the manager money for the ale and wasted food, she slipped a note into her own purse and returned the wallet to Alfie's pocket.

'Come on, Alfie, I'll tak you hame.'

Slipping her arm into his, she managed to pull him out of the inn. It was a mild, but breezy evening. The fresh air blowing round him revived Alfie. His head swayed forwards and back as he tried to bring Lisa's face into focus. He reached to touch her face with his fingers.

'Are you feeling better?' Lisa asked. 'Whit happened in there?'

'Didn't you see her?' Alfie asked.

'See whau?'

'She was behind the waiter, mocking us.'

'You dae need tae tak time aff,' Lisa said. 'I'll mak you a nice hot toddy and tuck you in bed.'

'Don't patronise me, girl.' Alfie pushed Lisa aside. 'There is nothing wrong with my health. Clearly you are the one who needs your eyes examined. I am going home. To my wife. Tomorrow I shall write a letter of complaint to the restaurant owner. I did not imagine seeing anyone and I most certainly asked for fish.'

With a day spent playing golf, away from his workshop and the clock warehouse, Alfie realised that he could not have seen Maggie in the inn, at the warehouse, or in the church. Lisa was right, it was the stress of trying to please Templeman and meet Farquhar's deadline, coupled with his concerns about the women in his life. There were too many of those, but what to do about them confounded him. Who to keep and who to get rid of. Lisa and Nancy could be kept hushed with money. The immediate problem, he realised, as he swung his iron into the grass and received a tut from Walter McLeod, was Dotty.

He replaced the divot and stamped it down with his heel. The operation was a success, or so Matthews said. She hadn't taken a fit for six months. Her mind was as healthy as his. Better, considering his behaviour in the inn. The doctor was keen to have her released into society. What would happen if she was?

Alfie organised events in his head as he lined up the ball. Clearly, he knew Dotty was still alive now, but it should be possible to convince the authorities that he married Winnie in good faith, at the time, believing Dotty to be dead. Dr Lutheral was in a clinic in Switzerland in declining health, taken to the bottle. He wouldn't be called upon to admit his misdemeanours, and if he were, nobody would believe the ramblings of a demented old fool, even if sworn on the Bible. No, the vital question was, which one of them would he wish to be married to?

He had the twins to think about. If he wasn't married to Winnie, he would either have to take full custody of them, or risk Winnie and her mother whisking them somewhere inaccessible.

Winnie had relatives in the Borders, somewhere near Dumfries. He could divorce Dotty and remarry Winnie.

On the other hand, with Dotty, he would enjoy stimulating conversation in the evenings. Despite her years in the hospital, Dotty's mind was sharp and inquisitive. She was young. She could give him a son to inherit the business. They might even travel together.

'Are you going to hit the ball or not?' McLeod asked. Alfie had been swinging the club in mid-air. He swiped at the ball, grazing the top. It trickled a few feet along the grass and came to rest.

'Let me demonstrate,' McLeod picked a club from the bag and stationed himself to take the next shot. 'Your hands should be positioned thus, your feet planted square, spreading your weight.'

Alfie wasn't listening. He tightened his grip on the club.

'No, no. You must relax your shoulders.'

Alfie was thankful he wasn't in the army. Following orders was not for him. The one consolation about the golf club was that it admitted men only. He stood McLeod a drink in the clubhouse, listened to tall tales of impossible shots and made his mind up to sell his clubs the following day. He also decided that if he did tell Winnie about Dotty, it wouldn't be until after his birthday party. Nothing would spoil his plans for that.

Chapter 18

Weir was in a fankle, jumping around as if he had fleas in his long Johns. His voice was higher than Jenny Lind's top 'C'. Alfie wouldn't say he was shouting, but he heard him berate one of the workers when he was ten yards outside the door.

'Had a bad night, Jonas?' he greeted Weir with a touch of mischief. 'Did Mrs Weir have a headache?'

'My domestic life is none of your business,' Weir snapped. '*This* is the problem.'

He waved his hand towards the finished clock with a theatrical flourish that didn't suit him.

'We have completed it ahead of time,' Alfie said. 'And it looks immense.'

'It not only looks immense, it is. Too immense,' Weir grumbled. 'When you built it, you didn't consider the hotel dimensions.'

'We did indeed,' Alfie answered. 'It will fit perfectly in the hallway.'

'Aye, if you can get it in there. Nobody thought about the doorway, did they?'

'Sorry?'

'There is no way on God's good earth that this clock will fit through the entrance doors to the West Tay Hotel.'

Twenty two words. The man needed to calm himself.

'Why, it would be easier for a camel to go through the eye of a needle.'

'Don't mock me,' Weir threatened.

'Have you spoken to Templeman?' Alfie asked. 'There will be a way of dismantling parts of the casing and re-assembling them inside the hotel.'

'Maybe you would like to suggest that to him. He told me I was an incompetent nincompoop and he intends to speak to Mr Squires with a view to having me replaced.'

'Much good that will do him,' Alfie offered. 'Where is Giles?'

'The hotel, I imagine. He wouldn't deign to tell me.'

'No problem is insurmountable,' Alfie declared. 'I shall take a stroll to the hotel and see what can be done. There may be a servant's entrance at the back we can widen without disrupting the running of the establishment. Make yourself a cup of tea and I swear we'll laugh about this when I get back.'

Alfie couldn't imagine Weir laughing about anything, but the disgusted look on his face was worth the comment.

Giles was indeed to be found at the hotel, standing on the outside steps, arguing with the doorman.

'You know who I am, man. I've been staying here for six months.'

'You have, sir, yes, but I still can't allow you to enter.'

'I am engaged to Mr Squires' daughter. I should think he will have something to say about this.' Giles attempted to sidestep the man, but he was too slow.

'What is this about?' Alfie asked as he strode up the steps to stand beside Templeman.

'Your silly British customs,' Giles answered. 'McKenzie here won't let me into the hotel without a tie.' He turned back to point a finger at the doorman. 'If your Prince of Wales turned up without one, you'd let him in, wouldn't you?'

'I doubt that very much, sir,' McKenzie answered. 'Not that His Highness would ever appear in public in a state of half dress.'

'There is nothing wrong with our customs,' Alfie agreed with the doorman. 'It's typical of an American to make a scene for no reason, other than to hear his own voice.'

'I'm not being churlish. I need to get into the hotel. Now.' Giles slapped his fist against his thigh.

'And you shall,' Alfie laughed. He gave a nod to McKenzie, who reached into the pocket of his uniform and produced a tie.

'You expect me to wear that?' Giles said.

'It's a little plain,' Alfie agreed, 'But it is silk.'

Templeman snatched the tie from McKenzie and fastened it round his neck. It clashed with his orange shirt and reminded Alfie of the travelling circus folk that visited the city every year, but rules were rules.

'Come on, I'll stand you a whisky,' Alfie said. 'After that rawhide stuff you drink in the States, this will be nectar.'

'I prefer bourbon and we don't have time for a chit-chat. You must have spoken to Weir or you wouldn't be here. The clock won't fit through these damned doors.'

Alfie waited until they were inside and alone before continuing the conversation. 'Have you considered the back entrances?'

'The doors are too narrow and most are below street level. There is no way we could manoeuvre the clock up to the hall.'

'Then we shall have to remove a panel or two from the casing,' Alfie said.

'We can't do that,' Templeman spluttered. 'Good Lord, man, have you lost your senses?'

'It wouldn't take more than an hour to re-assemble the parts.'

'But it would interfere with…' Giles looked round the hall. The reception clerk was occupied attending to three gentlemen about to go out shooting. '…You know what.'

Alfie gave a laugh.

'It isn't a joke,' Templeman reminded him. 'Weir is asking awkward questions about the positioning of the pendulum and the space behind the fulcrum.'

'He is an expert on clock making is he?'

Templeman looked back at the doorway. 'It's these god-awful columns that are the problem. Whoever designed them should be horsewhipped.'

'Harsh.'

'They are neoclassical junk.' Templeman walked across to the door. 'Not even real marble.'

'Granite. This is Perth, not Rome. Sensible Scotland, not idyllic Italy.'

'Sodden Scotland, more like. I can't believe this is April.'

'You are in a foul mood today,' Alfie said.

'And you are unusually jolly.'

'Leave Weir and the hotel door to me. Take a couple of hours away to clear your head? See some of our sodden scenery. The palace of Scone is lovely at this time of year with the daffodils out. I'm sure Miss Emily would be delighted to act as your guide.'

'Emily, yes, you may have something. You'll deal with Weir?'

'I'll have him saddled and bridled and ready to comply with

whatever we wish.'

'Good man.'

Templeman left and when he was gone Alfie made his own measurements. Giles was right about the pillars. Granite or not, they were too flimsy to be of structural importance, but he couldn't see Farquhar or Squires agreeing to have them removed. Back at the warehouse, Weir was finding fault with everyone and everything. He was scribbling notes with his American pencil when Alfie returned.

'What is there to whistle about?' He turned on Alfie.

'Would you prefer me to sing?'

'I would prefer you to work rather than parade around like a marching bandsman.'

'I have spoken with Templeman. We have found a solution that involves minimal disruption to the running of the hotel.'

The foreman was listening in to the conversation. 'How much work does it mean for us?' he asked.

'I have measured the dimensions. If we remove the clock face, the body will pass through the main door.'

Weir looked to the foreman.

'The face is held by twelve bolts. There should be no problem dismantling it,' the foreman agreed.

'We will also need to remove the...the.. Alfie struggled to think of a word for his time travel chamber.

'Yes?' Weir was peering into his eyes, keen to know what the empty space behind the clock face was for.

'The gumplestroff zimmer,' he invented.

The foreman looked blank.

'Can I ask what that is for?' Weir said. 'It takes up a good deal of space for no purpose.'

'No purpose? No purpose?' Alfie stamped his foot. 'If there was no gumplestroff zimmer, there would be no clock.'

'It isn't something I have read about in the clock making literature,' Weir persisted.

'It wouldn't be,' Alfie answered. 'It is the newest technology. State of the art. Everyone was talking about it at the conference in Glasgow. Even the American delegates.'

'And what exactly did they say?'

'The zimmer allows for a balance between pressure and temperature. The equation is complicated.'

'I have a knowledge of science,' Weir said. 'We are talking about a clock, not an engine.'

'A clock? This is no mere timepiece, sir,' Alfie feigned offence. 'Have you understood nothing of our work? Why, even Mr

Squires appreciates the hydraulics necessary for controlling the water flow, the friction generated by the moving models, the weights needed to stabilise the casing. The clock workings, sophisticated as they are, constitute a fraction of the intricate machinery of this masterpiece. And you are concerned about what you deem to be a waste of a few cubic feet.'

Weir spluttered a few syllables in response, but he was stunned into silence.

'You'd better show me which bolts you want unscrewed,' the foreman said.

'And be careful with the paintwork,' Weir grumbled. He tapped his pencil against his notebook, breaking the point, and walked off.

The parts were harder to remove than Alfie anticipated and it took two days to dismantle the clock face, wrap the parts carefully without snapping the hands or chipping the paint, then box everything up. Several carts were required to transport the boxes to the hotel. A good part of the reception hall was sealed off for the arrival of the pieces and a crowd gathered to watch. The foreman and door attendant kept them under control while the men wrestled with the boxes. Alfie and Giles supervised the unloading and reattachment of the face.

'Careful with it. This isn't some girder for the Forth Bridge,' Alfie remonstrated with the men as a box banged against one of the columns.

The boxes were laid to rest below the reinforced ceiling. Templeman took a crowbar to the smallest of the crates, while the guests gathered round to watch.

'Get them back,' Giles instructed. 'We are not a seaside peep show.'

Alfie moved to stand in front of the watchers, shielding their view of the clock. The guests moved a few feet, but didn't leave the hall.

'I knew it,' Giles pulled the straw away from the clock face.

'Knew what?' Alfie stepped over and crouched on his haunches beside Giles. His knees clicked.

'There is a scratch on the gilding.'

Alfie looked where Templeman pointed, but couldn't see the defect. 'Will it take long to repair?'

'Repair? What do you mean by repair?' Giles pulled at his hair. 'I have spent months perfecting the face and you talk about a repair.'

'We don't have the time or money to replace it,' Alfie reminded him.

292

'I am working with Philistines.'

Giles glared at the onlookers then back to Alfie. 'I will need absolute peace to work on it. The area will have to be cleared.'

'This is the main hotel thoroughfare. Clearing it would involve closing the building,' Alfie warned.

'Then close it.'

'What about the guests?' Alfie asked.

'I don't give a pumpkin pie about them.'

Templeman's words were heard by the spectators and were not appreciated.

'How long will you need?' Alfie asked.

'As long as it takes,' Giles tossed a bundle of the packing straw across the hall.

Temper, temper. What are you going to do about him, Mr Clockmaker?

Alfie jumped. The voice was in his head, but it sounded like Maggie. He stood up and rubbed his back. The duty manager was pretending to arrange papers behind the reception desk, while keeping an eye on events in the hall. Alfie walked over to speak with him. The man was foreign, across from Paris to learn how a Scottish hotel was run. When his exaggerated shouts of 'non' didn't influence Alfie, he gesticulated with his arms. His face was darker than a beetroot.

'I shall speak with Mr Squires,' Alfie said.

'Monsieur Squires is not here,' the manager said. 'He and Monsieur Farquhar are travelling to Edinburgh.'

'Really? They both traipse off to Edinburgh on the day when the clock arrives? A clock they have been waiting on for months.'

'I do not know why they went there. I only know they are not here.'

Alfie looked around him. His eyes were drawn to the gong standing on the right side of the staircase. 'I will trouble you no further.' He gave a smile and walked towards the stairs.

'Monsieur?' the manager called, 'Non.'

Alfie picked up the stick, drew it back and banged on the gong. He jumped at the reverberation, as did the gathered crowd. Even Giles stopped nursing his clock face to look over.

'Fire,' Alfie shouted, his voice trembling. 'Clear the hall, fire.'

There was murmuring from the guests. Alfie hit the gong again.

'Fire, you must leave the building. Now.'

People sniffed the air for smoke.

'It's coming from the kitchens,' someone called.

'Fire, fire.'

The cry was taken up by a porter, staggering under the weight of a society lady's luggage. He dropped the cases and ushered the fur clad grandee towards the exit before she could complain.

Alfie watched the commotion with amusement. Guests rushed to grab valuable possessions then pushed to reach the doors. The manager's protests of 'Non, non. Il n'y a pas de feu', fell on deaf ears.

'You'll need to shout in English, man,' Alfie advised him.

'Come back. It is a false alarm. There is no fire.'

The people who had congregated in the hallway had already shoved their way out, but the residents in the lounge were unwilling to give up their easy chairs. A little smoke might influence their actions. With the attention elsewhere, Alfie slipped a box of matches from his pocket and edged towards the curtains separating the entrance to the restaurant from the reception hall.

Go on, light it, I dare you.

Maggie's voice again. He hesitated then struck the match to produce a flame and shielded it with his palm. There was a bucket of water, discreetly positioned behind the curtain, in case of accidents. Alfie made sure it was within reach before moving the match towards the material. He waited until he smelt the velvet smoulder before sidling away. Templeman marched towards him as he walked across the hall.

'What on earth is going on? I said I needed peace.'

'You said you wanted the hotel reception cleared.'

'Fire, fire.' One of the drinkers in the lounge spotted the flames edging up the curtains. He was some yards away, but threw his whisky towards the fire in a misguided attempt to soak the flames.

'Templeman gaped at Alfie. 'Is this your doing? Are you off your head?' He shoved Alfie aside and rushed towards the curtains. He yanked at the material, hoping to pull it down and extinguish the flames before the fire spread.

'What do you mean "my doing"? I saw the fire and beat the gong, trying to warn everyone,' Alfie spluttered as he retrieved the bucket of water. 'I may have saved lives.'

'Rubbish, you were trying to clear the hotel,' Templeman accused. 'There was no fire until you came over here.'

The curtain material didn't catch and the fire burnt itself out. Alfie threw the water at the smoke. Most of it landed on Templeman's sleeve.

'Idiot, look what you've done. This jacket cost twenty dollars.'

'Sorry.'

'The panic is over, Messieurs et Mesdames.' The manager danced around the hall reassuring the guests. He spotted

Templeman shaking off the water from his jacket and fetched a towel from the bar. Giles snatched it from him and wiped his sleeve.

'Do not worry, gentlemen. I have arranged for screens to be brought to separate the clock from the main hall while you work on it,' the manager explained.

'I've a mind to report you to Farquhar.' Templeman rounded on Alfie once the manager was gone.

'What for? You can't go making accusations without proof, not here in Britain,' Alfie answered. Templeman looked ridiculous with his sodden jacket and hair. Alfie couldn't hold back his snigger.

'You think this is funny?'

'Of course it's funny,' Alfie said. 'Look at yourself.'

Templeman didn't look amused.

'Let's get back to work on the clock.' Alfie turned, but Giles put out a hand to stop him.

'You are not going anywhere near my clock in the mood you are in. For all I know, you might think it a lark to reassemble it topsy-turvy or inside out.'

'Don't be daft, man.'

'I'm serious. You have been acting strangely since I returned from America, possibly even before, for all I know. You need to lie down. Take this. It's the key to my hotel room. You'll find sleeping pills in the top drawer of my dresser. I advise you to use them. You'll feel better after a peaceful sleep.'

'Yes, doctor.' Alfie gave a mock salute. He took the key.

'It's two five..'

'One,' Alfie finished for him, before realising his mistake. Giles raised an eyebrow. 'It says so on the tab,' Alfie smiled.

He didn't expect to find anything of great interest in Templeman's room, but that wasn't going to stop him from having a good look, including in the bathroom cupboards and under the mattress. The maid had completed her rounds and the room was cleaned to Farquhar's impeccable standards. Alfie bounced on the bed. The springs met with his approval. He wouldn't need pills to send him to sleep. First though, he felt Giles had given him carte blanche to rifle through the dresser.

Templeman kept his papers in the bottom drawer, beneath his socks. The important documents would be in the room safe, but Alfie spent a few minutes examining the snippets he found. There were bank slips that indicated Templeman was being paid three times what he was for half the work. The rest were letters from relatives in the States and cuttings from newspapers applauding the American and his amazing clock. Alfie tossed the papers onto the floor the way Templeman had tossed the straw from the packaging. He gave the pile a kick, as if the notices were autumn leaves, and watched them swirl around the room. He would have to pick them up and return them to the drawer, not good for his back, but Giles would never suspect him if a few of the cuttings were torn, or if water was spilt on the ink.

He was bending to pick them up when there was a knock on the door. He hadn't locked it. It would be typical of his luck for Giles to come in and see him with the cuttings.

Too late to think of an excuse.

'Wait a second,' he called, but the door opened and a girl's face peeped in.

'Oh, sorry sir, I thought this was Mr Templeman's room,' she said.

'It is. Mr Templeman is downstairs, working on the clock.' The girl looked at the papers in Alfie's hands. 'He sent me to fetch his sketches.'

'Would you like me to take them to him, sir?' the girl asked, stepping into the room.

'No, thank you. I will deliver them myself.' Alfie tightened his grip on the cuttings.

'Is there anything I can do for you, sir?' The girl moved towards the bed and ran her hand over the cover.

She was a pretty thing with an inviting bust and swaying hips. The offer was tempting. Alfie put the papers on the dressing table and felt in his pocket for his wallet. He opened it and brought out a note. The girl slipped it into a little purse in her pocket. Alfie reached for her blouse, but she tapped his hand away.

'I've got to be careful with the uniform, I don't want buttons popping off. Repairs have to be paid for.'

Alfie removed his waistcoat and set it on the chair beside the dressing table. He unfastened his tie and laid it on top, then unbuttoned his shirt and moved to lie on the bed. The girl locked the door.

'I've got to be downstairs to report to Mrs Walker in fifteen minutes,' she said.

'Who is Mrs Walker?'

'She's in charge of the chambermaids. A right dragon. If I'm a minute late, she'll dock an hour's wage.'

'Then you'd better stop talking and start undressing.'

There were times when Alfie regretted being a few days short of half a century old, but Sarah had given him his money's worth. She was a good girl. He lay on the bed and watched her straighten her uniform.

'You look fair bonnie,' he said.

'I'd better go. You had too, if Mr Templeman is to get his papers.'

'Don't worry about that,' Alfie said.

'Will Mr Templeman want anything later?' Sarah asked as she unlocked the door.

'You're an eager one.'

'Saving up to get married, sir.'

'Does your intended husband know about your fund-raising activities?'

'Oh yes sir. It was his idea.'

Alfie thought to advise her that no good would come of marrying a man like that, but she was gone before he could think of a way of putting it. He rested his head on the scented pillow and lay there for a while, listening to the rhythm of Templeman's bedside clock. It had a loud tick and an inaudible tock. That was American craftsmanship for you. Soon even the tick was barely more than a background vibration.

A herd of American buffaloes were stampeding through Alfie's skull when he woke. The clock was ticking like a war drum. He rubbed his eyes. It was ten to five.

Ten to five, ten to five.

'Bother.' Alfie sat up. It took a moment to realise where he was. Had he dreamt about the coupling with the maid? His body told him otherwise and when he managed to rise and check his wallet he was sure of it. Luckily she seemed a good girl, not likely to blab. He put on his shirt and trousers and as he was knotting his tie he spotted the newspaper cuttings and bank slips on the dressing table. He had better replace them before Templeman came looking for him, fearing an overdose on the sleeping pills. While he was at it, he could have a look in the drawers to see if Templeman kept any laudanum, before whatever was thumping in his head burst its way out through his eyeballs.

He stuck the newspaper cuttings beneath a pile of garish American socks and worked his way through the other drawers in the dresser. He found what he was looking for in the top drawer – a medicine bottle with 'laudanum' printed on the label. Alfie opened the bottle and held it to his nose. The contents smelt like laudanum.

He gulped down a mouthful then exhaled deeply. He took another sip before replacing the lid and slipping the bottle back into the drawer. As he did so his hand displaced a sheet of paper. It was a letter from a doctor in Edinburgh, the address was printed at the top of the sheet. Alfie lifted it out. The writing was virtually illegible. He was trying to decipher it when the door opened.

'You're up at last,' Giles said, walking into the room. 'What's that you're reading?'

'Nothing. I was looking for laudanum. I've got a splitting head.'

Templeman took the letter from him and put it in his pocket before reaching in the drawer for the bottle of medicine. 'Looks like there isn't much left,' he said.

Alfie accepted the bottle, but didn't open it. 'That letter, it was about a termination.'

'I didn't take you for the type of chap to read another man's mail,' Templeman answered.

'I couldn't help noticing.'

'And you expect me to give you an explanation?' Giles took the opportunity to check his appearance in the dressing table mirror. He flattened his hair and whisked a lock behind his ear. Alfie didn't answer him. 'You know what maids are like,' Templeman continued. 'You met Sarah.'

'You arranged a termination for her?'

'Not for her. Sarah has more sense than to get herself pregnant, but some of the others don't take precautions.'

'Some of the others? Like Maggie?'

Templeman had lifted a comb from the table. He brandished it in front of his chest.

'Maggie?'

'Miss Emily's maid.'

'What about her?'

'Did you arrange a termination for her?'

'Of course not,' Templeman couldn't prevent the colour in his cheeks. He looked away, but his reflection in the glass betrayed him. 'Because she decided against it.'

'You knew she was expecting your child?'

'I couldn't help but know she was with child, but there was no proof that I was the father. The bitch tried to blackmail me. She said she would tell Emily. I told her I would have her arrested for slander.'

'There's no smoke without fire.' The words were out before Alfie realised they weren't the wisest choice. 'You must be glad she is out of the way.'

Templeman shot Alfie a look that could have downed Goliath.

'I didn't kill her, if that is what you are suggesting. You are one to talk. Maggie told me she knew all about your little secrets.'

'What secrets might those be?'

'She wasn't specific, but I know she expected to get money

from you. Was she getting greedy, asking for too much?'

'This is utter nonsense.'

'You were on the same train as Maggie.' Giles set the comb down and turned to face Alfie.

'How do you know that?' Alfie asked.

'I saw you, with a young lady that wasn't Mrs Peters.'

'My niece.'

'Yes. Look, all I'm saying is that we are both men of the world.' Giles straightened Alfie's tie. 'We understand each other.'

'Do we?'

'Of course we do. After all, what can't be sorted out with a little extra time?'

Chapter 19

The atmosphere between Alfie and Templeman was colder than a polar bear at the North Pole. The assembly of the clock suffered due to needless disagreements, but both men were keen to see the work finished.

'The paintwork on the hands needs to be touched up,' Alfie noted.

'You would do better to concentrate on aligning your cogs and wheels rather than complain about my art,' Giles countered.

'Gentlemen, if you please, the workmen have set up their levers and chains and are ready to lift the clock.' Weir stepped between them for the seventh time.

'One moment.' Giles dipped a paintbrush in a tin of blue paint and scribbled his signature at the bottom of the clock face.

'Do I get to write my name?' Alfie knew what the answer would be, but he put aside his grievances to stand with Templeman as they watched the labourers hoist the massive clock aloft.

'This is it,' Giles said. 'The first of its kind.'

Squires and Farquhar were back from Edinburgh and the clattering brought them out from Farquhar's office. Squires looked on, wide-eyed. Farquhar felt he should assert his authority by taking over the supervision of proceedings. He held a gold-handled walking cane, which he pointed at the foreman and his assistant, who were balanced at the top of ladders, one on either side, ready to fix the clock in place. The ceiling beam creaked and the massive structure swayed.

'Tilt it to the left,' Farquhar called up.

The men shifted the position of the clock. Water in the model reservoir rippled, overflowed and dripped onto the Persian carpet at Farquhar's feet.

'Fools, couldn't you have filled the tank after the clock was in position?' Farquhar said.

'It wasn't clear how easy that would be,' Alfie answered. In truth, simple as the idea was, he hadn't thought about it.

Ropes were pulled and the workmen managed to even out the clock before it was bolted into place.

'Splendid,' Squires clapped. A few of the workmen joined in the applause, but this was stopped by a look from Farquhar.

'Well, do we get to see it in action?' Farquhar demanded.

'We agreed we would wait until the official unveiling,' Squires said.

'Humph!' Farquhar looked up at the clock. 'What if our invited guests are gathered for the show and this ugly lump of wood and metal doesn't work?'

'Hardly ugly,' Squires objected. 'It is magnificent.'

'I can promise you, nobody will be disappointed,' Templeman said.

'Although a trial of the workings may not be a bad idea.' Alfie sided with Farquhar for once.

'We can't start the clock for a two minute show,' Templeman objected, purely for the sake of argument, in Alfie's opinion.

'Sir, you are forgetting it is my clock,' Farquhar said.

'For the time being, it is *my* clock.' Squires' remark took Farquhar by surprise. 'I have the receipts to prove it.'

'If you are going to be pedantic,' Farquhar banged his cane on the floor, 'You can have the receipt for the cleaning of the carpet too.' He marched across the hall to his office.

It was unusual for Squires to publicly stand against his partner and all eyes were upon him. His face reddened. 'Well, yes, quite,' he mumbled, rubbing his bottom lip in the hope that more profound words would come.

'If we are to have an unveiling,' Alfie said, 'We will need a cover.'

'A cover, yes, indeed.' Squires turned, searching for something suitable. There was nothing in view. He called one of the hotel porters over.

'A veil? Like on a lady's hat?' the man queried.

'Something larger.' Squires made a rippling gesture with his right hand.

After a few minutes a sheet was found and the foreman and his assistant manipulated it over the clock.

'That had better not stick to the fresh paint,' Templeman warned.

'We shall need a cord to enact a swift removal,' Alfie said. 'It won't augur well if the cover tangles in the metalwork, not with the newspapers taking photographs and writing reports.'

'See to it,' Squires instructed the men.

It took time for the workers to rig up a system enabling the smooth removal of the cover when the time came.

'It looks like a prop from an amateur production of Hamlet,' Weir complained, smarting from Farquhar usurping his role.

'It will do,' Templeman said. 'It is the clock that is important. That's what the folks are coming to see.'

'All ready for you, sir,' the foreman presented the rope to Squires.

'Not me,' Squires answered. 'The Duchess of Argyll is visiting the county next week and has kindly agreed to do the honours.'

This brought about appreciative murmurings from the workforce.

'The gal's one of your Queen's daughters, ain't she?' Templeman was heard to ask no one in particular. No one answered him.

'You don't feel we should have a trial run?' Weir asked. 'To make sure the cover pulls off without injury to anyone watching below.'

'I have confidence in your men,' Squires answered. 'You have all done well.'

The workmen were given a coin each from Squires before they left. Templeman followed them out. Weir muttered something about organising a plaque to mark the unveiling and headed out. Alfie stayed behind to look at the clock. Squires stood beside him.

'It will work, won't it?' Squires asked.

'Yes,' Alfie assured him, 'Still, I would have been happier to see it tested, what with Royalty and the press due to arrive. Perhaps if the ladders could be kept in place, I might be able to check individual parts before the Duchess's visit.'

'The ladder will have to be removed in good time before the Duchess comes, but if you think it necessary we can leave it here until the morning of the unveiling. Now, I would like to speak with you about arrangements for your party.'

The conversation was one sided. Squires had organised everything and Alfie was happy to nod in agreement with his plans.

'I know we talked about having the party on Monday evening, but the Duchess would find it convenient to visit on Monday morning,' Squires said. 'I propose we hold the party on the Saturday evening, before the unveiling. A grand thank you to those involved with the clock, as well as your half century.'

'Saturday will give your staff time to clear up before the official ceremony,' Alfie noted.

'A minor point,' Squires stammered.

It didn't bother Alfie when the party was, but Winnie was flustered by the new arrangements.

'I shall have to find someone to watch the twins. I have no shoes to wear. My hair is a mess. Will there be a cake?'

'Calm yourself, woman.' Alfie watched Winnie rush round the room like a headless bantam and for an odd moment he was tempted to tell her about Dorothy. That would give her something real to lose her hair over. Winnie was called away by the sound of Sylvia crying. Alfie settled at his desk to compose an invitation list.

311

Everyone connected to the clock would be invited by Squires, but it was nominally his party and he could ask whom he pleased. He wrote Walter McLeod's name at the top of the paper, followed by the other committee members of the golf club. It wouldn't be possible to omit his mother-in-law's name from the list, but he would leave that invitation for Winnie to send. His clock making colleagues were falling over themselves to get invitations. They weren't interested in his fiftieth birthday. They wanted an opportunity for a sneak preview of the clock.

It didn't surprise Alfie when Forbes McGregor turned up at his shop the next day, pretending he had found himself in the city on business. He was surprisingly vague about the details of this business when Alfie queried him.

'I heard you were having a party in the new hotel.' Forbes lifted one of Alfie's stopwatches to examine the workings.

'Yes, this Saturday. I thought I should mark my half centenary,' Alfie agreed.

'An excellent idea. Saturday, you say? I should be able to extend my stay until then.'

'It is by invitation only.'

'Of course.'

Alfie took the watch from him. 'I am glad you like this piece. It is accurate to a hundredth of a second. The problem is, it's overly sensitive to touch.'

'A disadvantage for use on the sports field,' McGregor said. 'You need something robust for that.'

'Aye,' Alfie waited for a further response.

McGregor nodded. 'I see. I may be able to help you. I have been working on stabilisation mechanisms. I'll send you the diagrams.'

'Thank you.'

'I'm staying at the station hotel. You'll need to know where to send the invitation.'

Alfie heard Lisa trundle down the stairs. She waited until McGregor left before entering the shop.

'Wha wis yon?' she asked.

'Nobody special. He was after an invitation to the party, to see the clock.'

'Will you send him one?'

'Maybe.'

'Whit aboot me? Dae I git an invitation?'

'I didn't think you were interested in society dos,' Alfie said.

'Whit made ye think that? I can galop and gavotte wi' any o' your fancy ladies or gents.'

313

Lisa took the opportunity to twirl around the floor of the shop, knocking over a display of lacquered pens. She stopped and glanced at Alfie. Before he could speak, she burst out laughing. 'You look so funny when you are angry, Alfie.' She bent to pick up the pens that had rolled below one of the cabinets. Alfie admired her behind.

'You would have to stay out of Winnie's way,' he said.

'Oh Alfie,' she leapt towards him and Alfie narrowly missed having the nib of a pen stuck up his left nostril.

The next few days were taken up by preparations for the party. Although his mother was a McDonald, Alfie was delighted there was no Peters' tartan or Winnie would have him kilted up like a Highland fusilier, knobbly knees and all. As it was, she insisted he wear a tailcoat and cummerbund.

'I'm a clockmaker, not a count,' he argued.

'You need to look smart. Wait until you see my new hat.'

'Another one. How much did that cost?'

Winnie was adept at evasion and Alfie never found out. On the Saturday afternoon before the celebration, he escaped the house and Winnie's flapping. After a short detour to his shop, he strolled to the hotel. The clock was aloft, but hidden from the guests by the cover, like a ghostly galleon sailing in the sky. A screen surrounded the area beneath the clock where a ladder was still in place for final maintenance in preparation for the unveiling. It would be removed in good time for the Royal platform to be erected.

Alfie slipped behind the screen and paused with his right foot on the first rung of the ladder. He looked up, feeling a weight in his stomach as he did. He hated heights, since falling from a tree as a lad. It was his own fault for scrumping apples. The ladder wobbled. He paused on the third rung and gripped the side with his left hand. His right hand held his toolbox. One slow step at a time, he reached the level of the casing.

The cover the hotel porter had found was a bed sheet from the laundry. Thankfully, it was a clean one. After three attempts at reaching over, the first two with his eyes closed, Alfie managed to take hold of a handful of the linen. Manipulating it out of the way was like trying to stack blubber. The moment one fold was drawn back another would drape itself over the casing. The more frustrated Alfie got, the harder the task. Force didn't help, as he found to his disadvantage. He gave up and stuck his head under the sheet, reaching in his pocket for the key.

His hand shook as he slid it in the lock and opened the door to the small chamber built into the side of the clock. He tossed his tool bag into the chamber and paused before attempting to enter. The gap was less than two feet, but it was no easy feat, hampered as he was by the cover. The ladder shook and his feet slipped. He grabbed onto the door and swung in the air until he scrambled to regain his footing on the ladder.

'Are you having problems?' A hotel guest was watching his antics. 'Would you like me to steady the ladder for you?'

'Everything is under control.' Alfie managed to get the words out through the sheet. They sounded like a dog whining as he caught his breath. 'Thank you.'

'Good show.' The man stood for a moment then departed.

Alfie freed himself from the material and waited until the guest was out of the hall before trying to enter the clock again. This time he removed a pen knife from his pocket and stuck it through the cover, ripping a slice of the sheet with satisfaction. The torn material drifted to the floor, but he caught the end and pulled it up. The linen refused to fold, so he stuffed it inside the chamber in a bundle. Filling his lungs and holding the air in, he stuck out his right leg and eased his weight across. He expected the clock to sway under his feet, but Alfie had underestimated the workmen. They had done their job well and the clock was stable, although he misjudged the height, failed to bend his head and banged his crown.

'Ouch.' Rubbing his head, he looked round to get his bearings before reaching for his tool bag.

He had practised the job in his workshop until he could do it bent double with limited light, but his workshop wasn't twenty feet in the air and his hands hadn't been trembling. He factored in an extra five minutes, but that came and went without the job being completed. When he started the hall had been empty, but people were returning from their day's activities and the staff were busy preparing the suites for the evening. Numerous pairs of eyes were ogling him as he reached once again for the ladder.

'Making final adjustments,' he told the manager who held the ladder for him. 'If your wine is of the usual excellent quality, I may not be in a fit state tomorrow.'

'Of course sir, but shouldn't you be getting ready for your party?'

Alfie checked his pocket watch on the way out. The first guests would be arriving in half an hour and he should be there to greet them. Winnie would be fuming.

Winnie hadn't regained her figure, such that it was, from having the twins and a layer of flab had made camp round her midriff. It was a struggle for her to get into her costume, even

317

with her corset tighter than medically advisable. She was busy arranging petticoats when Alfie returned to the house.

'Where have you been? The cab will be here any moment.'

'It isn't booked until seven,' Alfie reminded her, stopping to do up one of her buttons that she couldn't reach.

'If the driver remembers to come at all. Help me with the catch for this necklace, will you? Is that Fred crying? Mrs Allendale should be in to look after them.'

'I hope she isn't bringing her cats with her.'

'It was kind of her to offer. Be nice when she comes.'

'I am always nice, especially when it is my party.'

They heard the door knocker.

'That will be Mrs Allendale now,' Winnie said. 'I'll go. You had better get dressed.'

'I will if you give me peace.' Alfie gave Winnie a kiss on the cheek and she left to let Mrs Allendale in.

'I'm sorry I'm late, but poor Puss got stuck half-way down a rabbit hole and…'

Alfie heard the beginning of the tale, but he was not interested in puss. He had barely finished knotting his tie when the cab arrived, on time, despite Winnie's fears. The twins were settled and Alfie's appearance met with Winnie's approval.

'It's a bonny evening, we could have walked,' Alfie moaned as he paid the cab driver.

'Not with these shoes on.' Winnie put him in his place.

Walker Squires was waiting for them at the entrance to the hotel.

'You look wonderful Mrs Peters. Maude and the girls are waiting for you in the Atholl Suite. Upstairs on the right.'

He took hold of Alfie's arm to hold him back as Winnie made for the grand stairway. 'I was told you were working on the clock this afternoon. There's nothing wrong, is there?'

'A minor adjustment,' Alfie assured him. 'To do with balance.'

'Everything will be perfect for the Duchess?'

'The clock will do everything we promised it would. It may even tell your guests the time,' Alfie answered.

'This is no joking matter. There is a great deal riding on the success of this venture.' Squires' voice was unusually severe.

'Your investment is safe, if that is what you mean.'

'Good. Good. I just wanted to get that straight.'

'Of course, now, I think I had better join my wife and guests.'

The Atholl Suite consisted of three upstairs rooms. At the last minute Alfie decided against proclaiming his age in large letters, so instead of a banner declaring the number fifty, the staff had decorated the main hall with clocks; pictures of clocks, models of clocks, broken clocks, enormous hands, pendulums and even some working timepieces. They had gone too far, in Alfie's opinion, by unearthing a Regency carriage clock from the stables and thinking a coat of paint would restore it to its former glory. Still, it was a talking point among his horologist friends and it was the clock that had drawn people to the party, not the celebration of his half century. His plan had survived its birthing. It was ready for further schooling.

Winnie abandoned him to drink pink champagne with Maude and Lucy Squires and chat about the latest Gilbert and Sullivan operetta. Set in Japan, or so he picked up from the gossip. Where would they think of next? The resident hotel band was playing and the more light-footed gentlemen had invited their partners to dance. Soon the floor was crowded. Alfie spotted Giles and Emily coupled in a waltz. He couldn't mistake Templeman. The American was wearing a jacket the colour of spring grass, with brown trousers to match. The effect made him look like an elm tree. Emily was doing her best not to look embarrassed. She was nifty on her feet, a necessity as Templeman's clodhopping could have broken her toes on several occasions.

Alfie watched the parading couples spin past and gave a

laugh. Surely that wasn't Lisa waltzing with Forbes McGregor? He didn't recognise her at first. She could have been taken for a rich, young lady in her silk dress, which he assumed he had paid for. McGregor couldn't believe his luck. Not only did he have a partner on his arm, but one that would make half of the assembled company jealous of him. He mucked up the steps and was still twirling Lisa when the music stopped. As Alfie applauded the musicians and dancers, he spotted Weir approaching with a formidable woman glued to his side.

'I don't think you have met my wife,' Weir said.

If he hadn't been told, Alfie would have imagined the lady was Weir's mother, or great aunt. A man could have a younger wife, that was sensible, but to have an old maid was against nature. Her make-up, demeanour and dress were suited for a funeral. Possibly her own.

'Delighted to meet you, Mrs Weir.' Alfie accepted her hand and pretended to kiss the glove. 'Can I get you a drink?'

'Adelaide is a member of the temperance society,' Weir answered.

'Admirable.' Alfie forced a smile. 'I meant soda water or squeezed apple juice.'

'No thank you,' Mrs Weir answered.

'Yourself Jonas?'

'I said, no thank you,' Mrs Weir repeated. 'Plain water is good enough for plain folk like us. This clock you have been working on, it seems rather an extravagance.'

Alfie thought to mention it was paying her husband's wages, but decided to be a little more tactful, at least until later in the evening. 'Perhaps the same could be said of the Sistine Chapel or Westminster Abbey,' he countered.

'These are dedicated to God, Mr Peters.' A hint of colour pushed onto Adelaide Weir's cheeks. It took years off her, but she still looked like she could have been the Queen's nursemaid.

'Who is to say that our clock isn't also, simply because it is sited in a hotel rather than a cathedral?' he asked.

Mrs Weir screwed up her entire face, from her wrinkled forehead to the hairs on her chin. She so resembled a drained prune, that it made a spoken response superfluous.

'If you will excuse me, I must greet my friends.' Alfie made a show of waving to Lisa and Forbes McGregor. They didn't see him, but some other lady waved back and he walked off.

Mingling with people and making pointless small talk wasn't Alfie's idea of a pleasant evening. He smiled, waved and accepted best wishes without stopping to converse with anyone until he reached the buffet table set out in one of the smaller rooms, accessed from the hall. It was a relief to rest the corners of his mouth. He was afraid they might have jammed in a constant grin.

The hotel kitchen staff were renowned for their spreads and they hadn't let him down. The aromas of cheese and grilled chicken set his mouth watering. A waiter carved him slices of ham and his cheeks were stuffed with cold meat, bread and chestnut butter when Templeman appeared at his side. The American didn't speak and Alfie sensed the icy barrier between them.

'Shouldn't you be with your fiancée?' Alfie asked. His voice was pleasant, but he managed to splutter crumbs over Templeman's shirt. Templeman wiped it before answering.

'Emily has retired to the powder room with her sister. They have a lot to talk about. You know what girls are like.'

'I hope she doesn't need her sister by her side when she is married,' he answered. The comment was spoken light-heartedly, but Alfie was afraid it sounded facetious. He didn't want Templeman to take offence and create a scene. Luckily, Giles grinned.

'That might be interesting. Two for the price of one. Miss Lucy has enormous assets.' Giles rolled his hands over his chest. 'Don't

323

pretend you're shocked, like Jonas Weir. We're both men of the world.'

'So you keep saying.' Alfie took a bite of pork pie. He swallowed before speaking again. 'But we live in different worlds.'

There was silence as the conversation faltered. 'Will Miss Lucy be travelling with you to America on your honeymoon?' Alfie asked, unable to think of anything more suitable to say.

'Sadly not, but I need to talk to you about America,' Templeman lowered his voice. 'Looks like I'm going to have to set off for New York again pretty soon.'

'Will you be bringing forward the wedding or do you and Miss Emily intend to marry in the United States?'

'Emily won't be coming with me.'

'It's a short visit then. When will you be back?'

'The commission shouldn't take more than a couple of weeks, but I have contacts and hopes of better projects. I may be away for some time, but that's no concern of yours. The thing is, I have to leave tomorrow evening.'

'On a Sunday?' It took a moment for Alfie to realise what Giles was saying. 'What about the unveiling? The press? The Duchess?'

'You'll be on your own for that, I'm afraid.'

'But it is your clock. You are its creator. The press want to photograph you.'

'I'm the designer, that's all. Anyone can scribble on paper. You are the one who created it.' Giles put an arm on Alfie's shoulder. 'And an amazing job you have done. It is time you got the credit you deserve.'

'Are you in trouble?' Alfie asked.

'Of course not,' Giles turned away to admire the buffet table. 'This looks fantastic.'

'Is it a girl? Do you need money?'

'You met James Bailey, I believe,' Templeman said, his eyes fixed on the roast chicken.

'An unpleasant chap. He said you owed him money,' Alfie answered.

'He is a lying scoundrel.' Giles picked up a chicken leg and tore it with his teeth. 'Why, this is delicious.'

'What about Bailey? I thought he had been arrested. Is he causing trouble?'

'He has a loose tongue and thinks telling tales will lessen his sentence. I can handle things.'

'By running away?'

'Steady on, I didn't say that.'

325

'But you're not coming back, are you?' Alfie said.

'Not in the foreseeable future, no.'

'What about Miss Emily?'

'Hell, there are prettier gals in any New York salon. And richer ones. She'll find somebody else. Don't look at me like that. I'm not ready for marriage. Once I'm gone she'll soon forget about me.'

'Her father won't. He'll have the clock to remind him,' Alfie said. Templeman didn't reply. Alfie rubbed his chin. His plan was working better than he had hoped. 'Wouldn't you like to try it out, before you go?'

'Try it out? What do you mean? Don't we have to wait for the Duchess to unveil it?'

'The clock, yes, but I meant the time travel chamber.'

'What have you been drinking Alfie?' Giles laughed loud enough for the lady opposite them to look over. 'That was a joke, wasn't it?'

'Steady on,' Alfie repeated Templeman's terminology while feigning surprise at his disbelief. 'I have never been more serious. The screens are up and a ladder is in place. This would be the perfect time.'

'You are an odd fish,' Templeman answered.

Templeman gave no sign of any willingness to oblige Alfie. The issue could not be forced, though. The door from the buffet room was open and Alfie spotted Squires in the hall. He turned away when he caught Alfie's eyes, but not before Alfie saw the look he gave Templeman.

Things might not yet be lost.

'I can't imagine Walker was happy when you told him of your plan to leave,' Alfie said.

Templeman's ruddy complexion paled. 'He doesn't know. Neither does Farquhar. You don't mean to tell them, do you?'

'Of course not, but Squires seemed out of sorts when I spoke to him. You may wish to lie low until you leave the city.'

Giles took out his cigarette case while he thought. He offered Alfie a cigarette.

'I'm a pipe man,' Alfie said, refusing the cigarette. 'Look, if you do need to hide for a short while, there is maintenance space inside the clock.' Alfie retrieved a key from his waistcoat pocket and dangled it in front of Giles.

Templeman laughed, but he returned the cigarette case to his pocket without taking a cigarette and took the key.

'I have to go. There are things in my hotel room I need to recover.'

'If you do wish to test the time travel apparatus, turn the key in the central panel. Clockwise for the future, anti-clockwise for the past. Simple, even a child could use it.'

'Or an American?' Templeman joked.

'Touché.'

Giles headed towards the side door and out of the room, avoiding Squires. Alfie popped another slice of pie in his mouth before he returned to the dance hall. He found Winnie and led her onto the dance floor. The musicians played a jig, which involved a great deal of stamping and cheering. Alfie was out of breath by the time the dance ended. He escorted Winnie to a chair and went to fetch a glass of good, plain water.

'Mr Peters, have you seen Giles?' Emily Squires had returned from the powder room and was looking for her beau.

'I was speaking to him at the buffet table,' Alfie said.

'I've searched there.'

'He mentioned fetching something from his hotel suite.'

Emily made her way across the room, brushing aside a young man keen to dance with her.

She was better off without a cad like Templeman, Alfie thought.

He was only ever after her father's money and goodwill. The

328

music had started again and some of the livelier couples were taking to the floor. Winnie signalled to him that she was sitting the dance out. Alfie looked around for Lisa and spotted Giles in the far corner of the room dancing with a young lady.

Side-tracked by the first bit of fluff he saw.

The couple's heads were turned away from him, but no-one else in the room was wearing such a garish green jacket. The lady had on a scarlet dress with a fur trim. She must have been someone Templeman picked up in the lobby. Alfie would have remembered seeing that skirt before.

Keen for a better look, Alfie tried to keep pace with the couple, but however hard he tried, he never quite managed to reach them. He followed them to the window, concealing himself behind the curtain, only to see them dancing towards the door. By the time he escaped the folds of the curtain and reached the door they were skipping round the music stand. The girl had the nerve to duck under the band master's outstretched arms. The maestro seemed oblivious to her. He waved his baton to bring the tune to a close. Dancers moved apart or fell into one another's arms. Giles gave his partner a bow and she curtsied before turning round to catch Alfie's eye through the crowded room.

He stopped breathing. It was Maggie. Her belly was rounded

with child, and her dress was scarlet with blood. Giles put his hand on her abdomen. His fingers dripped with blood when he lifted them away. He laughed as drops fell to the floor in gruesome patterns. He was at least twenty feet away, but Alfie heard the cruel chortle. He saw Maggie's crazed look. Blood squeezed from her flaring nostrils. Templeman's face changed from that of a gavotting young man to that of a cadaver, mouth drawn in horror, with eye sockets as hollow as his life.

'AAARGH'

The crowd hushed as the strident noise echoed around the room.

'What was that?'

'It sounded like a scream.'

Questions bounced off the walls. One of the violin players screeched his bow down the strings and somebody laughed. The gentlemen pretended they hadn't been concerned and the ladies fanned themselves as if screams were a normal occurrence at parties. Only Squires left the group of businessmen he was with and rushed to the door. Alfie made his way to the exit and followed the hotel owner into the corridor and down the stairs, keeping a distance from him. The hall appeared deserted until he noticed Emily Squires collapsed next to the fallen ladder. Squires ran over to kneel beside her.

'Has she fainted? Winnie will have smelling salts in her bag. Would you like me to fetch them? Or some water, perhaps?' Alfie offered.

Squires stared over at him, his face expressionless. There was blood on the carpet. It was dripping from the ceiling. A rhythmic plip-plop. It was then Alfie realised the clock was ticking as the pendulum swung and the hands moved. He looked up and gasped. Templeman's body was hanging from the open casing by his legs which had jammed in the door. He wasn't wearing his jacket and his shirt was covered in blood. His head was dangling at an angle, almost detached from his body. On his neck was the deep cut made by the pendulum slicing through his flesh.

The night manager ran. He stopped when he saw Squires and was too shocked to do anything but stare. Emily gave a groan as she began to revive. The stench of blood clawed at Alfie's nostrils and throat. He raised his hand to his mouth, but the contents of his stomach spewed onto the Persian carpet. Squires looked from Alfie to the clock and shuddered.

'What have we done?' he muttered. 'What have we done?'

Chapter 20

The rest of the evening was a blur punctuated by screams. The hotel staff ran around carrying glasses of water and police officers ran around telling everyone to stay calm. An ambulance arrived for the body, another for the shocked guests. In the midst of it, Squires called for Farquhar then departed from the scene with his family. There was more screeching and a rather delicious peach flan, which Alfie scoffed while the others were fainting. The police were keen to ask questions.

Who spoke to Templeman last?

Was he in sound mind?

The most important question was what on earth Templeman was doing entering a clock suspended from the ceiling at some ungodly hour, while his fiancée powdered her nose.

'Are we to understand that the deceased gentleman made the clock?' the inspector asked.

'Templeman didn't have anything to do with the internal clock workings,' Farquhar assumed the role of spokesman as soon as he arrived. 'That was Peters' department.'

The inspector turned his attention to Alfie.

'You are the gentleman, whose party this is?'

Policemen couldn't or wouldn't speak plain English. It took

Alfie a moment to get his befuddled head round what the man was asking, if indeed it was a question.

'Jumping into a moving clock wasn't one of the party games,' he replied. The officer frowned and wrote something in his notebook. 'I believe Mr Templeman had been drinking more than his share of the wine,' Alfie added.

'We will need to take a statement from you. We will need statements from everybody before they leave.'

'That is ridiculous,' Farquhar argued. 'The hotel is full. We will be here all night. I have left a dinner party with several important dignitaries.' He named names, including senior police officials.

'A man has been killed in unusual circumstances, sir.'

'I understand that, in my hotel, with the Duchess of Atholl due in less than two days. We'll never get the stains out of the carpet in time.'

'It has been a shock, but this is no time for sarcasm, sir,' the policeman reprimanded him.

Those may not have been the exact words of the conversation, but Alfie felt he had caught the general gist when he told Winnie a few days later.

'Farquhar's face was like a burst balloon,' he laughed. Winnie didn't appreciate the humour.

He had given the police their statement. Yes, he had worked on the clock that afternoon, preparing the pendulum for the unveiling and starting of it. He hadn't imagined someone with no knowledge of the workings would squeeze inside. Yes, he had spoken with Giles shortly before he disappeared. They talked about New York. Templeman gave no indication he wished to end his life although if he had, he may well have chosen such a fanciful manner.

Winnie had been anxious to get back to the twins before Mrs Allendale fed them milk from a saucer and put bells round their necks. Lisa and Forbes McGregor had sneaked out early, down the fire stairs and through the serving staff's quarters. Alfie hadn't seen either of them since.

There had been a newspaper reporter and a man taking photographs. The grainy pictures were on the front page of the paper the next day. Funny, Alfie thought, how the editor now decided that he was the clockmaker. His name was in bold letters, even his age. Naturally there were repercussions. The windows of his shop were smashed, although nothing was stolen – who would touch a clock that had the capacity to kill its owner?

Alfie nailed boards across the windows and the next day there was a gruesome drawing of Templeman hanging dead from the clock painted on them. The likeness was remarkable. He had it painted over and now there was a police officer standing guard outside. There were no customers. It was hardly worth him being there at all.

The Duchess found that she didn't have the time to visit Perth. There was no need for her trip anyhow, the clock was under police guard. Farquhar was fuming. He called Alfie, Weir, Davidson and whoever else he could blame into his office on the Monday morning after the incident. He refused to pay outstanding bills. Alfie had his salary safely in the bank, but the workmen were owed money. The skin on Squires' face was virtually see-through. He had plenty to say about the finances, but not in front of the others.

'The clock has suffered only minor damage,' Alfie said. 'It can be repaired.'

'If only Mr Templeman could be too,' Farquhar spat. 'I want nothing to do with the clock. It has been a curse from the start. It shall not stay in this hotel a minute longer than it needs to. When the police have finished their investigation, it can be sold for scrap as far as I am concerned.'

'But wait...'

Squires sent the rest of them packing before he finished the

335

conversation with his partner. Alfie had to rely on the snippets gleaned from Maude Squires, via Winnie. She wasted no time before going to visit, to enquire after Miss Emily.

Squires had lifted the tab for the material and work on the clock himself in a bid to hurry things along. He assumed he would be able to reclaim the money from hotel funds, but oddly for a man of business, he had nothing in writing. His friendship with Farquhar went way back. So far back it meant nothing to Farquhar, who refused to pay for a useless chunk of metal and wood. It was rumoured, Winnie told him over tea, that the Squires faced financial ruin. They would have to sell their fine house and most of the art Walker had collected.

'Even Miss Lucy's upright piano will have to go,' Winnie said.

Alfie sipped his tea. 'That certainly would be ruinous.'

'Miss Emily is taking things really hard.'

Winnie assumed a tone of concern, but Alfie knew she was revelling in the Squires' misfortune. Women were like that.

'What with seeing the body, hanging there with barely a head and covered in blood, having no prospects of marriage now and having to sell her gold watch.'

'She had no prospects of marriage before Templeman got himself killed,' Alfie confided. 'He was about to go off to New

York and leave her in the lurch. Not quite at the altar, but near enough.'

'You don't say.'

'He told me himself at the party. His ticket was booked. I thought it wiser not to tell the police that, in case it got back to Emily.'

'That was thoughtful of you, dear.'

'I can give her a good price for the gold watch too, if she wants. I made it. I know what it is worth.'

'You are being very considerate today, Alfie,' Winnie said. 'If I didn't know you better, I might think you had something to hide.'

'I'm as open as a clock face.'

Alfie hadn't told Winnie about his vision of Giles and Maggie dancing before the body was discovered. It squeezed his lungs of their breath at the time, but he hadn't thought about it since. The picture came back to him as he spoke; Giles' green coat and Maggie's blood red dress. He choked on the biscuit he was eating and the crumbs splattered over Winnie.

'What is the matter with you?'

'I've remembered the police inspector wanted to see me this afternoon. I've agreed to meet him at the shop. We don't want a police officer at our front door.'

'It was a tragic accident,' Winnie said. 'I don't see why the police are so interested. They would do better to be out catching the hooligans who broke your windows.'

'Perhaps that is what it is about.'

The inspector was waiting at the door when Alfie arrived.

'Not open today, Mr Peters?' he enquired.

'Business is slow and my wife needed me at home. Her nerves…'

'Of course.'

The inspector looked at the boarded windows before entering the shop.

'We would like to get this case closed as soon as possible,' the inspector said. 'It isn't good for the hotel, and what isn't good for the West Tay isn't good for the town.'

'How can I help you?' Alfie asked.

'The clock has been taken down, as you no doubt know. I had my men examine it.'

'With no further incident, I hope,' Alfie put in.

'One of them did get soaked by falling water from some sort of reservoir.' The inspector wasn't overwhelmed by Templeman's design. 'We found this in the chamber behind the clock face.' He reached in his pocket to bring out the key Alfie had given Giles, with a torn leaf of paper he had wrapped around it. 'Do they mean anything to you?'

Alfie pretended to examine the objects. 'The key may well be for winding up a clock,' he said. 'But not the one it was found in. As for the scribbling on the paper, it looks clever, but it is gibberish. It may as well be Egyptian hieroglyphs.'

He made to put them in his pocket, but the inspector held out his palm. Alfie handed them back.

'You have no notion as to why Mr Templeman would have taken them into the clock with him?'

'Did he?' Alfie feigned surprise. 'I can think of no reason he should do so, but then there was no reason for Templeman to enter the clock in the first place. He was not a clockmaker. He did have some weird ideas though. He was an American.'

'So I gathered.' The inspector slipped the paper and key into his pocket. 'I won't trouble you further. If anything comes to you, let me know.'

'Of course.'

The inspector stopped to examine Charlie's grandfather clock on his way to the door.

'Hooligans,' Alfie said, referring to the scratch marks. 'I shall make repairs today.'

'My grandfather had a clock like this one,' the inspector said. 'I remember being allowed to wind it up when I was a lad.'

'What happened to it?' Alfie asked. 'If you inherited it, I would be interested in seeing it.'

'Lost in a house fire,' the inspector answered.

A trader's cart must have trundled past the shop as he spoke because the grandfather clock shook.

'Which reminds me,' the inspector continued. 'I wanted to ask what the purpose of the chamber behind your clock was. I've asked other clockmakers, but they don't seem to know.'

'They wouldn't. It was part of an innovative design. It worked as a counterbalance, but its main function was for maintenance. You can imagine, with such a complex piece of craftsmanship, we needed access to the interior. Why should a fire remind you of that?'

'My grandmother was trapped in her parlour during the fire.'

'I trust she managed to escape,' Alfie said.

'No, she suffocated.'

'Ah. My condolences.'

'It was some years ago now. Thank you for your help, Mr Peters.' The inspector lifted his hat and left.

Alfie walked over to the grandfather clock and gave it a kick.

He stubbed his toe and for a second he thought he heard old Charlie laughing at him.

Thanks to Templeman, Alfie's business was ruined in the city. He had decided to shut up shop and take his stock elsewhere. Dundee, perhaps. Winnie didn't like Dundee. She thought it smelt of jam, jute and whale oil. But he needn't take Winnie with him. Her company was tedious, she was always ill or too tired for exertions in the bedroom and he was sick of wailing babies who got more from Winnie's breasts than he did.

He would have to visit Dorothy again. There had been a letter from Dr Matthews that morning, not only requesting an interview, but returning the payment for Dotty's hospital fees for that quarter. Strange, since there was no indication that she had died. The money was welcome, though. It would take time to build the same reputation in Dundee as he had enjoyed in Perth. Moving there would have the benefit of being rid of Nancy, though. He was tired of their liaisons. She hadn't bothered him since Maggie's funeral, but she knew where to find him.

The door of the shop opened. He had his back to it, but he heard a familiar voice.

'I'm glad ye're here. I came earlier, bit ye were closed,' Lisa called.

'Where have you been?' Alfie asked.

'Wi' Forbes, your fancy friend frae Forfar,' Lisa caught her tongue round the twister and laughed.

'He is older than I am and has far less hair. What do you see in him?'

'He treats me like a lady. I've come tae collect ma stuff.'

'Have you? Who is to say I haven't sold it, or thrown it in the dustbin?' Alfie walked over to stand beside her.

'You'd better no hae.'

'Fancy Forbes from Forfar can afford to buy you new clothes.'

'Open the door,' Lisa instructed. He heard a tremor in her voice.

'You're not frightened of me, are you?'

'Course not. I dinnae listen to whit folk say.'

'What do people say?' He stepped back.

'They say you had a thing tae dae wi' Mr Templeman's death. They say you pit a curse oan the clock.'

Alfie gave a laugh and let her go. 'A curse? On my own clock?'

'People say you arenae richt in the heid.'

'Is that why you have taken up with McGregor?'

'There wis yon incident in the inn,' Lisa reminded him.

Alfie reached in his pocket for the key to the apartment. 'Here.

Get your things and be gone by the time I get back.'

Alfie collected his coat and hat and left Lisa to get on with it.

He didn't intend going anywhere in particular, he wanted time to think, without Lisa bustling around upstairs. His path led him to his usual drinking den, but he didn't go in. He wasn't going to be some fairground attraction for the locals to goggle at. It wasn't far to the park. He would stroll round and return to lock up the shop, assuming Lisa had departed.

It was a pleasant late afternoon and a number of the good people of the city were stretching their legs or walking their dogs. Alfie tried to steer clear of the nannies with their bawling charges, but in doing so he found himself outside the West Tay Hotel. Emily Squires was stumbling down the steps from the hotel towards him and he could see she was crying. Her hair was unwashed and in disarray. From the state of her dress Alfie found it easy to believe she had spent the night in it. She wasn't wearing a coat.

'Good afternoon, Miss Squires.' Alfie raised his hat in greeting.

She didn't recognise him at first, but she stopped and peered into his eyes.

'Mr Peters? I was looking for my father, but nobody has seen him. The man at the desk was rather rude. He said he had no time to look for papa. He suggested I try asking at the lending banks. I don't suppose you have seen him?'

'I'm afraid I can't help you,' Alfie said. 'Can I escort you home?'

'I need to find papa.'

'You need to rest, child,' Alfie said.

'I wish Giles were here. He would know what to do.' Emily stood helpless.

'Perhaps Mrs Peters is visiting your mother and sister. We could go to the house together and find out.' Alfie offered her a hand.

'I want to be with Giles. I'm wearing the perfume he bought me in New York.' She raised her hand for him to sniff her wrist. There was a clawing aroma of jasmine.

'Lovely,' Alfie said.

'Giles isn't here. I need to find papa.' Emily pulled her hand away.

'So you said, my dear.' Alfie reached for her arm and she didn't resist. He patted her hand. 'We'll soon have you feeling better.'

He attempted gentle conversation as he guided her through the park towards the Squires' house, but her replies were the same. Giles was gone and she needed to find her father.

'The loss of a loved one is never easy, but time heals some of the hurt.' He tried to console her.

'You don't know what it is like.' Emily's voice was more of a shriek.

'I lost my first wife,' Alfie said. 'She was younger than you at the time.'

'Oh, I'm sorry. I didn't realise. Did you love her so much you wished it was you who had died instead?'

Alfie couldn't honestly answer yes to that. He hesitated before answering, 'I have Winnie now. You will find someone else, someone different.'

He resisted saying 'someone better'.

'I don't want anyone else,' Emily sobbed.

They walked on in silence until they reached the gate to the Squires' house. Emily stopped.

'I don't want to go in,' she said. 'I can't bear listening to mama and Lucy with their silly platitudes.'

'They are trying to help you. I'll go in with you, if you want.'

'I want Giles. I need papa.' Emily reverted to her whine.

Before Alfie could react, she turned and ran down the path. He followed hastily, but she was faster than he was and his pursuit attracted looks from the passers-by. He stopped and watched her disappear round a corner. He had done his best, he had to let her go. She was of age, and could find her own way home when she was hungry enough. A day or two on the streets wouldn't be such a bad thing for the likes of spoiled brats like Emily Squires.

He had been gone longer than he intended and didn't expect Lisa still to be in the shop, but she was coming down the stairs as he entered.

'Got everything you wanted?' Alfie growled.

'I think so. By the way, there wis a wifie looking for you,' Lisa said. 'A gave her your home address.'

'A woman? What was she like?'

Lisa shrugged. 'She had a bairn wi' her. A pestering wee lad.'

'That is my son,' Alfie answered.

'Weel, he brak your display and three o' your pens. Goodbye. I micht see you aroon, if ye're ever in Forfar.'

'I don't think that likely.'

Alfie watched her leave. His mind was on Nancy. What was she doing in Perth, with Teddy? Whatever it was, he had better get home before there was a cat fight between her and Winnie.

Chapter 21

There was some commotion near the railway bridge as he passed, but he didn't have time to cross the road and investigate. Walking up the garden path, he suspected he was already too late to avoid a battle. Teddy was pulling up the flowers Winnie had planted while his mother battered on the door with her fists, shouting obscenities that were not appreciated in the residential neighbourhood. She didn't hear him approach and she spun round and aimed a fist at his chest when he put an arm on her shoulder. She missed and he grabbed her wrist.

'Please, the lady next door is of a nervous disposition,' Alfie chided.

'I'll give you a nervous disposition,' Nancy answered, before realising it was Alfie. 'Who is that demented trollop in your house?'

Alfie didn't answer. He looked towards Ted. 'Stop ruining the flowers boy, or I'll give you a good thrashing.'

'Don't speak to him like that,' Nancy answered.

'The boy is delinquent. It's no surprise. I can see where he gets his unruly behaviour from.'

'Why are you acting like this, Alfie? We haven't heard from you for ages. I was worried and came to see how you were and this is how you treat us.'

'You came for money and to find out how Dotty is,' Alfie countered. 'Dotty is doing well, apparently. I'm afraid things aren't so good with me, financially speaking. What did you say to Winnie?'

'Is that her name? I didn't tell her anything she shouldn't already know.'

'I'll be the judge of what Winnie should know.' Alfie had an urge to strike Nancy, but Teddy was watching him and he desisted. 'Here, take this money and find a hotel for you and the boy.' He thrust Nancy some notes from his wallet. 'There is a reasonable one on Methven Street. I'll be along to see you when I can.'

'Will you take us for dinner?'

'You, maybe, but not him.'

She snatched the money and called Ted to her.

'Don't come here again,' Alfie called after her as she made her way down the path, holding the folds of her skirt in one hand and a struggling Ted in the other.

Winnie was in, but he used his key rather than knocking. She was in the hall waiting for him by the time he opened the door and stepped in. She cradled one of the twins in her arms. It looked like Fred.

'Who is that slut?' she spat the words across the entranceway.

'A friend I knew before I met you. You weren't very polite to her.' Alfie tried to walk past towards the living room, but she blocked his way.

'You expect me to offer her tea and cakes, after what she said?'

'If I knew what she said it might help.'

'How can you be so calm about this?' The baby began to cry and Winnie lowered her voice. 'She called me a kept woman.'

'No one is keeping you here,' Alfie answered. 'It is not a prison. You are free to leave.'

'That is not what I meant and you know it.'

'You are making yourself ill. We should have tea and forget about Nancy.' He didn't feel it was safe to put a hand out to Winnie, so he leaned over to make a face at the baby.

'Don't touch him.' She swirled the babe away from him. 'That whore claimed the child with her was yours.'

'He may be,' Alfie agreed. 'Like I said, I knew Nancy before I met you.'

Winnie made a face, as if trying to work out how old Teddy was. 'How often do you see him and his mother?'

Alfie hesitated. 'As often as is proper,' he replied.

'Proper? That witch…'

'Her name is Nancy.'

'That witch told me I wasn't your wife, because you already have one.'

Alfie imagined if he denied it, shrugged it off as one of Nancy's mad fantasies, Winnie would believe him, but his temper was fired.

'That is true. I have a wife in Edinburgh. A wife who doesn't bombard me with accusations and complaints when I walk in the door. A wife who is glad to see me. I am going out.'

He turned and stormed out the door leaving Winnie to make of it as she wanted.

If he walked fast he could catch up with Nancy. With Teddy to mind, she couldn't have gone far. There was a gathering at the bridge and he spotted police officers trying to disband the on-lookers. Alfie's curiosity was aroused. He didn't want to be the last to know about something happening in his own neighbourhood.

'If you don't mind moving on, sir.' A policeman stepped in front of him before he could see anything.

'What has happened?' Alfie asked.

'There has been an incident on the island. We are dealing with it, so if you would continue along the road, thank you.'

Alfie was ushered from the scene. He waited a short way off, expecting developments. Whatever the police were doing, they were taking their time about it. Alfie was getting bored and a little cold when he saw Jonas Weir approach the police sergeant. He said something to the man and wasn't ordered away. Jonas pointed and the policeman nodded. They headed in the direction indicated.

'Hello,' Alfie called, making his way towards the men. He waved to Weir. 'Is something the matter? Can I be of help?'

'We're waiting on Mr Squires,' Weir answered and Alfie noticed his face was ashen. 'It's Miss Emily. She has drowned.'

Emily drowned, dead. It didn't sink in. He had been with her. He let her run off. Could he have saved her?

He had saved her, escorted her to the door, waited until her mother came.

No, she was dead. Drowned. The river weeds tangling her hair green.

'I need a drink.' Alfie staggered away from Weir.

His favourite watering hole was off Methven Street. With the shock of the news, he had forgotten about Nancy, but as he turned into the street he spotted her and Ted outside the hotel. It wasn't difficult. Ted was scrawling on the wall with a piece of chalk. Nancy saw Alfie and ran up. She took hold of his jacket.

'The hotel is full,' she said.

'No room at the inn for a mother and child,' Alfie mused. 'No matter. It will save money if you stay in the apartment above the shop.' He held out his hand for the notes he had given her, but she didn't give them back.

'It is too far for Teddy to walk. The poor darling is tired out,' she said.

The poor darling was about to throw a stone at a cat. Alfie grabbed him and lifted him off his feet. Teddy hit out at Alfie's shoulder.

'Do that again and I'll toss you in the river,' he warned. Nancy gasped, but his warning did the trick and Teddy allowed himself to be carried.

'You can show Teddy the guinea pigs,' Nancy said.

'Guinea pigs?'

'You said you kept them for showing.'

'Did I? They died.'

They walked the rest of the way in silence. Once in the apartment, Alfie poured himself a drink. He didn't offer Nancy a glass of his whisky. Alfie felt a desire to make love to her, but not

352

with Teddy in the apartment, getting up to mischief and asking questions. After a second glass of whisky he had an idea.

'Teddy, come here. There's something I want to show you downstairs in the shop.'

'A boring old clock,' Teddy answered. He didn't come over.

'You like clockwork toys, don't you?'

'Have you got a toy for me?'

'You'll have to come and see.'

Teddy stopped pulling at the curtains and came over.

'We won't be long,' Alfie told Nancy. He took hold of Teddy's hand and led him down the stairs and into the shop. Five minutes later he was back in the apartment, removing his waistcoat and tie.

'Where's Teddy?' Nancy asked as he unbuckled his belt.

'He's playing downstairs. He won't bother us.' Alfie moved to kiss her. She let him for a moment then pulled away.

'I have to check on Teddy,' she said.

'Can't you think of me, for once,' Alfie tried to stop her passing him, but the whisky and the events of the evening made him unsteady. She pushed him and he fell onto the bed. He listened to her dashing down the stairs and calling her son's name. He waited for the reaction with a smirk.

Five, four, three...

Her scream was louder than he expected. Enough to rouse the neighbours. He got up, picked up his belt and took deliberate steps down the stairs, fastening his belt as he did. When he arrived in the shop, Nancy was beating the casing of Charlie's grandfather clock with her fists.

'What are you doing?' Alfie called. 'That is a valuable clock. It belonged to Auld Charlie.'

'I don't care if it belonged to Auld Nick. Where is Teddy? What have you done?' She stopped thumping the clock to speak and there was a faint thudding noise from inside.

Alfie walked over to her and she slapped him on the face.

'Do you want me to release Teddy or not?' he asked.

'I'm going to call the police,' she threatened.

'You do that. When they arrive I shall tell them I caught some ragamuffin stealing a gold watch and apprehended him. Who do you think they will believe?'

'He is your son.'

'He is not my son. A son of mine would not act the way he does. If he is flesh of my loins, I disown him. I disown both of you.'

He took a key from his pocket and unlocked the casing of the

354

clock. Nancy pulled the door open to reveal a tearful Teddy, squashed beside the pendulum.

'My darling,' she reached to help him out. 'Are you hurt?' Teddy put his arms around his mother and she hugged him to her chest.

'He put me in the clock.' Teddy pointed to Alfie when Nancy released him. 'Like the man in the paper.'

'He could have suffocated. The pendulum could have slipped.' Nancy caught her breath, 'O my God, the man in the paper, the one who died. You are a monster, Alfie Peters. I hope you rot in hell.'

Picking Teddy up, she strode to the door. It was locked and she glared at Alfie until he walked over to unlock it. 'A heartless monster,' she repeated as she marched out, stepping on Alfie's toes as she did.

Alfie took a deep breath. The boy was unscathed. It would teach him respect, or set him up for prison where he no doubt would end up.

He had enjoyed good times with Nancy, before Maggie and Teddy were born, but life was too short to dwell on the past. The future was what mattered. It was time to take a final trip to the hospital and claim Dotty as his lawful wife. He turned to go back upstairs and caught a shadow out of the corner of his eye. His heart jumped.

'Who's there?' He lifted one of the heavier, but poorer quality, mantel clocks, ready to throw, but the room was still. 'Come out and show yourself.'

The room was silent. Alfie put the clock down and lit a lamp. He set it on the counter, but the far side of the shop was dark. As well as the ticking of the clocks, Alfie heard a dripping noise from the back shelves. He lifted the lamp and made his way over. The wood creaked and he swiped the shelf clear of the watches to see behind. The wall was damp and he detected the subtle scent of jasmine. Alfie's heart pounded and he staggered back.

He regained his balance and hurried towards the door of the apartment. He locked it behind him and dashed up the stairs two at a time. After another glass of whisky he told himself he was imagining things. When the bottle was empty he collapsed on the bed and fell asleep.

Chapter 22

His head pounded the following morning. It took a pot of tea before he recalled the events of the previous day and that was only after allowing the kettle to boil dry and having to restart the process. Nancy knew about Winnie, Winnie knew about Dotty, Lisa had left him for Forbes of Forfar and Emily Squires had drowned herself.

He assumed she had drowned herself, but as he recalled, Weir had merely said she had drowned. It may have been an accident or, God forbid, foul play. She had been in a sorry state when he left her. She could have lost her footing or some rogue may have tried to take advantage of her. He wondered whether he should inform the police about the talk he had with her. An accident was shocking enough. The Squires would not want suggestions of suicide.

His plan had been to travel to Edinburgh that morning, but he had overslept and it was touching noon by the time he finished breakfast. He went downstairs to the shop and heard a banging at the front door. Customers weren't so urgent in their knocking and he wasn't surprised to see a police officer when he opened the door. It was the same man as before.

'Inspector…'Alfie couldn't recall his name.

'Jamieson,' the man obliged.

'Well, Inspector Jamieson, what can I do for you today? Is it about Emily Squires?'

'You heard of her unfortunate accident. So young, such a tragedy, but no, I'm here on another matter. Do you know a man called Bailey? James Bailey.'

Alfie ran his tongue around his mouth. 'The name doesn't sound familiar, I'm afraid.'

'He claims to have spoken to you in the lounge bar of the West Tay Hotel.'

'When was this? I haven't been in the hotel since the accident. Is he one of the clock labourers? I don't remember all their names.'

'This man was a prison officer.'

'I certainly am not acquainted with anyone from that profession.' Alfie pretended to laugh. 'You said "was". I hope nothing has happened to him.'

Alfie was playing games. The inspector knew it and he was aware the inspector knew.

'What is this about?' Alfie asked more seriously.

'He is helping us with our enquiries regarding Mr Templeman,' Jamieson said. He lifted a ladies' pocket watch and examined the bracelet. 'Did you know Miss Margaret Gillespie?'

'Maggie - the girl who was murdered on the train? Yes, I know her mother.' He couldn't deny it. 'I have spoken to an officer before about that incident. The newspapers said the culprit was a sailor. I read he had escaped from prison. Have you caught him yet?'

'That is a police affair. I am here, because according to Bailey, Miss Gillespie's death may have had something to do with Giles Templeman. You spoke with Mr Templeman before his death. Was he agitated? Did he say anything to you about her death?'

'The girl, Maggie, was a maid to his fiancée, Miss Squires,' Alfie answered. 'He was naturally distraught about her death, as was fitting. I have been over this with the other policeman.'

'Miss Squires is now dead. Three deaths in three months, all connected through Mr Templeman.'

'As you said, a tragedy.'

Inspector Jamieson put the watch he was fingering on the counter. He looked as if he wanted to ask something important, but didn't quite know what. 'Mrs Jamieson would like this. It's her birthday soon.'

Alfie knew the inspector couldn't afford the watch. He named a price less than half its value. The inspector sucked his top lip and

Alfie took two guineas off the price. He would have given him the watch for nothing to get rid of him, but that would be seen as bribery.

'You drive a hard bargain,' the inspector said, reaching for his wallet.

'Would you like it boxed?'

It was the first sale he'd made since Templeman's death. He imagined it should be something to celebrate. Shutting up the shop, once the inspector had departed, Alfie took a stroll to one of the less salubrious drinking houses near the docks. He propped up the bar until the landlord rang his bell for last orders. The street was empty when he left. He wasn't familiar with the part of town and in the dark he wasn't sure where he was. He wished he had a stick, for protection rather than a walking aid. He heard light footsteps behind him.

'You're out late. Looking for a good time?'

The voice was familiar. He turned and in the shadow of a distant street light he saw Maggie.

'Get away from me.' He waved his arms. The spectre moved closer.

'Is he causing trouble?' Alfie heard a man's voice, but he had his hands over his eyes. It was an American accent. A New York twang, like Templeman's. 'Maybe he prefers a bit of class.'

Maggie laughed. Alfie felt water dripping onto his raised arm. He opened his fingers to peek out and saw Emily Squires hovering above him, her clothes soaking and river weeds tangled in her hair. He gave a scream and lurched into the gutter. The ale and malt in his stomach spewed over his shirt sleeve.

He woke in the same gutter the following morning. The town was going about its business, ignoring what they believed to be another down-and-out who trusted alcohol as the answer to life's problems. His palm was grazed and there was a tear in his trousers. His wallet and pocket watch were missing, but the thieves had left his keys.

'Need a hand?' A girl selling flowers helped him up.

Alfie rubbed his head. 'Where am I?'

He was given directions to his shop and the girl stuck a carnation in his top buttonhole.

'My wallet has been stolen,' he said.

'Aye, that's whit they all say.'

'It's true. Come to my shop this afternoon and I'll set you right,' he said.

'I don't think my man would approve of that,' she answered and strolled off down the street.

Alfie couldn't remember the directions the girl gave, but he came to a street he recognised and found his way back to the shop. He locked the door behind him and went upstairs to the flat, where he collapsed onto the bed and lay there, counting his breaths. At a hundred, he got up, washed, changed his clothes then made a cup of tea. The morning was young and he had business to attend to. He would go to Edinburgh unannounced and surprise Dotty. He spotted the crushed carnation lying on the floor where it had fallen from his jacket. He would take Dotty flowers.

The train was full and he had a choice of sitting next to a mud covered spaniel or standing in the corridor. He chose the corridor, near the door, and wondered which compartment Maggie had fallen from, or been pushed from. There was a young couple arguing along from him. About money, he gathered from what he overheard. The woman's voice was shrill and the man was trying to appease her. If he took Alfie's advice, he would take his belt to her, although possibly not on the train. The man put his hand on the woman's shoulder. She stepped back, but he tightened his grip and raised his other arm to her neck.

'Tickets please.' The guard interrupted Alfie's view of the tiff. When he punched Alfie's ticket and moved on down the corridor, the couple had disappeared. Alfie didn't see them go.

It was a tedious journey. Alfie's back was stiff and a dagger-sharp pain shot up his spine. Walking might help. He was curious to know where the couple had vanished to and if they had resolved their argument without the need for violence. They hadn't pushed past him, so he strolled the opposite way down the train. A group of sailors blocked the passageway beside the next door. They had opened the window and one of the men was hanging his upper body out of it.

'Excuse me.' Alfie squashed in front of them. The overriding odour was carbolic, but there was also the scent of cologne. The effeminate stuff Templeman splashed on his chin after shaving.

Several passengers alighted at the next station and Alfie stepped in front of an elderly gentleman with a stick, to secure a comfortable seat beside the window. He half closed his eyes to shield them from the sun through the glass. There was a flash of red. Alfie jumped up, knocking the newspaper from the hands of the man seated beside him.

'Did you see that?' Alfie asked.

'See what?'

A girl has fallen from the train.

He couldn't be sure. If he had the train stopped and it was a trick of the light, the railway company would not be amused. Most likely they would demand compensation.

'I thought I saw... nothing, my mistake.'

He sat back down and stared out of the window, feeling the disapproving gaze of the woman opposite. Her husband smoked a cigar. Alfie had never liked cigar smoke. It clawed at his throat. He stifled a cough, but was forced to give up his seat and leave the compartment in search of air.

The couple had returned to their spot by the door. They were standing close and Alfie smelt the cologne. The woman was trying to speak, but the man had his arms around her neck.

'Steady on,' Alfie lurched towards them.

The man gave a laugh. The woman fainted and he lowered the window and reached for the door handle.

'No…' Alfie shouted. He was at the door, but the window was up and he was alone. One of the sailors came towards him along the corridor.

'Are you feeling alright?' the man asked.

Ship shape and Bristol fashion, he wanted to joke, but he felt drawn. His chest was tight and he imagined what he experienced wasn't far removed from a heart attack. The sailor took a flask from his pocket, unscrewed the lid and offered it to Alfie. The rum was strong and dark. It burnt Alfie's throat and he choked.

'Not so fast,' the sailor said. Alfie handed him back the flask. His hand was shaking.

'Have you seen a young couple? They were here a moment ago,' Alfie asked.

The sailor pushed out his lips, shook his head and moved on. Alfie's nerves were on edge for the rest of the journey. He watched for the couple, but he feared seeing their faces. The remainder of the trip was uneventful, though, and by the time the train arrived at his station he had recovered composure. He took his place on the ferry and looked out to observe the men working on the bridge. He didn't envy them their task. He wasn't good with heights. He heard someone had already fallen into the water, but it was unclear whether they were rescued or had drowned.

The ferry was approaching the bank and his eyes moved along the shore where a group of boys were throwing stones at driftwood in the shallow water. They may have been trying to show off their prowess, but none of them managed to hit it. Surprising, since it was really quite large. For sport, Alfie picked one of the boys as his champion, the red-haired one standing a couple of inches above the others, and willed him to succeed. The boy raised his arm and re-positioned the stone in his fingers before lobbing it towards the water. Alfie followed the arc of the stone. It would have hit the target, but the waves from the ferry had driven the wood nearer the shore. Alfie could make out the detail, except it wasn't wood, it was a body. His jaw fell open and he gripped the railing. It was a woman, floating face upwards.

'I used to play that game when I was young.'

Alfie turned to stare at a man beside him. The man pointed to the boys. 'I had a mean right arm. Never missed.'

'Shouldn't someone...do...something,' Alfie was lost for words.

'Harmless fun,' the man said. 'We have a winner. The freckle-faced lad has hit the wood.'

'The wood?' Alfie looked again at the water. The driftwood was bobbing and the boys were celebrating. 'Excuse me, I need to…'

Alfie covered his mouth and sped away from the man.

The coach was waiting. It bumped along towards the hospital. Thankfully Alfie's stomach was now empty, or the governess facing him would not be pleased. Alfie closed his eyes and tried to return his nightmares to the land of sleep. He woke as the driver pulled the horses up. As he struggled to get down, he realised he had forgotten the flowers. He would have to visit Dotty empty-handed.

'We weren't expecting you, Mr Peters,' the warden said. 'Your wife is in the garden. I'll call Nurse Smith.'

'Thank you, I can find my own way.'

He spotted Dotty as he made his way out the back door and stopped to watch her. She was wearing a yellow dress and gathering daffodils. Alfie thought he heard her singing. She looked so young, and happy. Alfie felt a mild regret when she waved at him, breaking the angelic vision he had of her.

'You've come at last.' She ran over to him, but halted before she was close enough to embrace him. If he looked hard he could see the scar cutting down from her hairline, but it didn't detract from her natural beauty. Her cheeks glowed.

'I meant to bring you flowers,' he said.

'I have these.' She showed him the daffodils.

Their conversation was stilted. It didn't feel like Dotty he was speaking to. This was an educated and attractive young lady. She fidgeted with the flowers and he ran the brim of his hat through his fingers.

'You look...wonderful. It won't be long before I can take you home.'

'Oh.' She turned away from him.

'I know it will be difficult adjusting, but I'll be there for you.'

'Alfie.' She faced him and he saw her grip on the flowers tighten. 'Haven't you been told?'

'Told what?'

She took a breath. 'I want a divorce.'

'What?'

'Don't be angry, Alfie. We've never really been married, not properly. Not in the way other couples are,' she said.

'What ideas has that doctor been putting in your head? If you mean our marriage has not been consummated, then we can soon put that right.'

'We have always been friends, I hope, but we don't love each other. Not as man and wife. I love John and he loves me. We wish to be married.'

'Dr Matthews,' Alfie grunted. 'Well, I refuse to grant a divorce and shall consummate our marriage straight away.'

Forgetting where they were, he grabbed her round the waist and pulled her towards him. She dropped the flowers and tried to push him away, but he was stronger. Taking hold of her arms, he held them down as he pressed his lips against hers.

'Let her go.' Dr Matthews was striding towards them. Alfie released Dotty and turned.

'Do you mind, I am trying to kiss my wife.' He emphasised the final two words.

'Dorothy wants a divorce,' the doctor said.

'So she said, but I don't,' Alfie answered.

'We can cite infidelity,' the doctor said.

'You may be guilty of taking advantage of a vulnerable patient, but Dotty cannot be blamed. You should be struck off the medical register.'

'I have not taken advantage of Dorothy. I was referring to your infidelity.'

'What do you mean?'

'I had a visit from Maggie,' Dotty broke in. 'She told me about you and her mother.'

'I knew Nancy Gillespie before we were married.'

'And you have been seeing her since,' the doctor added. 'Not only her. You are keeping a woman you call your wife in Perth. She has given you twins. That is without mentioning the girl you have in your apartment.'

'Maggie told you that? And you believed the little slut?' Alfie appealed to Dotty.

'I knew about you and Nancy. You were forty three when we married. I expected you to have known women, but I didn't think you would continue to see her after we wed.'

369

'I've had you watched,' Dr Matthews added. 'I also have written evidence that Nancy's son is yours.'

'Dotty has been in hospital for four years. A man has needs.'

'A bigamous wife, two mistresses and visits to a house of disrepute in Perth?' the doctor scoffed.

'I shall fight you on this.' Alfie backed away from the doctor, who moved to stand next to Dotty. The fallen daffodils were crushed beneath his feet.

'If it's about the shop, I don't care about that,' Dotty said.

'I don't need your father's business,' Alfie retorted. 'I have my own money and reputation to build on.'

'If you intend to fight us, I advise you to use your money employing a good lawyer,' Dr Matthews said.

'You won't be able to call Maggie as a witness. I'm afraid she is dead,' Alfie said. Dotty gasped. 'She fell from the train on her way back to Perth. Perhaps there is divine judgement.'

'Don't you have any feelings?' Dotty said. 'She was your daughter.'

'If we don't cite infidelity, we can claim attempted murder,' the doctor challenged.

'Attempted murder?' Dotty put a hand over her mouth. It took a moment for her to understand. 'Oh, you mean the accident with the clock…'

'I mean you, my darling,' Dr Matthews said, his temper forcing him to reveal the information.

Dotty stared at Alfie before falling against the doctor. He put his arms around her shoulders to support her.

'Maggie spoke with me, as well as Dotty,' Dr Matthews continued. 'We talked about various things. She seemed an intelligent young woman and I am sorry to hear of her death. She told me about the toffee.'

'The girl had a fanciful imagination. I have no idea what you are talking about.'

'I have had a piece analysed. It was full of lead filings. Useful in your line of work, perhaps, but fatal if ingested in large quantities. The amount in each toffee wasn't sufficient to kill outright, but as you know, lead accumulates in the body. It causes nervous disorders and epilepsy. No surprise Dotty's "condition" worsened after your visits. I was suspicious when the warden started taking fits after eating the toffee. Maggie confirmed that you sent her mother packages of lead filings to add to the toffee she boiled up.'

Alfie took a step towards the doctor, but decided against squaring up. 'I shall have you arrested for slander.'

'I'll look forward to that,' the doctor answered. 'It isn't slander if the accusation is true.'

The words rang in Alfie's head. Hadn't Maggie said something similar? He fumed and looked towards Dotty, but she had her head nestled on the doctor's shoulder. He could hear her sobbing.

'He's lying, Dotty. I would never do anything to hurt you. I promised your father.'

'I would prefer to settle this matter as quietly as possible,' Dr Matthews said. 'To spare Dorothy the distress of seeing you hang.'

'You haven't heard the last of this,' Alfie spluttered, thrusting a finger at the doctor. There was nothing more he could say. He strode across the garden towards the door, into the hospital building and along the corridor.

'Did you find your wife?' the warden asked as he walked past him in the hall.

'It seems I no longer have one.' Alfie spat the words at the man as he marched out.

He didn't stop walking until he rounded a corner and the hospital was no longer in sight. They had nothing on him. Hearsay and one contaminated toffee, that's why the charlatan wanted to keep things quiet. Once Dotty was free from the place she would forget about her doctor. They would build a new life, working together as well as living together. She would give him a fine clock making son.

'Got the time, mister?'

Alfie reached in his pocket, forgetting that his watch had been stolen. 'Sorry,' he looked round. The street was empty. He was sure he'd heard a woman's voice. He put his hands over his face, counted to five then ran his fingers through his hair. A clump fell out.

He sat in silence on the coach back, gazing at a stain on the man in front's jacket. He didn't dare look at the water on the ferry. When the American gentleman beside him asked if he knew a good hotel in Perth, Alfie felt a scalding of urine dribble down the legs of his trousers.

Chapter 23

He sat alone in the train, going over events in his head. His mind had been unsettled when he spoke with Dotty. If it hadn't been, he could have convinced her to go with him. He would write her a letter when he got home. The toffee was Nancy's idea. The witch had cast a spell on him, blinding him to Dotty's true worth. The nearer the train progressed towards Perth, the less likely it was that Dotty would believe him. Not with Matthews reading the letter over her shoulder, or censoring it before she was allowed to see it. It would be better if he avoided mention of the toffee.

The train stopped and a middle-aged lady entered the compartment. She glowered at him and he glowered back.

'Is this seat free?' she asked.

'No, it costs the same as the others,' he answered.

She thought about leaving, but sat down as far away from him as possible and brought a newspaper from her bag. The intention was more to shield her face from Alfie's than to read the news. She didn't turn the page once. The movement of the train and the sun through the window lulled Alfie to drop his head and close his eyes. He prised them open, but it wasn't long before his eyelids fell and images flitted before him.

There was the clock in the hotel lobby. He heard the striking of

374

the hour and saw the clock open as it was intended, but inside was Templeman, his head at an acute angle to his body. Before he could jerk awake, Maggie was there watching, laughing. Then he saw her on the train. Two hands were round her neck and she stopped laughing. Her skin was white and her lips were blue. They were man's hands, squeezing the life from her. In his dream, Alfie could only see the back of the murderer's head, leaning over Maggie. He released her and she slumped forwards, blood gargling from her mouth onto her killer's palms.

Alfie's eyes flashed open. He had his arms held out in front of him, his fingers spread like talons, ready to squash anything that came between them. The woman had lowered her paper and was staring at him with her mouth agape. Alfie turned his hands over to look at his palms. His fingers shook.

'No blood,' he said.

'A bad dream?' the woman asked.

'I've just killed a girl,' he answered.

The woman gathered her bag and stood up. 'I think you should see a doctor,' she said then left the carriage.

See a doctor?

Perhaps that was what was needed to stop the hallucinations and bad dreams that were hounding him, but Alfie was loath to admit his weakness. He wasn't some old woman with shattered nerves relying on a doctor's tuppenny tonic and trips to the seaside spas. A dose of laudanum doused down with whisky would do the trick. He would see to it when he got home.

His nerves weren't helped any by the sight of Inspector Jamieson lingering outside his shop when he got back.

'Have you been waiting long?' Alfie tried to be civil. He invited the inspector in.

'Long enough.'

'How can I help you?'

'You told me you knew nothing about this,' the inspector produced the sheet of doodles he had found in the clock compartment. 'Yet I believe you drew the diagrams. I have compared the writing to that on the receipt you gave me for the watch.'

'Really? Let me see it again.' Alfie took the sheet of paper and pretended to examine it, turning the paper ninety then a hundred and eighty degrees. He opened a drawer and withdrew a magnifying lens which he held over the sketches. 'It may be my work,' he allowed. 'A workshop sketch, no more.'

'Why would it have been in the dead man's possession?' the inspector asked.

'Templeman must have borrowed it. He was interested in the workings of the clock. He liked to know how his artistic ideas were transformed.'

'That is not what I have heard,' Jamieson rubbed his chin. 'Mr Weir informed me he often heard you arguing over the matter. Mr Templeman produced ever more fabulous plans without worrying about the practicalities. Mr Weir said you got enraged by it.'

'I wouldn't go as far as that,' Alfie said. 'His attitude annoyed me. We were constructing a clock, after all. It looks as if my words got through to him.'

'More's the pity for him,' Jamieson said.

'You can't think he would be influenced to enter the clock because of some unfinished sketches he found in the warehouse?' Alfie folded the paper and was about to put it in the drawer with his lens.

'We must consider all possibilities,' Jamieson answered. 'I shall have to keep hold of the paper for now, thank you.'

Alfie handed him the sketches. 'Was that all?'

'I would like to see the key to your grandfather clock, if you don't mind.'

'Certainly. May I ask why?'

Jamieson didn't answer. He made his way over to the clock.

'You have changed the winding mechanism since I was last here.'

'Yes,' Alfie agreed. 'A mother allowed her young boy to play with the clock and he managed to upset the workings.'

'I hope his parents paid for the damage.'

'You can be assured that his father footed the bill. You wanted to see the key?'

'That won't be necessary now, thank you.'

'This case is dragging on longer than I imagined. It isn't good for business,' Alfie said.

'Deaths are never good for business, but we in the police force are concerned with justice, not commerce. Good evening.'

Jamieson made his way out. Alfie locked the door behind him and returned to the counter. As he approached his foot slipped and he grabbed at one of the displays to stop himself falling. There was a puddle of water on the floor. It hadn't been raining. Alfie looked up to check for a leak, but the ceiling was dry. He waited, but there were no drips.

Odd, he hadn't noticed it when he was talking to Jamieson.

As he pondered the problem, a waft of jasmine reached his nostrils. His right hand twitched. He covered it with his left hand and both hands shook. For a moment he thought he heard the rush of water as the river passed the small island in the Tay on a windy evening. He put his hands on his head and pressed to squeeze the images out, but all he saw was Maggie and Giles dancing their ghostly galop. He rushed to the door and fumbled in his pocket for the key. Ghouls and goblins could not force him to stay another night in the apartment.

The air in the streets was nippy and Alfie was in need of warmth. He would go home, he decided. There would be explaining to do to Winnie, but she was a good wife. She would see the state he was in and succour him. She would prepare hot toddy and wipe his forehead as he sat by the fire. He lengthened his stride and kept his gaze on the paving in front of him.

There was no light to be seen through the windows as he approached the house. The curtains were drawn and for a moment Alfie wondered if he'd come to the right house. The key fitted the lock. One of Mrs Allendale's cats watched him enter the house from the safety of its garden. The hall was dark and he felt a damp chill.

'I'm home, dear,' he called, but wasn't surprised when no-one answered. He found a box of matches in his pocket and struck one. There was a gas lamp on the table which he managed to light after three attempts and a burnt thumb. An envelope was on the mantelpiece, propped against the wall. It was addressed to Alfie in Winnie's spidery handwriting. He ripped it open, cutting his burnt thumb on the paper, and held the note beside the lamp to read. Winnie wasn't an accomplished letter writer. The message was short, but he felt the gist of her anger from the pressure of her pen on the page. She had taken the twins to stay with her mother. He would be hearing from her lawyer in due course. Meanwhile he should send funds to them there.

'You'll be hearing from *my* lawyers, my good woman and there will be no funds.'

Alfie tore the letter in half, then quarters and threw it in the air. 'I am the father. The courts will award me custody.'

The threat made him feel bigger although he had no wish to take charge of a couple of unweaned babies. He carried the lamp into the kitchen. Winnie had emptied the cupboards of anything edible. She left a bottle of beer. He took a swig. It had turned sour and he spat it out.

When he succeeded in lighting more oil lamps, Alfie saw it wasn't only the twins Winnie had taken to her mother. The house had been emptied of everything moveable. Even the carpets had been rolled up and transported away. Upstairs he found his clothes and toiletry items scattered across the floorboards in the bedroom. His shirts had been slashed and holes had been cut from his trousers.

You won't get away with this, Alfie smarted.

He had a mind to call the police, except he didn't want the law meddling in his private affairs. He would go to the nearest public house for sustenance and decide what to do.

The steak and ale pie was lacking in steak and low on ale, but tastier than the treacle dumpling that was stodgier than Norma's stockinged legs. At least the food filled his stomach. Downed with half a bottle of whisky, it sufficed. He was unsteady on his feet and his vision was blurred when he left the inn. The thought of returning to the empty house wasn't pleasant, but it was a five minute walk away, whereas it would take him at least twenty to find his shop.

Mrs Allendale was watching him from behind her curtains. No doubt she had seen the removal cart, may even have spoken with Winnie. To hell with her, she could think what she wished. Her mind had feline-ised years ago. He intended heading straight upstairs when he entered the house, but there were voices coming from the living room. Alfie looked for something to protect himself with, a poker or stool, but Winnie had left nothing.

'Who's there?' he called.

He would have considered leaving the house and seeking help, but the drink made him bold. Lifting an unlit lamp he pushed the door open.

The room wasn't lit, but he could see four people standing in an informal circle; two men in breeches and two women in dresses. They were facing inwards and Alfie couldn't see their faces, but one of the men had on the same green jacket Templeman had worn at the party. The room smelt of jasmine. Alfie stood in the doorway watching, expecting to see a puddle of water. As his eyes adjusted to the vision he saw that the figures were holding wine glasses. Three of them raised their glasses to the younger man. They were speaking, but Alfie couldn't make out the words. The younger man seemed to be accepting the accolades of the others.

'What is going on here?' Alfie stepped into the room, expecting the figures to disappear. One of the women turned to stare at him. Her eye sockets were empty, but a red light beamed out from them, piercing through Alfie's skull. He felt a sharp pain and pressed his hand against his forehead.

He was going mad. He had visited the asylum too often and contracted some illness from one of the inmates.

'We are celebrating young Alf's success,' she said in a voice as clear as his own.

'Maggie?' Alfie squinted.

'You would be proud of him,' the green coated man added. 'Not many men in their twenties get to make a clock for a royal residence. Balmoral, no less. Of course, he has me to thank for his talent.'

'You?' Alfie mouthed.

The second woman wasn't listening to the conversation. She was tugging at the sleeve of the green jacket. The man wasn't happy about it and kept trying to shrug her off.

'We named him after his grandfather,' Maggie explained. 'Look at his hands. Hasn't he got beautiful clockmaker fingers?'

She reached out to lift the young man's hands and show them to Alfie. There were no muscles or skin on them, only whitened bones held together by some invisible ether. Alfie took a step back and swallowed the bile in his mouth.

'It's not his fault,' Maggie said, seeing his horror. 'He died before he was born, but if he hadn't, imagine what these hands could have made.'

'Get gone, you foul ghouls,' Alfie knew what he meant to say, but his words came out like geese gaggling.

Maggie and Templeman laughed. The wine glasses had disappeared. The other woman, Emily Squires, held Templeman's hand with her right hand and reached for Maggie's hand with her other. Maggie accepted it and gave Templeman her free hand. They formed a circle with the young man in the centre and danced round him. When they stopped, Maggie let go of Emily's hand to offer it to Alfie.

'Come, join our celebration,' she invited.

The room was cold. A draught blew from the group and rustled round Alfie's legs, rising to his arms and face. He could hear his heart beating, rapid at first, but slowing as he felt himself reach out towards Maggie.

'No,' he screamed and staggered back as he felt her ice hard fingernails and knew he was touching death. His head hit the wooden door and he fell to the floor.

Chapter 24

There was crashing in Alfie's skull and when he rubbed his head there was congealed blood on his hands. The sun was shining through the window, dazzling his eyes. It took him a moment to realise where he was and what he had seen the previous night.

He hadn't seen anything. His mind was playing tricks and no wonder with the trauma he had been through.

He needed a drink. It was too early to go to a public house, but he had whisky in the apartment. The need for alcohol made him forget the puddle of river water that had forced him to abandon the shop. He hadn't replaced his stolen pocket watch, but guessed from the empty streets and darkened houses that it was early. He avoided the path by the river, taking the longer route to his shop. As he approached he noticed some wag had painted over his sign. It now read: ALFRED PETERS – MAKER OF FINE TORTURE PIECES AND KILLING IMPLEMENTS. The sooner he shut up shop the better.

Alfie locked himself in the apartment with shaking hands, drew a set of drawers against the door and drank in his bedroom until lunch time when his bottle was empty. He made his way to the docks. Full of whisky, there were other pleasures his body craved. A gin seller directed him to a house where he was told the

385

girls had their own hair and teeth. He found the building, but a harsh chortle from across the street stopped him knocking on the door.

Would the girl he chose know Maggie? Or worse, would she be there watching him, with Emily Squire's ghost flooding the floor with river water?

'Don't be shy, my dear,' a wrinkled hag with painted lips and blackened teeth called from the doorway. Alfie assumed she was the brothel keeper. 'Are you looking for love?'

'I'm a married man,' he retorted. He was about to leave when a bonny girl appeared beside the woman. Her auburn hair fell in waves onto her face, covering her right eye. She was curvy, unlike most of the half-starved wretches in such houses.

'What's your name?' the girl asked, crushing past the woman to rub a finger down Alfie's cheek.

'Dougie,' Alfie answered. It was never a good idea to disclose your real identity. 'And you?' He reached to brush the hair from her eye, but she stepped back.

'No touching before terms are fixed,' the hag said.

'I want to see what I'm getting.'

Alfie rushed at the girl and pulled her hair back. Her eye was missing from the socket and Alfie half expected a red glow in its place. He pushed her away from him and she fell to the paving.

'No sae fast, mister.' A hand gripped Alfie's shoulder as he tried to leave. Alfie swung round and hit the man holding him in the chest. It made little impact. 'Like that is it?' The man let go and punched Alfie on the nose, sending him reeling. Before he could steady himself, the man crunched a blow into his abdomen. 'Come on then.' The man's fists were raised in front of his face.

Alfie took a moment to arrange his clothing, showing the man he wasn't afraid. 'I have no wish to partake of this girl's services,' he said. 'If you try to detain me I shall call for an officer of the law.'

The girl was lying on the paving where she had fallen and there was blood oozing from her head. The hag was kneeling beside her.

'He's right Tam, ca' the police.' The hag stared at Alfie. 'Catriona is deid.'

'Dead? No, that's impossible,' Alfie stammered.

The man, Tam, had hold of him again, trapping his right arm behind his back. Alfie struggled, but couldn't free himself.

'There has been a mistake. The girl fell. You saw it was an accident.'

'Save your tittle-tattle for the law.'

The law turned up in the form of a young officer, barely old enough to be out on his own. A doctor was summoned and Tam was happy to help frogmarch Alfie to the police station, twisting his arm until the bones creaked.

'Been drinking have you, Mr Peters? Causing trouble?' Alfie recognised Jamieson's voice, but his face was blurred.

'Killed a lass,' Tam answered. 'Cos she widnae let him hae his way wi' her.'

'Rubbish,' Alfie tried to sound confident, but his voice cracked.

'I'll decide on that,' Jamieson said. 'Meanwhile we have a nice cell for you to sober up in here.'

The officers pulled off Alfie's jacket and he was searched for weapons before being hustled into a cell; a stone-walled animal cage with a wooden bed and flat mattress. The door thudded shut. Alfie rubbed his arm then sat down on the bed. The wooden boards gave way and he tumbled to the floor to the sound of laughter. The noise was in his head. He scrambled to the mattress. There was a small window, high up, allowing a beam of light into the room to cast haunting shadows. Alfie positioned the mattress under the light and lay down. He closed his eyes, but his head spun. He thought he heard the door open and sat up. There was a man standing across from him in the shadows.

'Jamieson? I demand to see a lawyer.'

The man didn't answer, but took a step nearer. A slow step. Alfie felt a cold breeze.

'Who are you?' Alfie croaked.

'A fellow traveller.' The man answered in an American accent. He moved into the light and Alfie saw it was Templeman. He had a hangman's noose around his neck. 'I'm glad you're coming to join me. I have such great plans for a clock here. Red, to match the fiery walls.'

'Get away from me.'

Alfie pulled his legs up to huddle against the wall. 'The girl fell. I didn't mean to hurt her.'

'Nobody will believe you,' Templeman answered, pulling at the rope round his neck. 'You've got form.'

'What do you mean?'

'It's not the first time you've used violence against a woman.'

'You are the one who killed Maggie,' Alfie accused. 'You strangled her and pushed her from the train because she refused to have an abortion. She would have ruined everything for you.'

'She was blackmailing you too,' Templeman said. 'You killed her to stop her blabbing. Pity you were too late. You killed your own daughter, Alfie. I tried to stop you.'

'No,' Alfie shouted. 'No.'

Templeman fled like a coward, but the scene on the train remained.

Templeman and Maggie were there at the train door. The window was down. He had gone over. There was squabbling and pushing. Maggie had her fist in his face. A hand reached down and the door had flung open....

The door to the cell opened. Jamieson stood there.

'You'll be glad to know the girl isn't dead,' Jamieson said. 'Her mother does not wish to press charges.'

'If that hag was her mother, then I'm my dead granddad.' Alfie stood up. It took a moment for the words to sink in, but when they did he gave a chuckle.

'Is that it, then? Am I free to go?'

'Not yet. There is another matter I would like to question you about, if you don't mind.'

Alfie followed Jamieson into the interview room and took a seat at one side of the table. He looked around. 'I don't want him here.'

'Sergeant Munroe will be taking notes.'

'I don't mean him. I mean him.' Alfie pointed at the corner of the room. Jamieson looked where he pointed.

'Who do you mean? There is nobody there.'

'Him. Somebody stop him. He's going to jump.' Alfie leapt up, knocking the chair over. Sergeant Munroe stepped forwards to prevent him dashing past the table and into the wall.

'Mr Peters, please,' Jamieson righted the chair and indicated that Alfie should sit down. Alfie stood with his shoulders hunched, staring into space.

'I won't do it, you know.' Alfie side-stepped Sergeant Munroe, as the police officer motioned him to the chair.

'Do what?' Jamieson asked.

'Confess, of course.'

'Confess to what, Mr Peters?'

'I knew you were a fool, but I didn't think you were stupid enough to take me seriously,' Alfie addressed the wall.

'I would advise you not to call an officer of the law a fool,' Jamieson said.

'Not you. Him. Yes, yes, I meddled with the pendulum. Don't come any closer.'

'Are you feeling well? Do you require a doctor?' Jamieson asked.

'I'm as sane as any man here.' Alfie fell to his knees and pressed his hands to his face. 'Leave me alone. No, not you too.

What are you doing here?'

Jamieson signalled to his sergeant. Munroe moved over and the inspector whispered in his ear. Munroe nodded and left the room.

'Would you like to introduce me to your friends, Mr Peters?' Jamieson sat down and stretched out his legs.

Alfie looked up. His eyes were red and there were tears trickling down his cheeks. 'Take them away. I'll tell you everything you want to know.'

Between shielding himself from Templeman's threats, Maggie's accusations and Emily Squires' dripping clothes, Alfie related a garbled account of how he adapted the clock mechanism then persuaded Templeman to enter the casing.

'Let me get this clear, you admit that you fixed the pendulum to fall on anyone who disturbed it?'

'She made me do it.'

'Who did?'

'Maggie, of course.'

'Maggie Gillespie, the girl who was killed on the train? What has that to do with Mr. Templeman?'

Alfie had stopped listening to the inspector. He punched the air several times, dodging out the way of invisible blows.

'Mr Peters, I must ask you to sit down,' Jamieson said, but made no attempt to restrain Alfie. The commotion brought a young constable to the room. Jamieson nodded and the officer moved to take hold of Alfie's arm.

'No you don't, you scallywag.' Alfie swiped at the policeman who ducked to avoid a right cut to the cheek. 'On the ropes now, aren't you?' Alfie mocked.

Munroe returned at that moment and dashed to prevent Alfie throwing another punch at the constable. Alfie stumbled forwards and the young officer clunked him on the head with his baton. He crumpled to the floor, with Templeman leaning over him and Maggie sitting on Jamieson's knee.

When he regained consciousness, he was stretched out on the bed in the cell. His arms felt stiff. He tried to move them to sit up, but to his horror they were held fast by a straight jacket. He shifted around, but it was useless. His arms were trapped. After a minute he managed to roll himself onto the floor and get to his knees. His joints cracked and a burst of pain shot up his back forcing him to cry out.

'Quiet in there,' a man's voice called and there was banging on the cell door.

'I demand to see a lawyer,' Alfie shouted back. Nobody

answered and the door remained closed. 'I want to see my wife.' His throat was burning from the after effects of the alcohol. He shuffled towards the door, but with his arms immobilised it was impossible to knock for attention. He slumped at the side and waited, watching the light from the window move across the room, imagining figures lurking in the shadows.

'Have you seen my father?'

The smell of jasmine told him that Emily was with him, but he didn't see her.

'Get away from me you witch,' Alfie snarled, edging his backside along the wall.

'Why, that isn't a very pleasant greeting, my dear.' The voice was familiar. The cell door was open and Alfie could make out three figures. One of them was wearing red.

'Get away,' he stepped back.

As his eyes adjusted he made out the figures of two men and a woman. He recognised Jamieson first. A man and woman were standing behind him. The man was wearing a green jacket and had his right arm round the woman's waist. It was the woman's voice he heard.

'Maggie?' he croaked.

She moved into the cell and stood in the light, so he could see her. She was wearing a crimson coat and her hair flowed onto the collar. 'It's me, Dotty,' she said.

Alfie heard the man with her tut and realised it was Dr Matthews.

'What am I doing tied up like this?' Alfie addressed Jamieson, but it was Matthews who answered.

'Inspector Jamieson called me to ask for my advice on the matter of your mental health.'

'My mental health?' Alfie spluttered. His words echoed round the space until they were no longer his, but Templeman's.

'You are mad, Alfie. Completely out of your mind. You'd better come and join us or they will lock you up for good.'

'The inspector informed me of your confession and I have told him about the business we spoke of in Edinburgh regarding Dorothy,' Matthews answered.

'You can have your divorce, if that is what you want,' Alfie stared at Dorothy.

'I don't think you understand, Mr Peters,' Jamieson said. 'You are guilty of the unlawful killing of Mr Giles Templeman and, it would seem, the attempted murder of your wife, Dorothy Peters. From your behaviour, and from speaking with Dr Matthews, I have reason to believe you are not in your right mind.'

'I am as sane as you are,' Alfie replied. 'Or I would be if I wasn't pestered by these infernal ghouls.'

'You see what I mean.' Jamieson turned to Matthews.

'A classic imbalance of the temporal humours,' Matthews replied.

'The question is, did this start before or after the crimes?' Jamieson said.

Matthews muttered something which Alfie didn't hear because Maggie was singing a bawdy pub song in his ear. Dorothy bent down to speak to him. 'Alfie, you must allow John to arrange hospital treatment for you.'

'In an asylum? Never. I would rather die.'

'That is the alternative, Mr Peters,' Jamieson said. 'Either you are confined to an asylum or you will be hanged as a murderer.'

'It won't be so bad, Alfie,' Dorothy said. 'The doctors will know how to make you better. We will come and visit you whenever we can, won't we John?' She stood up and took hold of the doctor's hand.

'Of course darling.' He smiled at Dorothy and turned to look down on Alfie. 'We'll even bring you some nice toffee.'

Other books by Barbara Stevenson

The Organist
Where the Ocean Meets the Sky
The Dalliances of Monsieur D'Haricot
Travels with an Organ to Treacherous Lands

Printed in Great Britain
by Amazon